IN ANOTHER TIME

Also by Caroline Leech

Wait for Me

In Another Time

CAROLINE LEECH

HARPER TEEN

An Imprint of HarperCollinsPublishers

ISBN 978-0-06-245991-6

Typography by Aurora Parlagreco
18 19 20 21 22   PC/LSCH   10 9 8 7 6 5 4 3 2 1

First Edition

*To the lumberjills who served in the Women's Timbercorps in
the forests of Scotland 1942–1946*

*To Perryn, Jemma, Kirsty, and Rory
You are my everything*

John Anderson, my jo, John,
We clamb the hill thegither,
And mony a canty day, John,
We've had wi ane anither;
Now we maun totter down, John,
But hand in hand we'll go,
And sleep thegither at the foot,
John Anderson, my jo.

from "John Anderson, My Jo"
ROBERT BURNS, 1759–1796

IN ANOTHER TIME

One

Maisie's shoulders burned, her palms were torn, and her ax handle was smeared with blister pus and blood. Again.

The woods were airless today, and it made the work even harder than usual. As a bead of sweat ran down from Maisie's hair toward her eye, she stopped to wipe her forehead with the sleeve of her blouse, knowing she'd probably just added yet another muddy streak to those already across her face. Maisie wondered how on earth she'd be able to get herself looking presentable enough to go to a dance by seven o'clock. She'd only be dancing with her friends, but still, she didn't want it to look like she'd spent the week up to her knees in dirt and wood chippings. Which, of course, she had.

Perhaps it was just as well there was no chance that some handsome chap would ask her to dance. She would bet a week's wages—all thirty-seven shillings of it—that there were none of them left in Brechin these days, not since every man aged between eighteen and forty had been called up to the war.

Maisie stood and stretched out her back, pretending to study the tree she was attempting to chop down. When would this constant ache disappear? Even after two weeks of learning how to fell, split, saw, and sned, she still woke up each morning feeling like she'd gone ten rounds in the ring with a heavyweight champion. She had blisters on her hands from the tools—four-and-a-half-pound axes, six-pound axes, crosscut saws, hauling chains, and cant hooks—and blisters on her feet from her work boots. There were even blisters between her thighs where the rough material of her uniform chafed as she worked.

"I bet the WAAF and ATS recruits don't hurt this badly all through their training," she moaned to her friend Dot, who was working two trees over. "I still think the recruitment officer lied to me. She made it sound like the Women's Timber Corps would be a walk in the park."

"Or perhaps a walk"—Dot flailed her ax again toward the foot of her own tree—"in the forest."

"Very funny," Maisie replied, then blew gingerly onto her stinging fingers. "Bloody hell, that hurts!" She pulled out her once-white handkerchief and dabbed at her hands, hoping to feel some comfort from the soft, cool cotton, and watched Dot swing the ax a couple more times. Again and again Dot's blade seemed to bounce off the wood as if it were made of India rubber, exposing no more of the creamy flesh under the brown bark than had been visible five minutes before.

Maisie glanced behind her to see if their instructor, Mr. McRobbie, was watching, but he was talking to another recruit farther up the line of trees, so she let her ax-head rest on the ground. She had been issued this six-pound ax when training began, but right now, it felt like a forty-pound sledgehammer. She reached into her pocket and withdrew her whetstone, the smooth flat stone she used to set her blade. Mr. McRobbie had drummed into them the importance of having a whetstone with them at all times, to keep the cutting edge sharp and clean, but Maisie had discovered another use for it. She laid the stone, warm from her body heat, onto the blisters of her hands one by one, sighing as the discomfort was eased, if only for a few seconds.

Still Dot was hacking away at the tree.

Maisie sighed. "Do you want me to finish that off for you? We've got a dance to go to tonight, remember, and the way you're going, you'll still be slapping at it at midnight."

"Uggghhh," grunted Dot with one more swipe. "What am I doing wrong? I feel like I'm doing it the way he showed us, and I've got blisters a mile deep to prove it, but I don't ever make any difference at all! Bloody thing!"

Dot kicked the toe of her boot at the trunk and there was an ominous creaking sound, as if the tree were about to topple. Dot recoiled and jumped clear, but the tree stayed where it was.

Maisie burst out laughing. "Perhaps you should kick the tree into submission."

"Oh, get lost!" Dot retorted, but then she began to laugh too. "I only want to find one thing on this training course that I can actually do properly, because cutting down trees certainly isn't it."

Maisie felt sorry for Dot. She was shorter and slighter than Maisie, though certainly not the smallest of the women in their group, yet Dot couldn't seem to get the hang of any of the techniques Mr. McRobbie had shown them. After only two weeks, Maisie already felt quite competent at using the tools they had been given so far, but Dot was not progressing at all. That fact was not only making Dot anxious, it was starting to worry Maisie too. They were only two weeks into their six-week training course, but it had been made clear that anyone could be sent home at any time for failing to make the grade. She couldn't bear it if her new friend were thrown off the course. Who would Maisie have to talk with and work beside then?

The other women doing the Timber Corps training were all very nice, but that was the problem—they were all *women*, in their twenties and thirties. Only Dot was close to Maisie in age, and even then, Dot was already nineteen, almost two years older than Maisie. But it was comforting to have a friend of roughly her own age, someone who treated her like a teammate rather than a child.

Maisie had certainly felt like an adult last month when she'd walked into the recruiting office in Glasgow and told the sergeant behind the desk that she wanted to join the Women's Auxiliary Air Force, or even the Auxiliary Territorial Service. She was all ready to argue with him that since she was a grown woman taking control of her life, she didn't need to finish her final year at school because it was about time she did her bit for the war effort.

But the sergeant hadn't argued with her. He'd instead pointed her to the next office, where a friendly woman told her with a smile that, at seventeen, she was still too young to become a WAAF or a Navy Wren, or even to join the ATS.

Imagining the smug expression on her father's face as she returned home with her mature and independent tail firmly between her legs, Maisie tried not to whine. "So is there nothing I can do instead?"

"There's the Women's Land Army," the woman replied. "They take Land Girls from seventeen, if you'd fancy working on a farm. It's hard work, but if you like the outdoor life . . ."

Maisie could rather see herself walking through fields of golden corn swaying gently in the summer breeze, chewing lazily on a stalk of barley as the sun warmed her skin.

". . . you'd be working with crops and with the animals. You know, cows, horses, pigs, chickens, and the like. . . ."

Cows? Horses? Pigs?

A shudder ran down Maisie's aching back even now, remembering that conversation. She might enjoy working with chickens or maybe sheep, but not big animals like cows and horses. She especially hated—no, she *feared*—horses, ever since the rag-and-bone man's Charlie, a brutish Clydesdale, had taken a swing at Maisie with his huge head and left a nasty dark-red graze and a blooming bruise on her arm with his enormous teeth. How old would she have been? Eight perhaps? It still made her feel queasy.

"No, not animals. I can't do animals."

The woman had frowned at her.

"Well, I'm not sure there's much else other than munitions, dear," she'd said, "and a bright and healthy girl like you doesn't want to be stuck in a factory all day, surely. Oh, wait now, here's something. . . ."

She'd rummaged around in a drawer and pulled out a single sheet of paper. "This is quite a new setup, but according to this, they're taking girls from seventeen into the new Women's Timber Corps. It says here that because of the German sea blockade, supply ships can't get through to bring timber to Britain. Therefore, we need to get the wood from our own forests. Of course, all our foresters are soldiers now, so they've created this, the WTC. How does that sound?"

When Maisie didn't immediately respond, the recruiter had continued. "Would trees be more your thing, dear?"

Trees? Trees certainly didn't have teeth. "Yes, thank you," Maisie had said, "that sounds spot on. I think trees might be much more my thing."

From somewhere nearby, a whistle blew three times, long and loud. Miss Cradditch, the WTC training officer at

Shandford Lodge—known as Old Crabby to all the recruits—had a particularly piercing and insistent whistle, but right now no one cared since it signaled the end of the workday. Next stop, the Brechin dance.

As Maisie walked with Dot and the others down to the Hut C dormitory to gather her towel and soap, she knew she'd made the right decision at the recruiting office. After only two weeks on the course, Maisie was already proud to be training as a lumberjill.

Maisie stared down into the brown-speckled bathwater with distaste. The luxury of the long, deep baths she'd enjoyed at home before the war seemed so long ago now, since all she was allowed to bathe in these days were her strictly rationed five inches of water. And with so many women in the camp, and only three proper bathrooms upstairs in Shandford Lodge, the old manor house that had been converted into the WTC training center, there had to be a roster for who bathed when. It had been four days since Maisie's last turn to have a bath, and since those days had all been hard physical work, half of the Shandford woods appeared to have made its way into the bath with her.

The water, which barely covered her legs, wasn't even warm, but it was wet and soothing, and she felt herself relax immediately. After all, she was one of the lucky ones, having her bath on the same day as they went dancing, so she slid as much of her body down into the water as she could, while also trying to keep her hair dry. She considered her hands, not sure if she should risk putting open sores into such filthy water, but how else was she going to soap the rest of her body? Throwing hygienic caution to the wind, she picked up her small, pink WTC-issued bar of carbolic soap, just as someone banged on the bathroom door.

"Come on, Maisie, don't take all night." Dot's voice was muffled by the thick wood. "The truck's leaving in less than an hour. You need to hurry! Do you even know what you're wearing yet?"

So much for that long luxurious bath!

"All right," Maisie shouted back, quickly rubbing the soap up to a stinging lather between her hands. "I'll be down in a few minutes, and maybe you can help me decide."

Once she finished her bath, Maisie ran down to Hut C to get ready. She had only brought two dresses from home, so it wouldn't be hard to decide on an outfit. Many of the other women had worked the whole day with curlers under their decidedly nonregulation head scarves, but thankfully, Maisie only needed to brush out her shoulder-length blond hair and pin it up at each side. Dot's short dark hair was even quicker, just combed and tucked behind her ears, so the two of them were ready with time to spare.

As they waited for the truck to arrive, Maisie and Dot watched the older women fuss with whatever face powder, mascara, and lipstick they had saved from before the war—it was almost impossible to get hold of any makeup these days, especially in the wilds of Scotland. All Maisie had done was smear a little Vaseline on her lips to give them a shine. She'd only be dancing with the other lumberjills, so what was the point?

Even so, Maisie was excited to be going out. Two weeks after leaving home for her new adventure, tonight felt almost like a rite of passage.

Two

Brechin Town Hall, where the dance was being held, was a dour place, with dark marble columns and heavily ornate carvings on the walls and ceiling. To make things worse, the blackout blinds were already in place over the tall windows, meaning that none of the summer evening light would filter into the hall. The dance organizers had done their best to cheer things up by bringing in some spotlights and hanging some brightly colored banners from the gallery above the dance floor, so Maisie wasn't complaining. They were lucky to be allowed out from camp for any dance at all.

When the WTC girls had arrived, the band was already playing on a raised platform at the far end of the hall, and after a couple of numbers, Maisie had decided that the musicians were rather good. Brechin was a small town in the middle of nowhere, after all, not a metropolis like Glasgow. She was soon having fun, dancing either with Dot or with Mary, a red-haired girl from Aberdeen, and before long, Maisie noticed that her aches and pains had eased significantly.

Maisie couldn't help but notice that some of the other lumberjills were moaning about the lack of men to dance with. But what had they expected? With the war on, there were only a few locals left to go dancing, and they were only old men and young boys. Some of the boys were near Maisie's age, strutting around with gangly arrogance, even though it was clear they were not yet old enough to be called up, but Maisie studiously avoided making eye contact with any of them. She was quite happy to dance with her new girl friends. No pressure, no need to explain, they could just have fun.

However, not long before the end of the dance, the atmosphere suddenly changed, and heads began turning to look toward the front doors. Maisie was dancing again with Mary, and the two of them were forced to stand on tiptoe to see what was happening. Who had arrived, and why was it causing such a fuss?

Maisie strained to see over the other girls to the front, where more than a dozen men were standing inside the main door, nicely dressed, in suits and ties, each in turn handing his hat to the elderly cloakroom attendant, who was suddenly standing straighter and smiling wider than before, now that there were some handsome men in the room.

All right, not many of them were handsome, but even so . . .

A ripple of whispered excitement washed around the room as the first of the men reached the edge of the dance floor. "Americans, Americans, Americans . . ."

Maisie tugged at Mary's arm. "Come on—let's keep going. I like this tune too much not to dance to it."

All through the rest of that number, however, Mary kept glancing over her shoulder.

"They're Americans, though, Maisie!" she hissed, and then giggled. "Look, look! That one's asked Lillian to dance. And that tall blond girl from Hut B has nabbed one too. Oh my goodness, they're not wasting any time, are they?"

Mary was now so distracted that they were virtually at a standstill again, and Maisie found herself getting quite annoyed, though she wasn't sure if it was with Mary or the men.

"It's quite rude, really, turning up so late, don't you think?" Maisie grumbled. "There's only a dance or two left."

Clearly Mary didn't agree. She grabbed Maisie's hand and pulled her over to a table at the edge of the dance floor. "Then there's only a chance or two left to land a dance with one of them!" she declared, and leaned casually against a chair, pushing her chest out and pouting more than a little.

Maisie could feel the blush rising in her own cheeks at this blatant show of . . . of what, she didn't know, but she didn't much like it. She grabbed her handbag from the nearby table where she'd left it and headed for the ladies' to comb her hair, cool her face, and sulk a little. Her whole evening had been spoiled, thanks to those men.

Once she'd collected herself, Maisie realized she was actually feeling quite anxious. But that was ridiculous—it was only a bunch of men, for goodness' sake, even if they were Americans.

Back at the table, there was no sign of Mary. Maisie's neck was aching again, so she bent her head forward, pulling her shoulders down and back, to stretch out the muscles. As she did, she became aware of someone hovering nearby and, without lifting her head, she glanced sideways along the floor until she found a pair of polished black leather shoes sticking out from dark tweed trousers with wide cuffs.

"Go on!" she heard an American man say. "She won't bite, you know."

A woman giggled at his comment.

The shoes suddenly moved toward Maisie, a hopping, stumbling approach, as if their wearer had been shoved from behind. Maisie jumped back in alarm, whipping her head up to see who was about to crash into her.

The man attached to the shoes managed to catch his balance by grabbing onto the chair beside Maisie just before he bumped into her. Beyond him was a blond man, grinning widely, with one of the other WTC girls—Maisie didn't know her name—hanging on his arm.

The shoe man looked mortified, a frown furrowing deep lines across his tanned forehead.

"My apologies," he said, his voice deeper than Maisie had

expected, "I didn't mean to scare you. But some people seem incapable of minding their own business."

He glared over his shoulder, but the blond man only laughed and pulled the woman toward the dance floor. When Maisie didn't immediately reply, the shoe man coughed to clear his throat.

"My friend thinks that I should ask you to dance, since there can't be many more numbers left before it ends."

Maisie said nothing. What could she say? Certainly, it would be nice to dance for once with someone who was taller that she was, someone who didn't expect her to lead the whole time as Dot and Mary did. But she'd prefer him to ask her to dance because he wanted to, not because his friend told him to.

"I mean . . ." He looked embarrassed now. "It's not that I don't want to ask you to dance, it's just . . . oh hell! Pardon me! What I mean is . . . well, I don't dance."

Maisie's humiliation grew with each word.

"Well, why did you come then?" she asked, sounding snippier than she'd meant to. "It's a dance. What else did you think you would be doing?"

As she turned away, wishing the ground would swallow her up, fingers closed around the top of her arm, not tightly, but with enough pressure to stop her.

"Look, I'm sorry." He sounded like he meant it, so she turned to face him again. "We got ourselves off on the . . . er, wrong foot, so to speak, which is a shame."

He dropped his grip on her arm and shrugged apologetically. There was an earnest expression in his dark-brown eyes, now that she really looked at him, and the skin around them was like soft leather, tanned and supple, but with tiny wrinkles, as if he squinted into the sun too often. Or as if he were always smiling. Except he wasn't smiling now, he was grimacing. At her.

"And while I don't usually ask women to dance," he began again, "we've found ourselves into this rather embarrassing situation now, so perhaps I should make the effort. If you'd like me to, that is."

Though Maisie heard the words, she was wondering how an American like him could have ended up on a Friday evening in August in Brechin, of all places, and why he . . .

"Miss?" He was frowning again. "Would you like me to?"

Maisie startled. "Sorry. Pardon me? Yes! Erm, no, erm, sorry?"

His expression shifted into wry amusement at her embarrassment.

"I asked whether you would mind if I were to ask you to dance?"

In her blushing confusion, Maisie took a moment or two to work her way through the question.

"I think so?" she said. Was that the right answer? "Or . . ."

Then he smiled, and sure enough, the soft skin around his eyes wrinkled up in tiny folds. It was unnervingly infectious and Maisie couldn't help but smile back.

"You think you would mind?" He was clearly teasing her now. "Or you think I should ask you to dance?"

Maisie gave him an exaggerated sigh. "Is every question you ask this complicated, or is this how all Americans talk?"

"Not every question, no. But sometimes, it can be more fun this way." He held out his hand toward her.

Maisie hesitated. It might not have been the most romantic invitation, but it seemed like a genuine one after all that. And maybe this might be fun.

"Thank you," she said, laying her hand onto his. "I'd very much like to dance."

Her heart sped up as they walked the few steps to the dance floor and waited for a space to allow them to enter the dance. But then she noticed that his fingers were moving strangely against her own, and Maisie's delight quickly evaporated. She'd forgotten about her blisters, and could only imagine how unpleasant they must feel against his palm. Before she could pull her hand back out of his, however, he lifted it up and studied it, frowning again, as if trying to work out a puzzle. Maisie realized with a sinking feeling that he was trying to work out why a young woman would have the callused hands of an old crone, disgustingly rough, with hard-crusted blisters and sharp-edged cuts and cracks. Embarrassment again flooded through her and she snatched her hand from his grasp, tucking both her hands around her waist to hide them from his scrutiny.

"They're awful, I know," she burst out. "But it's the work, the tools. They rip up our hands, and there's nothing we can do to protect them. It's vile, I know."

"Tools?" he asked.

"Axes and saws, in the woods. I'm with the Women's Timber Corps." Despite her embarrassment, Maisie lifted her chin defiantly, already anticipating the same derision she had received from her father. "I'm training to be a lumber-jill."

"A lumberjill, eh? Hmmm." He seemed to be suppressing a smile, and Maisie felt her hackles rise. Why did men find that so ridiculous?

But instead of sneering, he took one of her hands back, resting it flat on his, and let his thumb rub gently across her palm and up her index finger, hesitating briefly by each blister, just disconcertingly long enough for her to feel the warmth from his touch.

"I mean, they issued us with gloves," she blurted out, "but they're all too big, so when you're using an ax, it feels like your hands are slipping on the—"

"Pig fat," he said.

What had he said? It sounded like *pig fat* to Maisie, but that was too bizarre, even for an American.

"Pardon?"

"You need pig fat and Vaseline," he said again, smiling now.

"I have no idea what you're talking about."

"Rub your hands with a mixture of pig fat and Vaseline morning and night, and this shouldn't happen anymore."

"But . . ." Maisie wasn't sure what to say. "But how would you know . . . ?"

Slowly he turned over his free hand and held it out flat

next to hers. Even in the low light, Maisie could see that he had once had blisters in almost all the same places as she had on her own hands—on all three pads of each finger, the two on the thumb, as well as across the bridge and the heel of the palm. His weren't fresh and crisp and sore as hers were, but there was a distinct whitening of hard skin in each place, the pale shadows of blisters where calluses lay as a permanent reminder of pain in his past. His scars matched hers.

He turned his hand over so it again lay palm to palm on Maisie's. A sudden wave of relief caught her by surprise. He understood and he wasn't repulsed.

"But how did your hands get like that?" she asked.

"You're not the only one who knows how to swing an ax," he replied with a wink.

The band had begun a new song. Maisie recognized the tune, but in the confusion of having her hand held by a stranger, she couldn't place it right then. He seemed to know it, though, because he glanced up at the band and grinned, squeezing her hand between his.

"Perhaps we can talk about my magic blister potion later, but while the band is still playing this lovely song, maybe we ought to dance?"

"Thank you. I'd like that"—Maisie let herself smile a little too—"and I'm Maisie, by the way."

"I'm glad to meet you, Maisie. My name's John Lindsay."

It became very clear, very quickly, that John Lindsay was a dreadful dancer.

When he had first guided Maisie into the crowd of slowly spinning couples, she'd enjoyed the reassurance of having his warm hand on her back. And once she had swallowed down the embarrassment of having this tall and rather handsome man holding her so close, Maisie almost relaxed. But then they'd stumbled, bumping into two other couples, and Maisie had had to fight to keep herself from falling. Whether it was because she'd lost her balance when she lifted her eyes to look up into his for a moment, or whether he'd simply tripped over his own feet, she wasn't sure, but either way, this was not how she had hoped her first dance as an independent woman would go.

As John tried again to swoop Maisie around the dance floor, she couldn't escape the feeling that she was risking life and limb, his larger frame and extra weight always pulling her off-balance. This was fast becoming a nightmare. How could a young and obviously fit man be so completely incapable of dancing?

She risked another glance up at his face, expecting him to be smiling apologetically, but there was no smile. In fact, it was as if the earlier sunshine had been smothered by the darkest of storm clouds. He was frowning, as if concentrating hard, and his breath came heavily now. Then she noticed that he seemed to be swallowing again and again. Was he unwell or in pain? Or was he drunk? She hadn't smelled any beer or whisky on him, but even so . . .

Suddenly, John took Maisie by the elbow and walked her to the side of the dance floor, where he let her go and staggered against the nearest chair, appearing to have difficulty catching his breath. Then, barely glancing up, he held out his hand, palm toward Maisie, as if trying to keep her away.

"I can't do this. I'm sorry, Maisie. I really can't."

"What's wrong?" Maisie wasn't sure whether to be embarrassed or annoyed. "Can I get you some water maybe?"

John didn't reply but turned and walked unsteadily toward the front entrance. Hesitating only long enough to proffer his cloakroom ticket and grab his hat from the attendant, John disappeared out of the door.

What the hell had that been about? He might not have been much of a dancer, and he certainly wasn't much of a gentleman either, but even so.

Maisie glanced around to see if anyone else had noticed her untimely abandonment, but everyone seemed to be paying attention only to their dance partners or to the friends they were gossiping with.

Luckily for Maisie, that had been the final number, and as soon as it ended, everyone clapped and the band began to pack up for the night. All the dancers made their way back to their tables, with much laughing and promises of more dances next time, and gradually they all crowded out the stained-glass front doors and into the mild evening.

Out on the street, however, it was clear that what had happened hadn't gone unnoticed by the other lumberjills after all, and Maisie found herself subjected to an inquisition from Dot and Mary. All the way back to the waiting truck, they demanded details.

"What did he do to you?"

"Nothing."

"Then, what did you do to him?"

"I don't know."

"Did he step on your foot?"

"No."

"Did you tread on *his* foot?"

"I don't know."

"Was he really as bad a dancer as it looked?"

"I don't know! Actually, yes. Yes, he really was. Simply terrible," Maisie said sadly, which caused much merriment for her friends.

"Talk about having two left feet!" chuckled Dot.

"You certainly pulled the short straw," added Mary. "Such a shame—he was good-looking too."

Even as they teased her, simply knowing that her friends were as indignant as she was that her partner had walked away like that made Maisie feel a little better.

On the drive home to the lodge, Dot and Mary delightedly shared with the other recruits the story of Maisie, the American, and their disastrous dance. At first, it was quite funny, even to Maisie, but as more and more of the women joined in, offering ever more hilarious comments at John Lindsay's expense, Maisie found herself becoming defensive. He didn't deserve this treatment. He'd been nice enough before they'd started dancing, even funny, and he was handsome, and until he had walked out on her, he'd been scrupulously polite and had shown such concern about her hands. It was only when they started dancing that he became . . . odd. Even so, he didn't deserve ridicule from people who hadn't even seen what had happened.

"Stop it!" she burst out. "Stop saying things like that."

After a moment's silence, somebody started a teasing "woo-hoo," and soon everyone was joining in, making jokes about Maisie having found herself an eligible bachelor at last, Maisie being in love, Maisie and John sitting in a tree.

Maisie put her head down and tried to ignore them. She knew they were only having fun, still riding their own wave of excitement from the dance, but still, she could do without a second, no, a *third* bout of humiliation in one night.

Only Dot, sitting next to Maisie, was not joining in the ribaldry and teasing. She nudged Maisie and laid her head on Maisie's shoulder, as the other women's conversation moved on to discuss their own dance partners instead of Maisie's.

"It's all right," Dot said so only Maisie could hear. "If he was thoughtless enough to walk away from a lovely girl like you, then it was his loss, not yours."

Maisie nodded, but couldn't force any words in reply past the knot that was tightening in her throat. Why had she let herself start to think that perhaps he might like her? And she might like him back?

But Dot was right. Walking away from her had been his loss.

Three

Maisie awoke with a start. A drum! Some blighter was beating a bloody drum inside their hut, and on the morning after a late night too!

The usual routine of being woken up at dawn by Old Crabby's incessant whistle blowing from outside the dormitory was bad enough, but being dragged from deep sleep after a dance by an apparent crash of drums from *inside* the hut was a hundred times worse.

And now there was shouting too.

"Come on, ladies of Hut C, up you get! Sooner you're up, the sooner it's over."

Maisie was still trying to cling to the last threads of a dream about dancing in the strong arms of a dark-haired man.

"What time is it, for goodness' sake?" Dot croaked from the next bed over, and Maisie's dream dancing was done.

"No idea," replied Maisie, lifting her head blearily from the pillow and squinting toward the far end of the hut, where she saw Phyllis Cartwright, the tallest, strongest, and most athletic of all the WTC recruits, striding along, banging on the end of each bedstead with a stick. So, no drums, after all, just Phyllis with a bloody thunderstorm on a stick. "But whatever time it is, Phyllis has clearly taken leave of her senses."

"We've all had enough of these aches and pains," Phyllis bellowed, "so from now on, we'll start each day with some calisthenic exercises to warm up the muscles and get us all ready to work."

Maisie dropped back onto her pillow with a loud groan. "But why today? We didn't get to bed until after midnight."

"None of that now, Maisie." Phyllis was standing over her now. "This was your idea, after all."

The groaning spread quickly around the room.

"My idea?" Maisie protested. "I didn't ask for this."

"Yes, you did, Maisie. Yesterday, you said to me how everyone was still aching, and how hard Dorothy here was finding the physical work each day because of her weak muscle tone."

"You said I was weak?" Dot glared at Maisie. "I'm *not* weak."

"No, of course I didn't say you were weak," Maisie said quickly, "I only said that you'd never done this kind of intensive physical activity before, you know, because you didn't play sports at school. That's what you told me the other day, that your school didn't even have hockey or tennis or anything."

"No, I didn't have much *tennis* during my childhood," replied Dot, and Maisie caught a very un-Dot-like bitterness in her voice. "But that doesn't mean that I'm—"

"Dot! Honestly, I didn't tell anyone that you're weak. This is just Phyllis—"

"This is just Phyllis doing her job," Phyllis interrupted, striding off around the room again, banging on any bed with an occupant still buried under the blankets. "I'm making sure you are all given the chance to develop your strength now, so that you won't struggle with the heavier stuff later, once you are out in a real camp, taking down real trees. I'm a fully trained physical fitness instructor, remember—five years teaching at Morrison's Academy in Crieff, then another six at the Edinburgh Ladies' College—so don't go thinking I'm only a pretty face."

Phyllis gave one of her wide rumbling belly laughs, and most of the women in the hut joined in. Phyllis's face would never be described as pretty—handsome, yes, even striking, but not pretty—but that was something she seemed quite proud of.

Phyllis's enthusiasm was infectious, because despite the early hour, soon everyone from Hut C was standing in uneven ranks on the wide expanse of driveway outside Shandford Lodge, stretching and jumping, bending and running on the spot.

Women from some of the other huts must have been disturbed by the rumpus, because they appeared up the hill in ones and twos to see what was going on, and some even joined in.

Finally, after half an hour that felt to Maisie like a week, Phyllis took pity on them and released them to get breakfast.

To Phyllis's credit, the atmosphere in the dining hall was far livelier and more engaged than it had been any morning so far. The women were chatting and laughing, and some were singing along to music from the wireless in the corner. Again, Maisie realized that the exercise, like the dancing, had warmed her muscles to the point where she wasn't even feeling the aches and strains that had been her constant companion since training began. Now, if she could just work out where to find some pig fat for her hands . . .

Just then Old Crabby appeared at the door, interrupting the merriment, her very presence demanding silence. She held up a wide, flat basket, tipping it forward for everyone to see.

"Postcards!" she shouted in a voice more suited to an army drill square than a dining hall. "If any of you want to do your family duty, may I remind you that recruits' mail will be picked up and taken to the post promptly every Saturday morning at nine o'clock. So if you want to write a postcard home, do it *now*, ladies. They're already stamped, which will cost you tuppence."

She slammed the box down onto the nearest table and picked up an old tobacco tin with a slot cut in the lid. "Honesty box is here for the tuppences. Of course, if you are literate enough to write a proper *letter* home, you can come now to my office. Letter stamps are tuppence ha'penny."

As Miss Cradditch turned smartly and left the room, there was a scramble of hands trying to grab one of the postcards and a stubby little pencil from the basket, and a tinkle of coins dropping into the tin. Several women got up and followed Old Crabby out of the door, each holding at least two or three thick envelopes.

Maisie stared at the basket, wondering if today was the day she should write a postcard home to her parents. She'd sent no word back since she'd walked out of the front door of the home she'd lived in for all seventeen years of her life, her father's hurtful words still ringing around the tiled hallway. She wasn't even sure they would know which part of Scotland she was doing her training in. All the letters from the WTC had been addressed to her by name, and since her parents had been so furious with her for signing up, they'd refused even to look at the information she had been sent. It was only at the last minute, as Maisie was standing in the front hall with her suitcase, that her mother had softened, if only marginally. She'd come out of the kitchen holding a brown paper bag, which she held out to Maisie.

"Here's a sandwich for the journey. It's only fish paste, but that's all there is. And I've given you an apple and your ration of cheese for this week. You can get a cup of tea at the station."

Maisie had taken the bag with a tight-throated thank-you and had stepped forward in the hope that her mother might embrace her, but her mother stayed where she was.

"Will you at least walk me to the bus stop?" Maisie had asked.

"The fact that you've chosen to leave home before you've even finished your schooling"—her mother hit the well-worn track without hesitation—"suggests you have no desire to spend any more time with us than you must."

"Mother, please let's not do this again." Maisie had tried not to sigh. "I'd like it very much if you'd all walk with me to the bus stop. Thank you."

Maisie's sister, Beth, had been the only one who had seemed in the slightest bit excited for Maisie. Perhaps she was already envisaging her own escape from their parents—she was almost sixteen, after all. As if to prove her support, Beth had already had her shoes on and had been grabbing her coat from the hall stand.

"Shall I get your coat too, Mother?" Beth had asked.

Father's voice from the dining room had not been loud, but it had been crystal clear. "Your mother will not be needing her coat. And neither will you, Elizabeth."

"But, Dad," Beth had begun, "what if there's rain?"

"Put. The coats. Away." Maisie's father's tone had been unmistakable, a command that was to be followed without question. But as she always did, Beth had pushed back.

"But surely—"

"Elizabeth! Your sister has decided she is mature enough to ignore the wishes of her parents and sign herself up for some ridiculous venture with women who clearly have no more sense than she does. She must therefore be mature enough to get herself there alone, so put the coats away, and go help your mother in the kitchen."

Suddenly he had been at the dining room door, and without even glancing in Maisie's direction, he'd stalked past his daughters and his wife to his study door. There he'd stopped, his fingers on the brass knob.

"I will not repeat myself again, Elizabeth. Your sister can see herself out. *You* have breakfast dishes to wash."

So Maisie had walked to the bus stop alone, and she had not written home since.

Maisie sighed as she looked at the basket of cards. She knew she ought to send something, at least to Beth. It hadn't been Beth's fault their parents had reacted so badly, but even so, that morning might have been the first time in years that quarrelsome and complaining Beth had ever supported Maisie in an argument. With two and a half years separating the girls, arguments had been routine, and it was usually Beth who started them.

No, Maisie did not even want to write to Beth.

Now feeling grumpy, Maisie picked up the plates and cups in front of her and Dot, and cleared them onto the pile of dirty dishes stacked on the serving counter. Dot's nose was still buried in a book, as it was most mornings over breakfast, and all the other women around her were scribbling on their cards. Dot didn't ever send mail home either, Maisie had noticed, though the one time she'd mentioned it, Dot had evaded her question and quickly changed the subject. Since

Maisie had no desire to share details of the misery of her own home life either, she'd let the matter drop.

A sharp stab of pain and a spurt of warm pus across her palm made Maisie realize that she'd been distractedly digging her thumbnail into one of the large blisters on her left hand. Hoping no one else had noticed, she dabbed at her palm with the corner of her handkerchief. She ought to wash her hands, but she was sure that the harsh carbolic soap was partly to blame for her blisters since it dried out her skin, which was already in trouble from its first exposure to an outdoor life. So if she wanted to avoid washing her hands so much, what she needed was . . .

Maisie changed course and sidled a little nervously toward the kitchen. Old Crabby had made it clear on the first day that Mrs. McRobbie's culinary domain was not to be entered without invitation. Mrs. McRobbie was the cook for Shandford Lodge, and was married to the old woodsman, Mr. McRobbie, who had been their primary instructor for all the ax and saw cuts, and also for tool care. He also had an encyclopedic mind when it came to all things flora and fauna in the woods around the lodge, something that Maisie had already found useful when faced with a patch of stinging nettles or if one needed to know, as Helen had the week before, whether the snake wrapping itself around one's boot was a venomous adder or a benign grass snake. Although Mr. McRobbie tried to be gruff and miserable with them, no one was convinced by the act. His wife's reputation, however, was truly fearsome, and so Maisie knocked gingerly on the doorframe before her toes had even crossed the kitchen threshold.

"Mrs. McRobbie?" she called tentatively.

There was a rustling and shuffling from beyond the pantry door, and the cook appeared, her tiny frame dwarfed by the enormous sack of flour she was carrying.

"Oh, here, let me help," said Maisie as she dashed forward and wrestled the sack out of Mrs. McRobbie's arms. "Where shall I put it for you?"

The cook pointed over to the far counter and Maisie laid the flour down. Hoping this favor might make Mrs. McRobbie more open to a request of help, Maisie quickly asked her question. "Do you have any spare pig fat I could have?"

The older woman gazed at her for a moment. "Pig fat?" she replied. "You mean lard?"

"Oh, well, if lard is pig fat, then yes, lard. Please, if you have some to spare. I have money."

"Show me," said Mrs. McRobbie, putting out her hand.

Maisie dug her sore hand gingerly into her pocket to find some coins, uncertain of how much pig fat might cost.

"Not your money, girl! Show me your hands."

Maisie could see now that the cook wasn't asking for payment but was holding out her hand, palm up, as John Lindsay had done. Self-consciously, Maisie laid her own hand on top as Mrs. McRobbie leaned forward, clicking her tongue and shaking her head.

"You're in a wee bit of a mess there, aren't you? But I'm sure I can find you some lard, if that's what you think'll work."

"That's what I was told would work," Maisie said,

following the cook into the pantry, "by one of the American chaps we met at the dance last night. He said I should mix it with some Vaseline and smear it on the blisters."

"An American, was it?" said the cook, as she drew back a white muslin cloth and cut into the large oblong of white fat it covered. "I didn't know that there were any Americans around here. Were they not the Canadians?"

"Canadians?"

Mrs. McRobbie had retrieved a crumpled sheet of brown paper and was folding it around the white block. "Aye, there's a whole bunch of Canadian lumberjacks up the road a piece, working on the old laird's estate, clearing it for another army camp, from what I heard."

"Oh, I'm not sure," Maisie said, "maybe."

She remembered that Mary had said that they were Americans, but had John said that himself? Perhaps not. And then it occurred to Maisie that she hadn't even bothered to press him further on what he'd been doing to get blisters that matched hers, or about where he was from. In fact, she hadn't asked him anything about himself at all. Her mother would not be pleased if she knew that, because according to her, a lady should always use the eighty–twenty rule when talking to a gentleman.

"Men like to talk only about themselves," Mother had said. "Therefore, a lady must ensure that eighty percent of the conversation should be by him or about him, and she should only ever talk about herself as an answer to his direct question, making sure to turn the conversation back the other way as quickly as possible."

Maisie had snickered with Beth through this lecture, but now, remembering that all that she and John had talked about was her wish to dance and her hands, she was left to wonder if that was why John had abandoned her.

Damn! She hated to think her mother might be right.

Mrs. McRobbie was watching her, and Maisie realized she was waiting for an answer to some question that Maisie hadn't even heard.

"Sorry?"

"I asked if the chap holding your hands at the dance was handsome." The old woman's eyes were sparkling with amusement. "You know, the Canadian."

"He wasn't Canadian, I don't think. And he wasn't at all handsome." Maisie tried hard not to blush under the cook's scrutiny. "Well, yes, he was quite handsome, but he wasn't holding my hands, other than to dance, obviously, since you have to hold hands to dance, but he wasn't *holding* them, not like *that*."

"Like what, dear?"

"Like *that*, like *you* mean, I mean," Maisie could feel herself getting flustered.

Mrs. McRobbie's smile spread wider. "Oh well, there's time yet."

As if realizing that Maisie was becoming anxious, the cook suddenly shoved the block of lard into Maisie's hand. "Off you go now—the others will be waiting for you, I'm sure."

"Oh, right. Yes. Thank you." Maisie waved the lard in the

air, and as she turned back toward the dining room, Mrs. McRobbie chuckled again.

"And best not put that on your hands just before you pick up an ax, dear. I don't want Mr. McRobbie being decapitated. He's to fix the tiles on our roof before the end of the summer, and he'll need a head for that."

Maisie smiled as she went back to the dining room. So much for the fearsome Mrs. McRobbie.

Dot, Phyllis, Mary, and Anna had already left the dining room by the time Maisie caught up with them.

"We wondered where you'd gone," said Dot. "Come on, back to the axes. According to Phyllis, Mr. McRobbie thinks we can move on to snedding tomorrow if we conquer chopping today."

"Lucky us!" said Mary.

As they passed the office, several girls were still waiting to get stamps for their letters. Beside them, on the table by the office door, was the basket of postcards, enticingly blank, other than the scarlet stamp bearing King George's head in the top right corner.

Maisie hesitated. Even if she put her money into the honesty box and took a postcard, it didn't mean she had to send it. Not today, anyway. She could keep it to send for Beth's birthday perhaps. Or even for Christmas. She didn't have to send it right now.

But then, why waste tuppence on it now if she wasn't going to send it till later? That made no sense.

Then it came to her. She would make a deal with herself. If she had exactly the coins to pay for the stamp, she'd get the postcard. If she didn't, she'd walk away.

Digging her hand into her trouser pocket, Maisie pulled out the small collection of coins and counted them off with one finger. Two shillings, five ha'pennies, and three farthings.

"Damn!"

She did have the right change to make two pennies exactly. With a resigned sigh, she slid four ha'pennies into the honesty box and picked up one of the cards, waggling it in her fingers for a minute or two before stuffing it into her back pocket.

No, she would not send the postcard today, but at least she knew she had it, just in case.

Four

Later that morning, Maisie and the others followed Mr. McRobbie for their final chopping lesson through the paths of the estate to where the old woods butted up to a wide stretch of pine plantation. Here the trees stood like soldiers on a parade ground, set at regular intervals, in rows and columns, each about five yards away from its neighbor. Maisie was pleased to see that here there was almost no underbrush or scrubby grass below the trees to get in the way of her ax, only a carpet of fragrant brown needles.

On Mr. McRobbie's order, the lumberjills all lined up along the first row of sturdy trees, one girl to each trunk, and set to work to chop it down. Although she was gradually figuring it out, chopping hadn't turned out to be as easy as Maisie had expected. But it was early days, she kept telling herself, because by the end of the course, she would know how to chop and saw, how to fell a tree, how to clear all the small branches off it—that was snedding—and also how to roll the logs using their cant hooks, and then haul the timber away with hooks and chains. They were also learning the uses for the different woods, and how to cut to a specific measurement. The trees the girls were chopping today were Scots pine, so they would probably end up sawn to short lengths as pit props for coal mines, or perhaps as fence posts, with the wastage going for charcoal. But for any of that to happen, the lumberjills had to get the trees down first.

"Don't swing so wildly, lassie!" Maisie heard Mr. McRobbie shout at someone farther down the line. "You've to let it sing. Hear the music in your head, and let it flow through your arm and into your blade. I told you that yesterday. Have you still not found yourself a chopping song yet?"

Maisie was relieved Mr. McRobbie had started at the other end of the line, because she hadn't found her chopping song yet either. Mr. McRobbie had been telling the girls for days now to find a song with good rhythm that helped them to time their ax swings. But Maisie was struggling to come up with a tune that worked. Nearby, Lillian had clearly found hers. She was humming a short musical phrase over and over as she lifted her ax away from the tree, *one*, raised it high on *two*, rounded it over above her shoulder on *three*, and brought it slicing down into the wood on *four*. Perfection, exactly like Mr. McRobbie had shown them last week. The motion was smooth and controlled, and Lillian's tree trunk was growing narrower at the waist with every cut.

"That's it, lass, you're doing a grand job," said Mr. McRobbie as he spotted Lillian's easy action. "Now get those cuts down as close to the ground as you can, so we don't waste that bottom foot of wood, not while there's a war on."

He stepped back a little and raised his voice to address the whole group.

"So, there's a bunch of Canadians"—Maisie stopped to listen, ax above her head—"working up the road right now, and do you know how they've been cutting down the trees over there?" Mr. McRobbie glared around him. "At knee height! And even, some of them I saw, at waist height. I couldn't believe how much they were wasting, so I went to have a wee word with them and I put a stop to it."

Canadians. Up the road. Not Americans then.

Lillian began to hum and swing again, and Maisie groaned in frustration. When he'd demonstrated what he meant by a chopping song, Mr. McRobbie had sung an off-tune "Auld Lang Syne" as he'd swung again and again in rhythm to the music, but when Maisie had tried the same tune, it didn't fit her action at all.

"Find some music that means something to you," he'd exclaimed passionately to the assembled recruits, "a song that flows from your breath to your ax, to your blade, to the tree." The old man had looked like he could have started to dance with his ax, right there, and a few of the girls had mocked him quietly from behind.

And yet, his strange method seemed to work. Each day

more and more recruits were swinging and chopping like professionals, and now the clearing was a cacophony of harmony and counterpoint, half-hummed dance tunes from Anna and Mary, and a medley of fully sung operatic arias from Phyllis. Everyone seemed to be singing except for Dot and Maisie.

As Maisie wondered about borrowing a tune from Phyllis, a thought popped into her head.

What song would John Lindsay hum as he was swinging his ax? Suddenly a tune came into her mind. It was the one she and John had danced to, albeit briefly and disastrously, last night, and it had been playing on the wireless in the dining room this morning too. What was it called? She could hear the tune quite clearly now, though she couldn't recall all the words.

Keep smiling through, just like you always do,
Something *blue skies* something something *far away.*

It was one of Vera Lynn's songs, she was sure. . . . "We'll Meet Again," that was it!

Before the music escaped her mind, Maisie lifted her ax and weighed it in her hands for a second or two. Then, as she began to sing the opening words of the song under her breath—"*We'll meet again, don't know where, don't know when*"—she hefted the ax away, curved it up and around behind her head, and brought it down sharp into the bark of the log.

Amazingly, it did the trick, and the blade cut cleanly

through the bark. She kept singing quietly to herself, and although her movements were not exactly effortless, they were certainly more synchronized, as if she and the ax were suddenly one effective machine, not two engines pulling against each other.

Maisie let out a cry of delight as the ax bit sliced cleanly again into the flesh of the tree.

"You've found it at last, have you?" Mr. McRobbie laughed as he approached, though he stayed a safe distance from Maisie's swing arc. "I knew you'd get it soon enough. And what about you, Miss Thompson?"

A grunt of effort, a thick slap of metal hitting wood, and a groan of frustration came from behind Maisie, as Dot failed yet again to make even so much as a dent in her tree.

"Well, lass, you maybe haven't found quite the right song yet," said Mr. McRobbie as he walked away. "But keep on trying."

"Grrrrrrr!"

Dot was holding her ax handle as if she wanted to throttle the life out of it.

"Did you just growl at your ax?" Maisie snorted.

"It's so bloody frustrating!" Dot cried. "How am I the only one who can't do this?"

"Oh, come on, you're not that bad."

Dot pointed at Maisie's log, and then held out her hand to her own, the surface of which could best be described as a little scuffed.

Dot suddenly lifted her ax up high over her head—not

the way they'd been taught at all—and brought it down hard on the tree in fury. The impact ripped the handle from Dot's grasp, spinning it straight at Maisie, who hopped to the side just in time. The ax buried itself in the ground close to where Maisie had been standing.

"Be careful!" she cried, but seeing Dot's torn face, she felt more sympathy than anger. "Remember to treat your ax 'as if it were your first-born bairnie, with love and with care.'" Maisie was mimicking their instructor's strong Angus accent so well that Dot eventually gave a wry smile.

"Sorry, Maisie. But I'm serious. I'm so rubbish at this, they're going to send me home."

"Oh, nonsense. They will not. We've got plenty of training yet before we get posted to a camp to do this for real, which is more than enough time to sort you out." Maisie put an arm around Dot's shoulders. "Anyway, you and I have our first lesson this afternoon, and I'm sure you'll be much better at that than me."

"Well, I'll have to be," replied Dot, "or you'll be looking for another friend by the end of the month."

Driving, however, proved just as elusive to Dot as swinging an ax. That afternoon, Maisie found herself pitched violently around in the back of an old Morris car as Dot did her best to coax it along. But just as Dot got it going, the engine's roar spluttered and died into judgmental silence. Dot smacked her hand onto the steering wheel and muttered "damn it" under her breath over and over.

Mr. Taylor had come up from his garage in Brechin to teach the recruits, two by two. He sat next to Dot with his hands on his knees, arms braced, as if he expected the car to take off again. Then he slowly exhaled, making his bushy black mustache flutter.

"Perhaps your pal should do the drive back, eh?"

Dot slumped forward in despair. "Why can't I get anything right?"

"It's fine, Dot, really." Maisie reached forward to lay her hand onto Dot's back. "Driving's a complicated thing to learn. I'm sure Mr. Taylor took ages to learn to drive too, didn't you, Mr. Taylor?"

The instructor turned to stare at Maisie with indignation, but eventually said, "Aye, well, maybe not quite as many problems, but I suppose it took a wee while."

Maisie flashed him a grateful smile. "See? So don't be down. It's really not easy, you know."

"But *you* took to it like the proverbial duck!" exclaimed Dot. "You only stalled the engine twice, and you certainly didn't almost put us in a ditch like I did."

"You didn't put us in a ditch, Dot—"

"*Almost* in a ditch, I said,"

"No, not even *almost* in a ditch." Maisie was trying not to smile. "We were still a good three feet from the actual ditch. Well, perhaps two feet. All right, we were six inches away. . . ."

There was a peculiar snuffling noise and Maisie realized that Mr. Taylor was chuckling, and though she didn't want to hurt Dot's feelings, it was hard not to join in. But then Dot began to giggle as she clambered out and opened the back door for Maisie.

"Get in the front then, Flash," Dot said, as she and Maisie swapped places, "and show me how it's done."

Maisie settled herself into the driver's seat and grasped the steering wheel again, careful not to bump her blisters. Thinking hard about everything Mr. Taylor had told her, about the steering and gear changes, she started the engine and moved the car forward. Thankfully it didn't stall, but after twenty yards, the engine began to whine and Mr. Taylor tapped his knuckle against the gear stick. "Come on, lassie, you can't stay in first gear all the way."

"Oh, right, yes, sorry," said Maisie, pushing down on the clutch and wrestling the gear stick into second as the car continued up the lane toward the lodge, and then into third.

"That's it, lassie, you've got it now," said Mr. Taylor, "which makes one of you anyway."

"I'm not sure I've really 'got it,'" said Maisie with a proud smile, "but with a little more practice, I might. Will we see you again tomorrow?"

"No, that's your instruction finished," said Mr. Taylor. "Miss Cradditch says you've got a lot to learn in a short time, so this is all you'll get from me."

Maisie braked a little too hard and the car slammed to a halt in front of the lodge. "But we've only had one afternoon's instruction. And on a car, not a truck."

"If you can drive a car, you can drive a truck," he said. "It's all just a matter of scale, after all."

"Scale?" Maisie could not believe what she was hearing. "A three-ton Bedford truck is not the same size as this car."

Mr. Taylor gave another mustache-ruffling sigh. "As I said, it's just a matter of scale. Now, don't you fret, lass. It's clear that you're smart and strong, and if you concentrate, you'll do just fine."

Smart and strong? Those were two words she'd seldom ever heard used about her. Quite the opposite. For years, her father had been telling her she was weak willed, lazy, and stupid. And her mother always said that while Maisie was handsome enough—"handsome" was Mother's word for Maisie; "pretty" was reserved for Beth—she'd have to shed some weight before she got too much older, if she wanted to marry. *That* was Maisie in her parents' eyes, lazy and fat, certainly not smart or strong.

Maisie turned and offered Mr. Taylor her hand.

"Thank you," she said, "I mean, for today's lesson. I enjoyed it, though I'm not sure if I could ever do it—"

"I told you, you'll do fine," he replied, taking her hand in his meaty fist. Then he leaned closer and whispered, "But perhaps your friend ought to take the train or the bus instead."

He gave Maisie a conspiratorial nudge and pulled a watch from his pocket. "I'd best be off. Mrs. Taylor will have my tea on the table at five o'clock sharp, and if I'm late, she'll feed it to the dog."

"If we get no more driving lessons," moaned Maisie as she and Dot walked back to the hut, "I won't have a clue how to do that again in a week's time, let alone four weeks, when we get sent out to our new postings."

"Well, as long as you remember enough by this Friday, you'll be able to drive me to the station when they send me home," Dot replied, misery clouding her usually bright voice.

Maisie nudged Dot's elbow. "Come on, mopey. We've got first aid training on Monday, which'll be interesting, won't it?"

Dot looked unconvinced. "I fainted when we dissected a frog in school," she groaned. "First sight of the blood, and I—" She mimed toppling over in a dead faint.

Maisie laughed.

"I'm serious," Dot said. "I might as well pack my bags right now."

"But first aid's not all about mopping up blood," countered Maisie, "or even bandages and slings. It's helping people, and that's what you're best at, after all."

Which was true. On their first day at Shandford Lodge, Dot had offered to help Maisie make up her bed with the stiff white sheets and thin gray blankets issued to them. By the time they had folded the corners in tight and smooth, and had helped some of the others too, Maisie already liked Dot very much. Dot had a genuine desire to get along with other people, though Maisie couldn't quite work out why such a shy and slight girl would have volunteered for this very physical lumberjill life.

"I suppose," replied Dot. "Just don't send me any injured frogs!"

The following week, even before the end of their first aid training, Maisie could see that Dot was a gifted first-aider. The visiting tutor, a retired nurse from Dundee, recommended that Dot do additional training so she'd be fully certified. Since every camp was required to have someone with a first aid certificate, Dot was thrilled. It meant that not only would she stay a lumberjill, she'd also earn an extra shilling a week in her pay packet once she was out in the field.

Maisie was delighted for her friend too, and had to smile when she overheard Dot reassuring one of the other more squeamish recruits over breakfast the next day.

"Oh, don't worry. First aid is more about helping people than it is about mopping up blood. I'm sure you'll be absolutely fine."

And suddenly it was the sixth and final week of training. This time next week, Maisie wouldn't be a recruit, and she wouldn't be at Shandford Lodge. She'd be a real lumberjill, working in a real camp, at last. The one thing, however, that dulled her excitement was knowing that she might be there alone. There was no guarantee that anyone from this group would be sent to the same place as Maisie, let alone a close friend like Dot, and they wouldn't find out where they were all going until the postings were announced on Friday, the day before they all departed.

Maisie tried not to think about it, and hoped that the coming week's sawmill training would distract her from the uncertainty of what was coming next.

On Monday morning as they trekked to Mitchell's Saw-mill in Tannadice, there had been nice breeze, but once they'd arrived it was clear that the cool air was certainly not finding its way inside the mill shed, even when the huge shed doors were propped open. It was hot, and it was loud.

Maisie stood with the others around an enormous bench saw and strained to hear the barked instructions from Betty Harp, who said proudly that she had been one of the very first WTC recruits, and would now teach them all her six months' worth of sawmill wisdom.

"There are four rules you *must* follow in any sawmill," Betty shouted. "*One*. No smoking. Cigarettes and sawdust are a bad combination."

Everyone nodded.

"*Two*. No hair. Your hair *must* be tied back at all times. You do not want this little beauty"—she slapped her hand down inches away from the vicious whirling vertical blade of the saw—"to be your next hairdresser.

"*Three*. Gloves. Please wear your leather gloves at all times. But be careful—gloves can give you a false sense of security around these blades, and even thick leather is no competition for spinning steel, so you still need to be careful. And remember, you'll never get to enjoy a manicure again if you have no fingers."

Maisie winced and immediately pulled her work gloves out of her pockets.

"And *four*. Communication. By that, I don't mean chatter and gossiping. In this mill, you are responsible not only for your own safety, but for the safety of all your team. If you tell them exactly what you are about to do *before* you do it, you'll all stay safe. Got it?"

The girls all nodded their agreement and followed Betty to the first machine.

Over the next two hours, Maisie watched Betty closely as she taught the group to adjust and feed big tree trunks into the big table and routing saws, and showed them how to use the edger, the jointer, and the plane. After a tea break, they were split into pairs, and Maisie worked alongside Helen at one station, then another, until they reached the routing saw. They both stood baffled for several minutes, until Betty came and gave them instructions again.

Just as Helen finally managed to get the engine turning over, though, a sharp scream rose above the din, and then another. Maisie shouted to Helen to shut off the saw again, waiting only until the blade started slowing before she ran to see what had happened. The others were already grouped around the big headsaw, and even from the back, Maisie could hear Dot's voice above all the others.

"Catherine! Press down hard on this, would you? Harder! Someone give me a belt. I need a tourniquet on her arm. And a cloth, I need another cloth. No, something cleaner than that. Your shirt'll do. Come on, give me your shirt, we need to get it wrapped quickly."

Maisie peered over the crowd. Lillian was lying flat on her back on the sawdust-covered floor, groaning and panting, her face ashen, her eyes squeezed tight shut. Dot crouched at her side, wrapping a bundle of green cloth around Lillian's hand—Catherine's blouse by the look of it—and as Maisie watched, the fabric slowly darkened as blood seeped through.

Betty shoved through the crowd, carrying a metal box painted with a red cross. Throwing open the lid, she grabbed a large paper packet and thrust it at Dot.

"Thanks, Betty," said Dot, her voice strong and decisive, "but I can't let up the pressure yet. Can you tighten the tourniquet around her upper arm to limit the blood flow first? And then carefully open that packet, but try not to touch the gauze as you hand it to me. I need to get the cut wrapped so it's kept clean. I'm sure they'll be able to stitch it up, but if the gash gets infected, then . . . well, let's just keep it clean, all right?"

Lillian whimpered at Dot's words, and Maisie tried to push past the people in front so she could give her some comfort. But Anna had already dropped to her knees and was laying her hand gently onto Lillian's forehead while she whispered soft words of reassurance.

Maisie glanced up at the saw table behind Dot, where the circular saw sat innocently still. Its guilt was clear, however, from its red-smeared teeth. A few inches away, a tan leather work glove lay abandoned, empty fingers curled as if in supplication. It was just like the ones Maisie had on, except that this glove's palm had been torn wide open—no, not torn, *sliced*. The cut across the smooth brown leather ran very neatly in a straight line from the bottom of the index finger to the heel. Its gaping edges were sharp, and were marred by dark-red staining of the pale leather all along their length. Someone beside her gagged, and Maisie realized that Lillian's glove had been no match for the cold steel of the headsaw, exactly as Betty had warned.

Within thirty seconds, the tourniquet belt was tight and Dot was wrapping the injured hand in its fourth layer of bandage. And then the truck was there by the open door of the mill shed, and Phyllis, Mairi, Helen, and Maisie were lifting Lillian onto the flatbed at the back while Dot kept applying pressure on both the well-wrapped hand and the pulse point on Lillian's wrist. As they laid her down, Maisie tried to reassure Lillian that everything would be fine, but the words felt hollow. After all, what did Maisie know about these things?

Once Lillian was settled, with her head lying in Anna's lap and with Dot still at her side, the truck pulled away. As she watched it go, Maisie heard someone say, "Well, still waters run deep, don't they? Who'd have thought mousy little Dorothy would step up and take over like that?"

"Just as well she did," another voice replied. "I was close to fainting at all that blood."

Maisie felt a rush of pride knowing she wasn't the only one who'd noticed the transformation in Dot. She'd looked so confident and in charge, and Maisie knew that Dot had finally found her place as a lumberjill. But what about poor sweet Lillian? If the cut was as bad as it looked to Maisie, perhaps Lillian's days in the Timber Corps had just come to a sudden and sorry end.

Five

The next morning, Betty Harp brought them news of Lillian, who was apparently doing well. She had been transferred from the cottage hospital in Brechin to the much larger Dundee Royal Infirmary, where surgeons had operated on her hand overnight. Betty praised Dot's quick thinking and determination, and told the group that because Dot had kept pressure on Lillian's hand all through the journey to the hospital, the doctors were hopeful that Lillian would not lose the use of her fingers, though only time would tell.

Once the lumberjills had applauded this good news, Betty repeated her lecture about safety in the mill, about wearing their gloves at all times—"Lillian might have cut her hand, but she's kept her fingers because she was wearing her gloves"—and about doing exactly what they were damn well told.

Once the lecture was over, all the girls gathered around Dot, patting her on the back and congratulating her. Dot tried to say it was nothing, that anyone else would have done the same, but Maisie could see that under the pink flush, Dot was thrilled.

And all through the rest of the week Dot was like a new person; rescuing Lillian had provided her the confidence to take on any number of tasks. And there were so many new things still to learn in the sawmill that even Maisie felt rather overwhelmed.

By Friday afternoon—the end not only of their sawmill training but of their Timber Corps training too—everyone was sick and tired of the work, as well as the stifling heat in the shed.

The unusually high temperature rather spoiled what should have been an exciting day. They had come to the end of their training at last, even if they were now looking at unknown futures. In fact, the weather was so unbelievably hot for September that at knocking-off time there were no cheers at all. Everyone just drifted wearily toward the track up to Shandford Lodge, wiping the dust and sweat off their faces and necks with scarves and handkerchiefs, not even bothering to congratulate each other for finishing the grueling training.

"Ladies!" Phyllis shouted from behind them, bringing them all to a stop. She was standing by the same Bedford truck that had carried Lillian to the hospital days before. "To mark this auspicious day, the end of our lumberjill training, we will be taking a little detour to do something we should have done days ago. Come on, up you get, and we'll be on our way."

With that, Phyllis pulled herself up into the driver's seat and beeped the horn twice as the ignition roared.

Maisie looked around for the truck's usual driver, a man named Eddie, but there was no sign of him. She clambered aboard the flatbed anyway, sitting down just as the truck lurched off toward the main road.

For the first time in hours—days even—Maisie felt cool, fresh air ruffle her sweaty hair and blouse. Was this what Phyllis had planned? A refreshing breeze for the trip home? But then Phyllis drove past their usual turnoff, and they were almost to Forfar before she suddenly swung the truck off the road and down a rutted dirt track. Maisie grunted involuntarily as she was thrown around with the other girls, bouncing on the hard truck floor every time Phyllis hit a bump. Fortunately, Phyllis soon slammed on the brakes, cut the engine, and jumped down from the cab.

"Follow me!" she cried, and was over a gate and off down a footpath beside a recently harvested field before anyone could ask her where they were going. Soon, Maisie was picking her way with Dot and the other lumberjills along the side of the barley stubble toward a wooded area at the far side of the field.

Maisie had long since given up trying to guess where they were being led when she heard excited cries followed by a splash. As she and Dot came through the thick curtain of young larches, an expanse of dark-blue water extended away from them. The sun dappled silver onto the surface, and ripples extended out across the long and slender loch. Suddenly, a naked Phyllis rose up from the surface, spraying water around her, and Maisie found herself clapping and laughing with delight.

"Come on in, everyone!" Phyllis cried through the sheet of water pouring over her face. "It's glorious!" Then she turned away and, bending double, gave a neat surface dive back into the water, a move that brought her bare buttocks up to the surface for a split second before they vanished again, followed by her legs, with a neat scissors kick of her feet.

Catherine, Mairi, and Mary clearly needed no second invitation, because they were already tearing off their sweat-soaked uniforms and charging over the soft grass into the water. The older women, Cynthia, Anna, and Helen, were a little more genteel, folding their uniforms neatly on top of their boots before tiptoeing down to the edge and easing themselves into the water with gasps and giggles.

"This is fantastic!" Maisie cried to Dot, as she tried to undo both bootlaces at the same time. "Why did no one think of doing this before?"

One boot came off, then the other, and Maisie was undoing the buttons on her blouse when she realized that Dot was still standing, fully dressed, staring at the women in the water, who were all splashing each other and laughing like children.

"Come on, Dot," said Maisie, "let's get in there quick. We're all so hot, I reckon we'll set the loch to boil like a kettle." Maisie was down to her underwear when Dot turned away from her, gazing instead into the trees behind them.

"Don't be embarrassed." Maisie lowered her voice a little. "It's only us girls."

Still Dot didn't move.

"Can't you swim?" Maisie asked gently.

"No, it's not that."

"If you can't swim, don't worry, it doesn't look deep. At least come in as far as your waist, so you'll get cool. I'll stay beside you, in case."

"It's not that I can't swim." Dot was now fingering the top button of her blouse. "It's . . . well, I don't have a swimsuit."

Maisie almost laughed, but stopped herself in time when she saw Dot wasn't joking, and it struck Maisie that she had never seen Dot get dressed or undressed in front of anyone else. Maisie, like all the others, got her uniform or her pajamas on beside her bed, without really thinking who else was around, but Dot never did. In fact, Maisie couldn't work out where Dot did dress—under the blankets, or in the ablutions block behind the dormitory huts? Wherever, she was always dressed ahead of everyone else.

"Well, neither do they," she said kindly, indicating the girls already swimming. "And neither do I."

"I know, but . . ."

Maisie was torn. She desperately wanted to swim, but Dot looked so upset. Either way, she was standing on a loch shore in nothing but her underwear, so she really ought to decide—

That was it!

"We can swim in our bra and knickers then." Maisie suggested. "It's so warm today, they'll dry out again in no time."

Dot glanced back at the cool water of the loch, and a faint smile began to break through the worry.

"I know I'm being ridiculous, but—"

"You're not being ridiculous, but you are wasting valuable swimming time. So come on, get those boots off!"

A minute later, Maisie grabbed Dot's hand and led her to where the soft mud at the water's edge cooled their feet even before the chilly water could make them gasp as it wrapped around their ankles, then their knees. There was a chorus of catcalls from the other women as Maisie took a deep breath and plunged into the water.

It felt wonderful, as if the water was sloughing off every bit of dirt and sweat that had caked her skin over the last few weeks, cleansing her in a way that no five inches of tepid bathwater ever could.

From somewhere a bar of soap had appeared—a very ladylike pale lilac soap that smelled wonderfully of lavender— and eventually, it was passed to Catherine, who then passed it to Maisie. For months now, the only soap they'd been able to get with their ration books was carbolic, harsh, bright pink, and sold in utilitarian blocks. So being able to rub this soft and silky, sweet-smelling lather over her skin and into her hair was sheer luxury, even if there was mud oozing between her toes, and pond weed—at least she hoped it was pond weed—grabbing at her ankles.

Tempting though it was to linger with the soap, Maisie

offered the bar to Mary, who was chatting nearby to Dot and Mairi. Dot, Maisie noticed, was looking relaxed now, but was also making sure everything below her shoulders stayed under the water.

Mary took the soap, sniffed it, and pulled a comically disgusted face. "What a choice to make," she said. "I can stay stinking like a sweaty cesspit, or I can use this soap and smell like my granny instead."

"Well, I thought it smelled lovely," said Maisie as she eased herself back under the water again, moving her head from side to side to clear the soap from her hair.

As Maisie surfaced again, she saw that Phyllis and Helen were now standing on the grass beside their clothes. Helen was squeezing the water from her long brown braid as Phyllis rubbed her short hair into a messy crown with her undershirt. Although Maisie wouldn't have hesitated to strip off to swim if it hadn't been for Dot, she was still struck by Phyllis's and Helen's complete lack of embarrassment. Neither seemed to find it the slightest bit unusual to be standing naked in the open air, whereas Maisie knew that she would soon be rushing to get her clothes on as quickly as possible. Even though her belt was these days pulled two notches tighter than when she'd first arrived at Shandford Lodge, proving how much flatter her belly had become from all the physical work, Maisie was still self-conscious about her size. Hadn't her parents been telling her she was fat—or "hefty," to use her father's expression—all her life? Perhaps Phyllis and Helen were lucky enough to have kinder, more sensitive parents.

Just then, something caught Maisie's eye from the trees beyond where Phyllis and Helen stood. A face peeked out, then another, and then a third. Maisie distinctly heard giggling and realized that they were being watched by three young boys of perhaps eleven or twelve.

Instinctively, Maisie ducked down into the water until her shoulders were covered, and called to Mary and Mairi, who were already wading out of the loch. "Girls, wait!" She pointed her finger toward the peeping toms in the trees.

There was a squeak from behind her, as Dot saw too, and within a second, Mary and Mairi were back under the water.

"Phyllis!" Mary called, her hand cupping her mouth, "Phyllis! We have visitors!"

Phyllis looked at Mary, and then at the boys Mary was pointing to. Helen grabbed her uniform and held it up in front of herself, apparently discovering her embarrassment at last. But Phyllis simply glanced back toward the women in the water with a wide grin.

The boys didn't seem to notice they'd been spotted until Phyllis was already heading toward them. One of them let out a shriek and ducked behind his tree. The others followed suit, but none of them reappeared from the other side to run away.

"Come out, come out, wherever you are!" called Phyllis in a singsong voice, and Maisie had to laugh. She'd bet these boys had never played a game of hide-and-seek quite like this one. "If you're so interested in female anatomy, lads, you might as well come and have a really good look while you have the chance."

There was the sound of a skirmish, and suddenly a boy was shoved out from behind the tree and held there by his friends as he tried desperately to fight his way back into cover. This boy was older than Maisie'd first thought, more like thirteen, though she guessed he had yet to hit the true growth spurt that came with puberty. Right now, however, he looked like a young deer caught in the beam of a ghillie's flashlight, quivering yet hypnotized.

"So, what's your name then, young man?" Phyllis asked in her best schoolmistress voice, as if she weren't standing stark naked in front of a boy young enough to be one of her pupils.

He swallowed before he croaked, "Davey," but when Phyllis placed her hands on her hips in what would have been a stern gesture in other circumstances, he corrected himself. "I mean, David Matheson, Miss . . . erm . . . Mrs. . . . ."

Phyllis nodded at him, the motion of which sent her breasts swinging, something that Davey seemed to find quite hypnotic. "You may call me Miss Cartwright. And now, young David, will you introduce me to your friends too?"

Davey continued to stare at Phyllis's chest but vaguely beckoned to his friends with one hand, in the manner of someone half-asleep. Five seconds of noisy shuffling later, the two other lads appeared. This pair, however, had no courage to look at the naked woman; they kept their eyes studiously on their boots. Glancing at them, Davey followed their example and dropped his gaze too.

"Poor little sods," chuckled Mary from where she was mostly submerged next to Maisie.

"This experience could scar them for life," replied Mairi.

"I think it's scarring *me* for life," joined in Dot, and they all laughed, sending out ripples around them. The movement of the water against Maisie's shoulders made her shiver, the delicious relief of cool water on her skin now turning into shivering cold, as goose bumps broke out on any skin that was still exposed to the afternoon breeze. She really wanted to get out of the water now, but there was no way she would stand up with those boys there.

"So, is it polite to spy on other people?" Phyllis was saying in a clear voice.

All three boys shook their heads solemnly without lifting their eyes.

"Then perhaps it's about time you got off home. I'm sure your mothers will be very keen to hear what you've been up to this afternoon."

Davey nudged his elbow against his friend, who did the same to the third boy, and all three of them shuffled sideways toward the tree.

"I'm sorry, boys, I didn't quite hear what you said there," Phyllis sounded very stern.

"Thank you, miss. Sorry, miss. Good-bye, miss," mumbled the boys as they moved.

"That's better," said Phyllis, as she shooed them away with one hand. "And good-bye to you too."

Sensing that they had been released, all three boys suddenly pelted behind the trees, reappearing three seconds later as they dashed toward the thicker bushes beyond. Maisie heard one of them let out a triumphant whoop, which was followed by a succession of cheers and yells, the boys clearly delighting in their narrow escape from the spitting venom of a naked Medusa.

Hearing the exultant cries, Phyllis put her head back and guffawed. "I don't think they'll be back anytime soon, do you?" she crowed.

"No, but their big brothers will be," called Mary.

"And their dads," added Mairi.

With relief, Maisie and the other girls left the water and pulled their clothes over their soaking bodies. Maisie wasn't about to let the presence of the boys disrupt her pleasant afternoon.

Walking back to where the truck was parked, Maisie tugged at the back of her trouser leg, pulling the fabric off her damp skin. With soaking underwear under dry clothes, it wasn't going to be the most comfortable ride home, but the swim had been worth it.

"Thank you for not laughing at me," Dot said suddenly.

"Why would I have laughed at you?" Maisie replied.

"You know, with the swimsuit thing. It's only that, well, I'm not used to being so open and uninhibited. I'm not very good around other women, I suppose."

"But that's nonsense—you've made loads of friends here."

"No, Maisie, *you've* made loads of friends, and they all let me tag along because they like you so much."

"That's not true, and you know—"

Dot put her hand on Maisie's arm. "I'm serious. I've got

four big brothers, and their favorite sport is to make my life miserable. My whole life they've been shoving me, and stealing my things, and tearing my clothes, and so I spent my time at home trying to be invisible. But then they started picking on anyone I tried to be friends with. It took a while, but in the end, no one at school or in our street dared talk to me because of what my brothers would do to them."

Maisie felt heartsick for her friend. "Why didn't you tell me all this before?"

Dot shrugged. "It's not something I'm all that proud of."

"But didn't your mother—"

"She died when I was little. I don't remember her much."

"Oh, I'm so sorry." Maisie felt a sudden wave of shame, never having considered herself lucky to have her mother and sister. They had always just been there.

Maisie and Dot were almost at the truck now, and everyone else was already clambering on board.

"I always wanted to be one of those pretty girls," Dot continued, "like Anna and Lillian. Or outgoing, like Phyllis, or someone who makes friends so easily, like you. But that was impossible. My brothers saw to that."

"But didn't your dad stop them?"

Dot slowed her steps. "My dad," she said quietly, "well, my dad's not a very nice man."

Maisie almost replied that her dad wasn't a very nice man either, but Dot's lowered eyes and stillness told her that her own family problems could not compare, so she said nothing.

"I've never really had a best friend before I met you,

Maisie, or any friend actually. And before coming here, I'd never really been around any women either, so I was terrified on the journey here."

"But if the idea of being with a large group of women scared you so much," Maisie asked, "then why would you join what is basically a large group of women?"

Dot looked at Maisie for several seconds, seeming to consider her answer very carefully.

"Because," she said eventually, "the idea of staying at home with a large group of men was worse."

Maisie reached for her friend's hand and squeezed it tight. "You're the best friend I could have hoped to find, Dot. I couldn't have survived the last few weeks without you."

Maisie was about to add how much she was dreading the postings being announced later that evening, in case she got separated from Dot, but why make it even worse? Even the thought of it made her nervous, so instead, she reached to put her arms around Dot.

Dot immediately shied away. "Best friend or not," she cried with a sudden grin, "you are not hugging me while you smell as bad as Mary's granny!"

Six

And then, training was over. The morning of the final day, the huts had been cleared, cleaned, and inspected before breakfast. Chores finished, Maisie stood with her suitcase, alongside all the other lumberjills, in front of the lodge waiting for the trucks to arrive to take them to their new camps. Maisie was looking forward to her next adventure, but was sorry to be losing so many new friends almost as soon as she'd found them.

When the postings had been announced last night, there had been squeals of delight as some close friends learned that they would move on together, but there had been tears too.

Miss Cradditch had read down the list of recruits alphabetically, each name immediately followed by one of the WTC camps around Scotland. Helen and Phyllis had learned almost immediately that they had been posted together somewhere in Perthshire, then Mary, Mairi, and Cynthia had found out that they would all be at the Advie camp, near Grantown-on-Spey. Maisie had grown anxious as Old Crabby reached the names beginning with *M*.

"McCall, Margaret," Old Crabby had shouted, and Maisie's stomach had lurched. "Auchterblair, Speyside."

Maisie had been sure she hadn't yet heard Auchterblair called out after anyone else's name, but if the camp was in Speyside, she would be close to Mary, Mairi, and Cynthia, even though they wouldn't all be at the same camp. But then, as Old Crabby had continued down the list, and no one else was assigned to Auchterblair, Maisie had grown uneasy. She didn't want to go somewhere by herself.

Finally, Old Crabby had reached the last name on the list.

"Thompson, Dorothy."

Dot had raised her hand. Maisie hadn't been able to breathe.

"Auchterblair, Speyside," Old Crabby had shouted, and a huge weight had lifted from Maisie's heart. She and Dot were moving together to Auchterblair, wherever that was. Scary though it was to leave Shandford Lodge, at least she'd have Dot at her side. Then she and Dot had hugged each other, and all the other girls had joined in too, everyone laughing and crying at the same time.

How ironic, Maisie thought as the first Bedford rolled up the drive, that she had shed more tears last night about leaving her new friends from Shandford Lodge than she had when she'd left her family in Glasgow.

The trucks, it turned out, were not only arriving to pick up, they were also dropping off. Down clambered a new set of fresh-faced lumberjills-to-be, all soft, silent, and clearly terrified. Watching the new arrivals, Maisie could see how much she had changed from the new recruit of six weeks ago. Not only was she slimmer and fitter now, more tanned and muscular, Maisie knew she was different inside too. She wasn't scared anymore to handle an ax or saw, or to drive a car—actually, she was still a little scared of the car—and she'd swum almost naked in a loch and had had her first dance with a man. She felt older, and wiser, and best of all, she had friends now, good friends, and these women loved and respected her. They treated her not as a child, but as an equal.

And that felt right. Maisie was not the spoiled child who had walked down Sutherland Avenue without a backward glance six weeks earlier. She was Maisie McCall of the Women's Timber Corps. She was a fully trained lumberjill, ready to go out into the forests to work—and to work bloody hard—to help her country win the war.

But suddenly, Maisie wished that her parents could see her now, and Beth too. They would be proud of her. Surely.

Maisie felt a surprisingly strong twinge of . . . something. Homesickness, or guilt? What if something happened to her? Or to her parents, or Beth?

Old Crabby interrupted her thoughts by calling for everyone going to Speyside, the camps at Ballater, Grantown-on-Spey, and Auchterblair, to board the truck on the far side, which was leaving shortly. Everyone else was to board the two nearer trucks to be taken down to the train station.

But as the other girls began picking up their luggage, Maisie quickly crouched down and clicked open her suitcase. Rummaging, she found the postcard she'd bought a month earlier. Even though it had been tucked inside a book, it was still crumpled and torn at one corner. But it would have to do.

Her only pencil was the thick-leaded one that she used to mark measurements on the cut timber, but that too would have to do. On one side of the bent card, Maisie wrote her mother's name and their home address, and then on the other side:

Completed WTC training. From today, Sat Sept 12, will be stationed at WTC Auchterblair Camp, Carrbridge, Inverness-shire.

Maisie

Entrusting her suitcase to Dot, Maisie ran over to where Old Crabby stood on the lodge steps and held out the postcard.

"Would you mind posting this for me, Miss Cradditch?"

Old Crabby grunted something as she took the card. Then she grunted again when Maisie grabbed it back and scrawled additional words.

Sending love to you and Li—

She had started to write "Lilibet," the sweet nickname for Beth that they'd borrowed from Princess Elizabeth, but writing that felt too . . . well, Maisie wasn't in the mood to be quite so nice to her family yet.

She wrote instead, "Sending love to you and Beth," handed over the card, and sprinted for the truck.

It wasn't comfortable, bouncing around on the hard seats in the back of the Bedford, listening to the engine whine and the gears grind as the driver urged the vehicle higher and higher into the Cairngorm Mountains, and Shandford Lodge was soon far behind them. They passed through pretty villages like Laurencekirk and Aboyne, and eventually reached Ballater, where they dropped off half of the lumberjill load, including Catherine and Anna, who tumbled out with hugs and promises to write.

It was certainly beautiful countryside, the road looping over steep and majestic hills, and through wide swathes of treeless wilderness. Soon, though, a thick fog rolled over the road, blocking the view.

They stopped for the driver to have a smoke, and so they could disappear behind a gorse bush to have a pee. As they climbed aboard again, the driver told them that it wasn't so much fog as a low cloud on a high road, which crested hill after hill as it rose and fell. Either way, they spent the next part of the journey peering into a thick curtain of mist. The air grew colder, and Maisie was glad to have her heavy WTC-issue coat. She'd been sitting on it to cushion the bumps, but since a bruised bum was preferable to frostbite, she now wrapped the coat tightly around herself, and Dot did the same with hers, as they huddled together on the bench. Had they really swum in a loch only yesterday? Maisie shivered at the thought.

The truck gradually wove down from the mountains, to where the countryside was flatter, warmer, and sunnier, with the road passing through dense woodland shade at times, and at others giving them glances of the sparkling River Spey. They dropped Mairi, Mary, and Cynthia at Advie, near Grantown-on-Spey, which left only Maisie and Dot in the back, and at last, they reached Carrbridge and Maisie felt a rush of excitement. In a matter of minutes, she would be a real lumberjill in a real forest camp, and her real life would begin.

Beyond the last stone house in the village, there was a hand-painted sign pointing to a track going off to the right, which said simply NOFU. Maisie would have thought no more about it but for the appearance of two men walking out from that track and onto the main road, talking animatedly and paying no attention to the three-ton truck hurtling toward them.

The quick-thinking driver threw the wheel, and the Bedford lurched, missing the men, but slamming Dot and Maisie hard against each other. The driver swore loudly, and Maisie heard shouts from behind. She looked back, expecting to see raised fists and angry faces, but instead, the two men were waving enthusiastically and shouting something at the truck. Before Maisie could stop her, Dot was waving back.

"Dot, don't!" Maisie grabbed her friend's hand.

"Why not? They were only being friendly." Dot retrieved her hand from under Maisie's and started waving again. "See?"

Maisie looked back as one of the men—the darker-haired of the two—lifted one hand in the air, flourishing a lit cigarette, and bent low in a deep, if slightly unsteady, Jacobean bow.

Neither girl could suppress their laughter at this ridiculous gesture, even as they were again bumped together when the driver negotiated a tight turn up another track between high hedges. Back on the road, the blond man shoved against his still-bowing friend, knocking him off-balance, though somehow the dark-haired man managed not to fall. As they disappeared from view behind a hedge, the two of them were wrestling like little boys after school, apparently having already forgotten about the girls in the truck.

Something dawned on Maisie then. She *knew* the dark-haired man with the broad smile and the deep bow. She'd seen him before, she was sure. After the swerve, the men were already some distance away, so she hadn't gotten a close look at his face. But his dark hair and his lopsided gait as he walked were triggering something in her mind. And that smile was somehow so familiar.

As they pulled up in front of two large log huts, set at

right angles to each other with other smaller huts beyond, the puzzle piece slipped into place. The man looked exactly like the American chap—or had he been Canadian?—who had danced with her a few weeks ago in Brechin, the awful dancer, the one who had left her in the lurch. But what were the chances of it being him? And if it was, what the hell was he doing here?

The driver killed the engine, and Maisie and Dot clambered down, stretching their aching muscles and looking around for any sign of life.

Maisie dismissed the idea that she knew the man. It couldn't be the same chap—that would be ridiculous. They were hours away from where she'd met him and the coincidence would be too great.

But what had that chap's name been again? James, or Jack? Maisie tried to tell herself she couldn't quite remember, all the while knowing that was a lie.

She knew his name. It had been John. John Lindsay.

Just then, a girl appeared, coming at a trot around the corner of the farthest hut. She looked to be only a year or two older than Dot, and she was tall, with a wide smile and a healthy tan, her brown hair loosely plaited into two thick braids. She was wearing WTC overalls, but also a brown leather jerkin, sleeveless and with wide pockets, out of which were hanging several leather straps.

Pulling the straps out of her pocket, she smiled and waved at them as she approached.

"Hello, everyone!" she called as if to a crowd, instead of

only three people, and Maisie could now see that what she held was a horse's bridle. "Come on, let's find you somewhere to dump your things. You all look exhausted, and I bet none of you would refuse a cup of tea. No sugar, I'm afraid. We haven't had any for a couple of weeks now."

She picked up Dot's suitcase and made for the hut on the left. "But we did get some honey on the sly from Mr. Macallan at the farm this morning, and that's almost as good, isn't it?"

She turned and grinned over her shoulder, clearly delighted to have found a way around the strict sugar-rationing rules. Dot followed along, apparently so mesmerized by the girl, she didn't even object to the girl carrying her bag.

At the door of the hut, the girl turned, seeing only then that the driver had followed too.

"Sorry, love!" she said to him cheerfully. "You can't come in here, since it's our dormitory hut, but if you go into the mess hut through that door there, I'll get this pair settled and come over to get a brew on. Is that all right?"

The driver nodded, and as he walked in the direction she had pointed, he pulled cigarettes and matches from his pocket and lit up.

Turning back, the girl said, "As I said, this hut is where we sleep, that one there is the mess hut and kitchen, and then at the back is the lavatory and shower block, or the Blue Lagoon, as we like to call it around here."

Maisie and Dot laughed at that and the girl looked delighted.

"Oh, almost forgot! My name's Nancy, and today, I'm your Auchterblair welcoming committee. On any normal day, though, I look after the horses." She waggled the bridle at them. "Actually, only one horse now, since we lost Elsie."

"Lost her?" cried Dot. "Oh no! How did she die?"

"Oh, no, she didn't die. No, we lost her to the camp at Grantown. But we've still got Clyde. You'll meet him in the morning, sweet old chap." Nancy pulled open the door. "Clyde's a big handsome Clydesdale—he'll pull anything that's too big to haul by hand, especially useful up on the hills, when the trucks can't always get close."

Maisie felt her mouth dry and her throat tighten. Why did it have to be a Clydesdale and not a donkey? The memory of her encounter with the rag-and-bone man's massive beast, Charlie, was making her pulse race.

But no, she was not a child anymore. She was a lumber-jill now, and she could handle being beside a horse without bursting into tears.

At least, she hoped she could.

"Do you two like horses then?" Nancy said as she waved them inside.

"Actually," Maisie said as she passed Nancy, "I'm not much of a horsewoman. I'd rather stick to my ax and saw."

"Please don't tell me you're scared of an old horse?" A strident voice came from the far end of the hut. "How silly!"

Looking around the gloomy room, Maisie saw a dozen or so neatly made beds lined up on either side, iron headboards against the walls. Two small windows let in only a little of the bright sunshine from outside. In the far corner, in the low light from a paraffin lamp, a woman was sitting in an upright chair at a table, shuffling several pieces of paper into a pile in front of her. As Maisie watched, the woman brought a rubber stamp down with two emphatic thumps—once on an inkpad and once on the top sheet of paper—and thrust the papers into a large envelope, winding the little string around the button with perfectly manicured fingernails to close it up. She was exquisitely made up, with perfect lipstick and primped blond hair neatly rolled, suggesting that she might not spend as much time with an ax and saw as Maisie and Dot had been. Maisie tucked her own cracked and crusty hands into her pockets and wondered what she should say in response.

Before she could decide, the woman stood up and consulted a typewritten sheet on a green metal clipboard before approaching Maisie and Dot.

"So, you're my new recruits, are you?" she drawled, reaching out a hand, giving Maisie no option but to shake it, blisters or not. Closer up, Maisie could see that the woman was probably only in her midtwenties. "My name is Violet Dunlavy, and I'm the WTC officer in charge around here. So as long as you girls do exactly what is expected of you, we'll all get along nicely. Isn't that right, Nancy?"

Nancy was now leaning against the doorjamb, and Maisie got the distinct impression that she was trying not to roll her eyes.

"That's right, Violet," Nancy replied, her friendly tone

sounding only a little forced, "we're all one happy family here." She walked up to the other end of the dormitory and set Dot's suitcase next to a pile of linen at the foot of a bare bed.

After a moment, Violet continued, her cut-glass accent betraying barely a hint of Scots. "And you must be, um . . ." She ran a long nail down her paper.

"That's Maisie McCall," said Dot, peering at the list on the clipboard. "And I'm Dot, I mean, Dorothy Thompson."

"Yes, here you are. Margaret and Dorothy." Violet noticed what Dot was looking at and snapped the clipboard tight to her chest. "Well, your timing is perfect, because I'm filling out the work schedule for the coming week. Generally, we all pitch in together at Auchterblair. Some of us are specialists, like me as the team leader; then we have Agnes in the kitchen, and you've met Nancy, who sleeps in the stables," Violet chuckled as she waved her pencil vaguely in Nancy's direction. "I'm only joking about that, *obviously*, though sometimes I think she would, if I let her. You rather enjoy spending your life ankle-deep in muck, don't you, Nancy?"

"At least it's honest muck," Nancy replied tartly as she disappeared through the door.

"Each to his own, I suppose," muttered Violet as she began to scribble on her paper. After a moment, she looked up again, giving them a beatific, but not quite believable, smile. "Get acquainted with everyone this evening, and you'll start work at dawn tomorrow. I'll post the schedule shortly, but bear in mind that it's for this week only, since next Monday, we'll be joining the noh-foo chaps for something big."

"Noh-foo?" asked Maisie. "What's that?"

"Noh-foo. N. O. F. U." Violet spelled it out with a sigh, and Maisie recalled the painted sign she had seen down on the road. "Canadian lumberjacks. They've a camp toward Carrbridge, and they call themselves the Newfoundland Overseas Forestry Unit. But that's such a bloody mouthful. Noh-Foo's so much easier."

"And do they—" began Maisie.

"Please!" snapped Violet. "You must stop interrupting me so I can inform you of your duties."

Maisie did as she was told, though not willingly, as Violet pulled her fallen smile back onto her face and turned to Dot. "This week, Dorothy—"

"You can call me Dot if you—"

"This week, Dorothy," Violet said, clearly determined to ignore Dot, "you will be helping Agnes, our cook. Breakfast preparation begins at four a.m., so don't be late. And you, Margaret—"

"It's Maisie, actually."

"You, *Margaret*, will be—"

This woman's manner was already riling Maisie, and seeing Dot shrink back from her sharp tone was more than Maisie would put up with.

"Violet," Maisie said, being overly polite, "I think you might have misunderstood. Please call me Maisie, and please call her Dot." Maisie couldn't remember ever being so assertive before, but she knew she could not let this snooty woman win even such a petty argument. "Thank you so much."

Violet stared at Maisie for a moment, her nose lifted as if to avoid a bad smell. "As you wish," she said eventually, then cleared her throat as if what she was about to say would choke her. "*Dot*, you'll be in the kitchen, as I said, and *Maisie*, you will be with Nancy in the stables. You'll only stay with them this week, just until you can follow the camp routine. Then you'll be out working with all the other girls in the woods. And Maisie, I do not want to see you wearing anything but your WTC uniform. Nancy is already on a daily warning about that hideous leather ensemble of hers, so please do not think you can copy her."

Maisie cringed. She certainly did not like Violet. Not only was Violet being rude to them, she had assigned Maisie to work in the stables even after Maisie had said she was uncomfortable around horses. Well, she could always ask for a change.

"Violet, about the stable duty, would it be possible for me to switch—"

Maisie's earlier assertiveness dried up under Violet's glare, as if she were trying to decide if Maisie was daring to be insolent yet again.

"Stables first, trees later. That's what it says on my schedule," Violet trilled, her voice tight and brittle. "And at Auchterblair, we *never* argue with the official schedule."

"But you only just wrote the—"

Violet dismissed Maisie's comment with a wave of her hand, and then pointed her clipboard toward the bed where Dot's case lay. "Pick any of the empty beds down there, and get yourselves unpacked. The rest of the girls will be back in about an hour or so, and dinner will be served at six on the dot."

She immediately looked at Dot and let out a loud, horsey laugh. "On the *dot*! And you're *Dot*! How funny! Oh, you know, I can be quite hilarious sometimes."

Violet tucked her clipboard and the fat envelope under her arm and looked at them, her face stern again. "By the way, HQ would not be happy to know that there was any *fraternizing* going on between a lumberjill and a NOFU chap. And neither would I." She frowned for a second longer, then her face brightened and she let out another horsey bray. "Especially if you were trying to fraternize with the particularly handsome chap with the dreamy brown eyes. Consider yourselves warned, ladies—he's mine!"

With a strangely tinkling giggle at her own hilarity, Violet disappeared out of the door, leaving Maisie and Dot to stare at each other before bursting out laughing.

"Well, she's not quite what I was expecting to find in a shabby wooden hut on the side of a hill." Maisie said. "Perhaps all the Swiss finishing schools are closed for the duration. I'm sure she's very efficient, but does she really have to be such a cow?"

"She's as bossy as Phyllis," replied Dot, "but without any of the charm."

"And if we're lucky, without the calisthenics too."

Maisie followed Dot down the room to the black metal bedstead with the bare blue-ticking mattress where Nancy had dropped Dot's suitcase. Beside it stood a wooden night-stand and small metal locker, also bare. Maisie glanced around, looking for another empty bed, but the nearest one was on the other side of the hut, two beds down. For a moment, Maisie was tempted to find Nancy or Violet to ask if there was any way that someone would swap, so that she and Dot could have beds side by side, as they had done from their first night in Hut C. But realizing that sounded child-ish, as if she were afraid of the dark, she carried her own case over to the other bed and lifted the pile of linen—two off-white sheets, one rather flat pillow, and the thinnest blanket that she had yet seen—onto the rough wooden nightstand.

Around the room, all the other pieces of furniture sported random selections of photographs of family and of movie stars, as well as fashion pages cut from magazines. Some col-orful quilts and blankets hung over the ends of beds, and for a second, Maisie wished that she had brought from home the lovely patchwork quilt that Mother had made for her shortly before Beth was born. But carrying a quilt on the train to Brechin in midsummer would have been ridiculous, so it was still on her bed at home, or at least it should have been, assuming Beth hadn't stolen it the second Maisie walked out of the door. Beth loved the quilt as much as Maisie did. They'd cuddled under it for years, telling each other stories on cold nights. At least, they had until Beth had turned into a whiny pain in the neck when Maisie was about thirteen.

Suddenly the yearning for Mother's quilt, and for Beth's silly stories, overwhelmed Maisie. She had felt so strong and so grown-up this morning, but now, the thought of the soft padded quilt, with shiny silk ribbons around its edge, made her want to crawl into bed—even *this* rickety bed—and pull her quilt up over her head.

But Nancy appeared through the door, and Maisie's fleeting homesickness vanished.

"Has she finished with you then? And you've both found a bed? Good. Your driver's already guzzling down his second cup of tea, so you'd best come quick or he'll have drunk the whole pot."

Seven

It turned out that despite Violet's haughty demeanor, Nancy and the other women of Auchterblair were great fun to be with, and Maisie soon wondered why she'd been so worried about arriving at a new camp knowing no one. Of course, she was thankful to have Dot there with her, but it felt good to know that if she ever had to move camp again, she'd probably fit right into life there, too, without much worry.

However, she still didn't like Violet, and had also decided to avoid Violet's two cronies, Evelyn and Claire. That wasn't difficult, though, since the three of them would rather have dyed their hair purple than spent time in the stables, and Violet had clearly arranged the schedule to make sure they never had to.

Maisie, on the other hand, had found that she was happy to help Nancy in the stables, mucking out, changing straw, mending and polishing the tack, and even brushing down the huge Clydesdale's hide.

And Clyde the Clydesdale was vast.

"He's bloody enormous!" she'd declared nervously when she'd entered the stables on her first Monday at camp.

"Gosh, I'd never noticed that," Nancy had laughed, clapping Clyde's shoulder. "But you don't need to worry—he's a big baby really. By the weekend, he'll be eating out of your hand. Literally."

Remembering her awful horse bite of years before, Maisie was not convinced, but sure enough, with Nancy's guidance, she soon felt confident enough to let Clyde nibble carrots and apples from her palm. Nancy also showed Maisie how to lead Clyde by the reins—though he mostly led Maisie—up the hill to where the other girls were working on an area of larch forest. Since larch trees were so tall and straight, and the wood so durable, they were mostly used for telegraph poles, so once the lumberjills had cut a trunk to the right length with the cross-saw, they used Clyde to drag the eighteen-foot log to the collection point for the large trucks to pick up. As Maisie became confident in attaching Clyde's harness and chain to each trunk, she was sure that she and the huge horse were already developing an understanding, or even a friendship.

It had been nice to get to know Nancy this week too. She loved pointing out interesting things about the trees, plants, and animals around them as they worked, all things that would have passed Maisie by otherwise.

Sitting under the stable lean-to on Saturday afternoon, polishing the mud off the harnesses, Maisie asked Nancy to tell her more about her life growing up on the Floors Castle estate, where her grandfather was head groom for the Duke of Roxburghe.

"But why on earth would you want to leave a real-life fairy-tale castle?" asked Maisie, only half joking.

"Fairy-tale castle? Hardly!" Nancy replied, "I'd always loved helping Grandpa with the horses, but as I grew older, the estate became quite . . . claustrophobic. So, when I heard the Timber Corps needed girls who could handle workhorses like Clyde, I signed up straightaway."

"And will you tell me about your leather jerkin?" Maisie reached forward and rubbed the soft, supple leather between her fingers. "Not exactly standard issue."

Nancy seemed quite pleased that Maisie had asked about it.

"It was my grandpa's, actually. He wore this jacket most of his adult life. But when I told him I was leaving, he gave it to me. It's far too big, of course, but he said that if I was going to work with horses like he did, I should wear his jerkin. He's such an amazing horseman, I suppose it's become a talisman for me. If I'm wearing it, Grandpa's looking after me."

"That's lovely," Maisie replied, just as a whistle blew. Three short bursts, the camp signal to call everyone to the yard in front of the huts. As Nancy and Maisie hurried to clear away the harnesses, Violet could be clearly heard shouting for people to "come along quickly, please. The post is here!"

Maisie heard Nancy muttering something under her breath. Maisie didn't understand quite what Nancy had against Violet, nor what Violet had against Nancy, for that matter. Of course, Violet hadn't been very kind to Maisie or Dot, either. While not being outwardly nasty, Violet had spent their first week making very certain that the newcomers knew their place in the group, and that was clearly, in Violet's opinion, on the lowest rung. And she also made it clear that she believed Nancy sat barely any higher.

"You don't like Violet very much, do you?" Maisie asked Nancy.

"No, I can't abide the woman," Nancy huffed in reply, now not even trying to disguise her contempt.

"But why ever not?" Maisie asked sweetly. "She's such an inspirational leader to us all."

Nancy spun to face Maisie in surprise, but seeing Maisie's grin, she started to smile too. Then she shrugged. "I don't like being told what to do, or who to be. My grandad had no choice but to take orders from the Duke, and even from the Duke's children—all privileged brats like Violet over there—and I saw how it wore him down, having to bow and scrape to those people.

"So, I swore that I'd never do the same. I want to run my own life, even my own business, one day. And I can't bear that all Violet does is issue orders. She's so full of herself, and she can be downright nasty too. Seriously, Maisie, watch out for that one. She'll turn vicious if she thinks you've got something she wants."

By the time they joined Dot and the others, Violet had already turned the distribution of letters and parcels into a major performance. She was standing in front of the group, a pile of letters under one arm and at her feet three parcels wrapped up with brown paper and string. She was making a great show of checking each envelope and proclaiming the name of the recipient.

"Susan Henderson!" Violet waved an envelope above her head, as if it were a Union Jack at a royal procession. "Come on, Susan, we haven't got all day."

A short, stocky woman in her late twenties, known to all as Wee Susan, trotted over and took the letter from Violet.

"Susan Johnson, two for you. Big Susan! Pay attention, and come and take these! And Rose Macarthur, just the one!"

Big Susan—who was actually shorter than Maisie and was only considered to be "Big Susan" in relation to "Wee Susan," who was positively tiny—stepped forward and took the three letters from Violet, passing one of them down to Rose, who was poking with a stick at the pile of ashes at the center of the cold campfire ring. Neither woman, Maisie noticed, opened the envelopes in front of the others. Instead, they continued to watch Violet.

Maisie hadn't received any letters in all the weeks she'd been away from home. How could she have? No one cared where she was enough to write. But even so, she found her anticipation building as Violet worked her way through the letters.

"Margaret McCall!" Violet declared, and Maisie startled. A letter for her?

"Who?" asked someone from the far side of the group. "We don't have any Margaret, do we?"

"That's me." Maisie stepped forward shyly.

"Two for you," said Violet, holding out an envelope and a picture postcard. When Maisie tried to take them, however, instead of handing them straight over, Violet held on a moment too long, meaning that Maisie almost had to yank them out of her fingers.

"Thanks," said Maisie. As she turned away, she glanced at the postcard first. It was a photograph of a neat little railway station. Below the picture was printed "Blair Atholl, Perthshire." Maisie flipped the card over. On the other side was a boldly scripted note from Phyllis.

Maisie,
Struan is heaven. Camp not far from pub.
Billet has chickens & a real bath!
Sending love to you, Dot, and the Highlands!
Come see us soon. Helen sends hugs, as do I,
Phyllis xxx

Maisie smiled to herself as she turned over the other envelope, expecting it to be from either Beth or their mother. She was not prepared for the surge of disappointment and irritation when she saw it was instead her father's elegantly looping cursive.

"Pardon? I didn't quite hear what you said, Margaret" Violet was saying, "I mean, Maisie." Violet snorted, as if Maisie's chosen name was some sort of joke.

Maisie turned and looked again at Violet, her irritation doubling. What was Violet's problem? Well, whatever it was, Maisie couldn't be bothered with it.

"I said 'Thank you,' Violet," she snapped, "and I know you heard me. Or would you like me to curtsy too?"

Barely registering Violet's indignant response, or the laughter from the other women, Maisie strode into the hut, kicking the door shut behind her.

A letter from her father. Even though she'd addressed the postcard to her mother, she should have known that her father would demand to read it too. But she hadn't expected him to write back to her himself. He could sulk for weeks about anything he perceived as a slight or as disrespectful, so receiving a letter from him within a week of sending home details of her new posting was unnerving.

Maisie sat on her bed, which squeaked under her, and regarded the envelope. Perhaps she needn't open it at all. She could stuff it into her locker and pretend it had never arrived. But what if something was wrong at home? What if something had happened to Beth or to Mother? Perhaps that was why Dad was writing to her instead of one of them? Maisie steadied herself, tore open the top, and pulled out a single sheet of paper.

39 Sutherland Avenue
Glasgow
17ᵗʰ September 1942

Dear Margaret,

"Dear Margaret"? Why not "Dear Maisie"? Maisie was the name he had always called her, in spite of her mother's pleas not to. They had originally christened her Margaret after his mother, even though she was a harridan who had made no secret of the fact that she didn't approve of her only son marrying a girl fourteen years younger than himself, a girl far more beautiful that she herself had ever been. And then the old bat had died, leaving her only son with none of the extensive inheritance he had been anticipating, but instead a moldy old house and a box full of debt notices. After that, *he* had insisted that they shorten it to Maisie. According to Aunt Jenny, Maisie's mother's younger sister, who delighted in sharing gossipy stories that Maisie would never have heard from her own parents, Maisie's mother had tried to suggest that Maggie might be a prettier shortening, or even Meg. But her father had been adamant that it must sound as little like the name borne by "that miserable old witch" as possible.

And so she had been Maisie ever since, although her mother had almost always continued to call her Margaret, especially out of her husband's earshot. Beth still used the infantile nickname *Piggly*, though now only because she knew it annoyed Maisie. But to her father, she was only ever Maisie. Until now.

Dear Margaret,

Your mother was relieved when you finally deigned to let her know where you are, albeit in a scrappy two-line postcard. I, however, expected little more from a girl who would so willfully abandon her home and family, to say nothing of the significant financial investment made by me in her upbringing and her schooling, in order to go off on some ill-advised jaunt to undertake manual labor for which she is wholly physically and temperamentally unsuited, and educationally overqualified.

At least we can be sure that your sister will be wiser in her choices, being less headstrong and less selfish than you. Her presence will continue to offer solace to her mother in your unforgivable absence.

Yours,

Father

Maisie's fingers trembled, crumpling the letter, resentment bringing the prick of tears. What a letter! This was not a snapped remark, or a dismissive gesture. She was well used to those. This was something he had thought about, had taken time to write, to put in an envelope, to address and stamp, and to walk to the post box at the end of the road. Or had he sent Beth to mail it, while he stayed locked away in his study? Either way, he had had more than enough time to change his mind about sending this vile thing, yet he had sent it anyway.

She was about to tear it into tiny pieces when she realized that perhaps this letter was something she should keep, something to act as a reminder that her decision to leave home, to escape from the smothering rule of her father, had been the right one. Maisie could now live her own life, according to her own choices, with no pressure from her father's expectations. She flattened the paper out again as best she could before folding it back into its envelope, which she then tucked with Phyllis's postcard inside one of her books.

Maisie rolled her head from side to side. The tension of disappointment and resentment was tightening the muscles in her neck and shoulders. She needed to get away, to walk it off. So instead of joining the others for dinner, she headed out the back door, through the tumbled-stone gap in the wall beside the Blue Lagoon, and across the field. At the trees, she followed the worn sheep path that wound roughly up the slope beyond the farm. She'd walked up this way with Dot and Nancy one evening during the week, but right now, she was happy to talk to no one at all.

There had been a sharp edge to the breeze when she'd set off, and she'd been glad to have her sweater on, but now that she was in the shelter of the trees and climbing the slope, she was warming up. She took off her sweater and tied it by the arms around her waist, something that Mother would have considered unladylike. But Mother wasn't here, so this small—and rather pathetic, Maisie acknowledged—act of rebellion felt good and even came close to making Maisie smile again. Close, but not quite.

By the time Maisie reached the place where they had

turned back last time, there was a sheen of sweat across her face—yes, *sweat*, not perspiration as her mother would prefer—and she was breathing hard. But she felt good, as if she'd achieved something more than just a hill climb. It felt as if she'd walked away from her father yet again, and she allowed herself to smile.

The hillside was bare of trees now, and she had to scramble over hillocks of stubbly grass and around boulders and gorse bushes. Soon she found herself on a natural shelf on the hillside and could turn around to look at the view behind her. It was worth looking at too. She'd climbed up far enough so she could see above the tops of the trees she'd just walked through. Ahead to the north the land rolled gently down, she thought, toward Inverness, and to her left, the sun was already deepening to orange as it sank to the western horizon, gilding the bare hilltop around her with a golden glow.

Having got her breath back, Maisie continued up the path, feeling the tension release with each step. By the time she reached the false crown of the hill where the path split in two, she could have burst into song, she felt so wonderful. But as she opened her mouth to sing out loud, she saw something that surprised her into silence.

It was a croft, or at least, the remains of a croft, nestled in a pocket across the slope, beyond an outcrop of rocks. She could see clearly the rectangular outlines of two buildings. Whatever thatch had made up the roofs had long gone, but the large, roughly square rocks forming the walls were still there, though they had tumbled down into piles in places. There was still a clear entrance into each of the dwellings through a gap about two feet wide.

What was this place? And how long since someone had lived here?

Nature was fast reclaiming the man-made, with tall golden grasses swaying their way through the doors and cushions of green moss tinting the gray stone on the shadowed side, away from the sunlight. Hard human labor had once cleared this space and built these huts from boulders. She doubted there would have been room to grow many crops up here, but perhaps there might have been enough soil on the rocky hillside to grow potatoes or turnips.

How hard it must have been for whoever had lived up here. It was still only September, yet the wind was already cold. Maisie could not imagine anyone living perched up here in the teeth of a winter gale.

And with that thought, she realized that the sweat on her skin was rapidly cooling in the blustery breeze, so as she crossed the slope to the croft, she pulled her sweater from around her waist. Once she'd jumped down a drop of about five feet onto the flatter ground, a few paces from the larger of the two buildings, she paused to put it on.

As her head pulled through the tight woolen neck, Maisie heard a noise, a single rasp, short and sharp, and then nothing. She couldn't work out which direction it had come from, but it was a familiar sound that only a human could make. It was a match being struck.

Maisie glanced quickly around. No one was there.

And then she smelled it. Smoke. But not woodsmoke. This was tobacco, a cigarette.

Then she saw a fine stream of gray rising from the other side of the low stone wall.

Maisie was not alone. Someone was smoking only feet away from her.

Eight

Maisie wanted to turn tail and run. It could be anyone up here—a vagrant, an escaped prisoner, a German spy dropped by parachute—all right, maybe not a spy, but even so, she should still run. But which way? Back the way she'd come might be safest, although then she'd have to climb up that steep drop without making any noise. But what choice did she have?

Without taking her eyes off the cigarette smoke, she backed toward the rock. She'd only taken a couple of steps, however, when her heel caught on something, and she stumbled, an instinctive "damn it!" escaping her lips.

Maisie caught herself before she crashed to the ground, but as she stood upright, she saw a man's dark head rise from behind the croft wall, followed by his dark-blue-sweatered shoulders. He turned, clearly searching for the source of the profanity, and Maisie immediately knew his dark eyes and frowning face.

It was John Lindsay. Of all the bloody people it could have been. It was John Lindsay.

Suddenly, Maisie found herself wishing it had been a German spy after all.

For a moment, he looked as shocked at seeing her there as she was at seeing him, but his expression turned quickly to something else, one eyebrow lifting, his lips pressing together in what might have been an amused smirk or a grimace of irritation, Maisie couldn't quite tell. He rested his forearm on top of the low wall and, flicking off the gray ash from his cigarette, he surveyed her.

"Maisie," he said.

"John," she replied, her voice cracking a little as she spoke.

Neither of them spoke again, but since the silence was becoming embarrassing, Maisie searched for something witty to say.

"Do you often lurk inside abandoned buildings—" she began, but John had started speaking too. "Pardon?" she asked, "I didn't catch . . . I'm sorry, go ahead."

God! She sounded like her mother.

"I said, we must stop meeting like this," John said. "And I only *lurk* inside abandoned buildings, as you put it, when I need some shelter from the wind to light my cigarette."

"But how come you're here?"

"I told you, I needed to light my—"

"No, I mean, why are you *here*," Maisie waved her hand in small circles across the view, "and not in Brechin?"

John nodded his understanding.

"I'm *here*," he mimicked her circling wave, "because I'm with the Newfoundland Overseas Forestry Unit at Carrbridge. I have the lumberjack's badges of honor, remember?" He held up his palm so she could see again the rough calluses that exactly matched her own.

"Oh, right. Well, then, why are you *here*?" Maisie pointed at the croft wall between them.

John seemed to consider his hiding place. "I'm *here* to find some peace and quiet, away from the crowd, to read and to think. And to write."

John rested his other arm on the wall too. He held two books, Maisie saw, one with a red cloth cover and one bound in black leather. That one bulged and Maisie could see the stub end of a pencil tucked inside. A notebook.

"You read and write?" she asked, innocently enough, though as soon as he smiled, she knew she hadn't expressed herself particularly well.

"Yes, indeed"—his tone was teasing and his eyes crinkled at the corners—"even in Nova Scotia, some of us can read *and* write."

"You know I didn't mean that," Maisie replied, embarrassed, but not beaten. "But I'm confused. You told me you were an American—"

"Actually, *you* told *me* I was an American, and I chose not to correct you."

"That certainly explains why you talk nothing like Clark Gable or Shirley Temple."

"That's good to know," John said, his face suddenly earnest, though he laughed a little as he spoke. "I'd hate to think I sounded like Shirley Temple."

Maisie lifted one hand to swat him for being cheeky but realized just in time how strange that would be, given she didn't really know him. Instead, she pretended she'd been planning to tuck her hair behind her ear the whole time. "And you'll be glad to know you don't have Shirley Temple's dimples either."

John grinned at her, and Maisie saw that she'd been wrong. He did have dimples after all, and now she'd noticed them, it was hard to look away.

Suddenly self-conscious, Maisie tried to change the subject. "So tell me something. You just said you're from Newfoundland, but now, you say you're from Nova Scotia. Please make up your mind. And I know they are not all the same place, because even in Scotland, some of us can read, write, *and* use an atlas."

"Imagine that! An atlas, eh?" John was still grinning, and still showing those dimples. "You're right, though. I come from Nova Scotia, which is not Newfoundland, and is definitely *not* America. And to warn you, you might get away with calling *me* a Newfoundlander, but never call one of them a Canadian, or even worse, an American. They're very proud of their heritage, those Newfoundland boys, so approach with caution."

He was still teasing her, a smile playing around his eyes. His face was different when he wasn't frowning, she thought, when his forehead was clear of the thunderous fret lines. He looked so much younger.

Maisie realized she was staring, and looked away before he noticed, trying to work out what to say next.

"So now we have established that you can read and write," she said, pointing at the books, "can I ask what you are currently reading and writing? Is that a notebook?"

John regarded the books in his hand.

"Yes, it's a notebook," he said eventually.

"And what do you write in your notebook? I'm intrigued."

"Some thoughts. Some ideas. Whatever comes to mind really. Nothing much." John shifted the books so that the red one was on top, as if he wanted to hide the black.

He didn't seem entirely comfortable, so Maisie didn't press him. "And the other book? Is that a novel?"

John ran his fingers across the other book, tracing the line of silver lettering pressed into the red cloth on the front. Then he lifted it toward Maisie, and she took a few steps toward him so she could read its title.

In Flanders Fields
And Other Poems

"*In Flanders Fields*," Maisie read aloud. "I know that poem. It's about the war, isn't it? The Great War. We studied it in English class. Mrs. Packham usually reads it out every

November during the Armistice service at school, though last year she made me read it instead. A soldier wrote it, I think."

John nodded. "Lieutenant Colonel John McCrae." A strange expression had come over his face, not exactly sad, but perhaps nostalgic? "First Brigade, Canadian Field Artillery, and the Canadian Army Medical Corps."

"McCrae, of course." Maisie was embarrassed to have forgotten that. "I'm not sure if I can remember it all, but I know it begins *In Flanders fields the poppies blow between the crosses, row on row . . .*"

He nodded, so feeling strangely brave, she went on.

"*. . . that mark our place; and in the sky the larks, still bravely singing, fly scarce heard amid the guns below.*"

John's gaze moved away from her face and over her shoulder toward the north.

"*We are the Dead . . . ,*"she continued, but his brown eyes were suddenly so far away, Maisie lost her train of thought. "*We are the Dead. . . .*"

"*We are the Dead,*" John took over, his voice low and resonant. "*Short days ago we lived, felt dawn, saw sunset glow, loved and were loved, and now we lie, in Flanders fields. Take up our quarrel with the foe: To you from failing hands we throw the torch; be yours to hold it high. . . .*"

He recited with such pathos, Maisie felt a shiver run through her, one that was caused not by the chilly air, but by the intensity of his voice. He was speaking the words as if they were his own.

"*. . . If ye break faith with us who die we shall not sleep, though poppies grow—*"

"*—in Flanders fields.*" Maisie joined in for the final words. "This poem is special to you, isn't it?"

John didn't reply immediately. A golden eagle was circling high over their heads, and his eyes followed its soaring flight in silence. But after a few moments, he turned and walked through the doorway in the tumbledown wall, past Maisie to where three large boulders lay. He sat on one, leaning his elbows on his knees, and stared out over the view.

Maisie followed him, and when she was close, he nodded slowly.

"John McCrae was my uncle."

"Your . . . ?"

"My mother's older brother, a doctor. He joined up when war broke out in 1914, and was sent to France. He didn't come home again. Died in one of his own hospitals, and is buried in northern France." John sounded strangely like he was reading from an encyclopedia entry.

"I'm so sorry. It sounds like you were very fond of . . ." Maisie hesitated as she tried to do a quick calculation. John couldn't be more than three or four years older that she was, and she had been born in 1925, so if his uncle had died before the end of the Great War in 1918, then . . .

"I never met him," said John, as if reading her mind. "He died before I was born, though he used to send letters from the front to my older brothers and my cousins. But after he died, my mother wanted the family to remember him, so—"

"She gave you his name," interrupted Maisie, suddenly making the connection. She tentatively sat down on the rock next to him, half expecting him to get up and move away from her, but he barely seemed to notice.

John nodded again. "She baptized me John McCrae Lindsay."

"That's such a lovely thing for her to do," she said, but John was frowning again. "Wasn't it?"

"Of course. It would have been an honor to bear his name even if he had only been Lieutenant Colonel John McCrae. But by the time I was old enough to understand that I bore his name, this book had been published by a friend of his from McGill University, and 'In Flanders Fields' had already become adopted as the poem of the Armistice. My namesake, my uncle John, was, to the world, 'Lieutenant Colonel John McCrae, war poet.'"

"And did that make a difference?"

John shrugged. "I suppose it shouldn't have, but it did. His name came with an expectation that I would become the same kind of man as him. It was as if my mother had already set out my life, sure that I would graduate top of my class, that I would study medicine in Toronto and lecture at McGill or Vermont as Uncle John had done. And she had no doubt that I would become as accomplished a poet as he had been."

Maisie was surprised to hear a bitter edge to John's voice. It was almost as if he despised bearing his uncle's name, and resented his legacy. But then again, how could any boy live up to the legend of such a man without wanting to rebel against it?

"So, you refused to become a doctor," she said gently, "and ran away to become a lumberjack instead?"

And that was the bit that didn't quite make sense. John was clearly intelligent and well educated, so how did he end up a NOFU lumberjack, especially since he wasn't even from Newfoundland?

"A lumberjack?" John looked at her as if he were genuinely puzzled by the idea, then seemed to catch up with her. "Yes. Yes, that's what I did. I went off and became . . . a lumberjack."

"But even so, you still write poetry." Maisie reached out and laid one finger on the black notebook. "May I take a peek?"

John looked at her then, really looked at her, as if trying to gauge her trustworthiness. Whatever he saw, he let her take the book from his grasp.

Maisie hesitated, giving him the chance to stop her, but when he didn't, she opened the notebook.

She flipped through the first two or three pages, not reading exactly, but marveling at how tightly he packed words, here in ink and there in pencil, into every space available, as if this might be the only notebook he'd ever own. Words were underlined or scored through, and he'd connected one line of text to another using arrows that looped across a whole page to what might once have been a blank space, but which was now covered in more words. John's handwriting was scrawling and haphazard, nothing like the elegant cursive of her father's letter—

Just like that, the pain of her father's loveless letter flooded back, overwhelming Maisie, and she closed the notebook.

"I don't blame you," John said, obviously misreading her thoughts. "It's nothing I'd want to read either."

"No, that's not why . . . ," said Maisie, opening it again, trying to make sense of all the scribbled markings over the throbbing in her head. She needed to recover, so she picked a page at random—the title underlined at the top of the page read "Sunset Songs"—and held the notebook out to him. "Would you read it to me?"

John looked like he wanted to refuse.

"Please?" Maisie said quickly. "I'd love to hear you read your own words. I've never met a real poet before."

"I'm not a real—"

"Please, one poem?"

John watched her tap one finger on the open page, then took the book from her. "Not that one," he said, and flipped pages until he came to one he seemed to find acceptable. Looking up at Maisie, he gave her a half smile. "You don't have to do this, you know. I don't write happy poems, I'm afraid."

"I'm not looking for sunshine or rainbows."

"Well, if you're sure."

When she didn't move or reply, John took in a breath and began to read.

You stand, salt-flecked, as evening's sun
Scalds golden tracks of Phoebe's ceaseless tears . . .

His voice, low and full, had a rich timbre that filled the air around them, resonating off the stone walls. He kept his eyes down, following all the lines around the page without hesitation.

As from sweet heaven's bed the angel flies . . .

As his voice rose, so did John, standing up from the rock and lifting the book as if he were on a stage, reciting Shakespeare or Milton.

To gather you in tainted silk, your hair adorned,
With bark-ribbed boughs and berried leaf . . .

Maisie was spellbound as he drew the verse down to its quiet and thoughtful conclusion.

Then lead you through your final hour.

She waited for him to continue with another verse, but instead, he closed the notebook and sat down again beside her.

"Will you read more?" she asked.

"The rest isn't worth sharing."

"But—"

"Not yet, anyway. It needs more work."

Without meaning to, Maisie found that she'd laid her hand on his arm. "I'd love to hear it all once you think it is finished. The first bit was so beautiful, I think your uncle would have been proud."

John shrugged, as if her compliment meant nothing, though Maisie thought for a second a pink flush was rising under his tan.

"I could never hope to write words like his," John said.

"But you've found your own words instead," she replied.

"That's kinder than I deserve." John glanced up at her, and then his hand was on top of hers. "Especially since I still owe you an apology."

Maisie stared at their hands. This was not what she'd been expecting. Men didn't ever apologize, did they, even when they knew they'd been wrong? Or at least, her father certainly didn't.

"An apology?" she began uncertainly.

"I mean, I'm sorry things went wrong at the dance." John's hand remained upon hers. "It was my fault entirely. It's only that, well, sometimes it's easier to walk away than to have to deal with things. Difficult things. That's why I write poetry, I suppose, as a way of dealing with the hard stuff."

Maisie was thrown. She'd been so hurt by him walking away from her at the dance with no explanation, and she had no idea what he was talking about now. Yet she found herself drawn to find out more.

"Difficult things? I'm not sure whether I—" She fell silent

as John appeared to be about to say more, to explain, but then he seemed to change his mind and said nothing after all.

And before Maisie could press him further, John pulled his hand away and ran it through the dark hair that had fallen forward over his forehead.

"Enough about me," he said, his face filling with an unconvincing smile. "Tell me about you instead."

"Oh, erm, well," she started. John seemed keen to change the subject, but why did his new topic have to be *her*? "I don't write poetry. I don't think I'd even know where to start. But I do love reading it. Actually, I won the diction competition at school last year for my recital of 'A Red, Red Rose' after my mother bullied me into entering."

John gave a soft chuckle, though it was barely more convincing than his smile had been. "I know that poem. Robert Burns. It's lovely. But why did you need to be bullied into it?"

"Because it meant that everyone would be looking at me. But it was my mother's favorite poem, and it seemed to mean so much to her that I did it."

"Do you remember it?" John's eyebrow was raised again. "Would you recite it for me?"

Maisie felt her breath hitch. It was one thing to recite "In Flanders Fields," which was about war and remembrance. But this one was a love poem, pure and simple. Reciting this one, and to John, wouldn't be the same at all. "Now? Here? Oh, I'm not sure if I—"

"I think you could, if you tried." John was smiling again, but this time it looked unforced and genuine. "How does it start? Let me think . . . *O my love is like a red, red rose that's newly sprung in June . . ."*

When Maisie didn't take over the line, he continued, *"O my love is like the melody that's sweetly played in tune."*

Now Maisie had no desire to join in. There was such sweetness in hearing Burns's words of love spoken in John's lilting accent that she found herself leaning toward him, willing him to keep going.

"So fair art thou, my bonnie lass, so deep in love am I"—and now John was leaning in toward Maisie too, his voice lowering until it went no farther than the narrow space between them—*"and I will love thee still, my dear, till a' the seas gang dry. . . ."*

John's face was now only inches from Maisie's and she wondered how hard it would be to cross those inches and place her lips against his. He was silent now, his lips still and inviting and . . .

And, oh God, what was she thinking?

Maisie jumped up from the rock, her face flaming. She was not the sort of girl who started kissing random lumberjacks because they could quote Robert Burns off the top of their heads. Was she?

"I need to get back to camp," she blurted out. "They'll be worrying about me. And it's going to be dark soon."

Stealing a quick look back, she saw John easing slowly to his feet, looking out to the west as if checking the time on the clock face of the setting sun.

"Yes, I suppose you're right," he said eventually, and

perhaps a little sadly. Or was she imagining that?

"Well, good night," she said, moving toward the rock face she'd jumped down earlier. "And thank you, I mean, for the poetry, and for . . . well, anyway, perhaps I might see you again soon. I think it might even be tomorrow, because aren't we teaming up with the NOFU men? Or am I wrong?"

She knew she was babbling, adding to her embarrassment, and it was made worse by the fact that he wasn't responding. Now, faced by a shoulder-height wall of rock, her words died in her throat. How could she climb it and retain any dignity?

"Hold on!" John said. Maisie turned to find that he'd crossed the space between them and was holding out the red book of his uncle's poetry.

"You could borrow this so you could read his other poems as well," he said. "If you'd like to."

He couldn't have looked more bashful if he'd offered her flowers.

"Of course I'd like to." Maisie felt her face flush as if he had. "In fact, I'd love to. But are you sure you'd let it out of your sight?"

"I trust you," John said quietly, and taking her hand, he placed the book onto her upturned palm. "And perhaps, when you are done with it, we can meet up again so you can tell me which one is your favorite. And I can tell you mine."

Maisie sensed that this gesture was important to him, so she laid her other hand on top of the book. "You could tell me your favorite now."

"*Or*—I can tell you when we meet again."

He was teasing her, and Maisie wondered if perhaps this was his way of asking to see her again. Her face burned even hotter. "I'd like that, thank you. And I'll look after it as if it were my own, I promise."

"I know you will. Now, shall I walk you back down to your camp? As you said, the light is fading."

"I'll be fine, really. But thank you for offering. And for the book, and for . . . the poetry."

Even before she'd finished, John was already walking back across the clearing, one hand raised, toward the path that would presumably lead him back down to the men's camp.

Maisie tucked the little red book into her pocket and hauled herself inelegantly up the rock face, glad he wasn't still watching her. She quickly reached the same path she'd followed earlier. Even before she reached the tree line, she found herself singing a song under her breath.

"Keep smiling through, just like you always do, till the blue skies drive the dark clouds far away."

Where had that come from?

Nine

Maisie set her ax down and glowered as she watched Violet bump her shoulder flirtatiously against John's and bray with laughter. Clearly, Violet's hands-off warning had not been theoretical. Violet had known exactly which handsome man with dark eyes she'd been warning them away from.

All week, the WTC girls had been working alongside the NOFU men, and all week, Maisie had been forced to watch Violet flirt with John.

It wasn't that Maisie was jealous of Violet, who had used her authority to put herself in the same work party as John each day—it was more that . . . actually, yes, Maisie *was* jealous, and she was big enough to admit it, if only to herself.

And it wasn't that she wanted to spend all day, every day,

with John, but she did think of him as a friend now. They'd met again on two evenings at the croft, and although they hadn't gained again that moment of intimacy she'd felt at their first meeting up there, she'd enjoyed hearing his thoughts on books and poetry, their tastes for which had proved remarkably similar. He took his poetry seriously, yet he also made Maisie laugh easily, and their friendship was already feeling comfortable.

So, when Violet announced that her little coven—herself, Evelyn, and Claire—would be working with John's group yet again today, Maisie could feel her hackles rise.

This was the fifth morning it had happened, and Haven, the short, bullish man in charge of the NOFU lumberjacks, had even made a joke about it as he and Violet announced the work parties.

"And the last group is Hanwell, Croft, and of course, Mr. *Lindsay*," he'd said with emphasis, and added with a chuckle, "and we all know which of you ladies will be teaming up with him, I mean, *them*, eh?"

There had been some laughter from around the assembly, but Violet didn't even look embarrassed. She had just swatted Haven lightly with that damned clipboard, winked at John— yes, blatantly winked at him in front of *everyone*—and said, "I can't imagine how that might have happened, can you?"

Maisie was so annoyed, she didn't even bother to hide it, and therefore wasn't surprised when Rose Macarthur nudged her elbow. Rose was probably Maisie's favorite new friend, after Nancy at least, even if she was English. She'd been sent from London to live with her grandparents in Scotland after war broke out, and had never gone back. Rose was also the one other person at Auchterblair to whom Maisie had talked about John, aside from Dot.

"You do realize that you're looking like a bulldog chewing a—" Rose began.

"If you say 'chewing a wasp,'" Maisie snarled, "I'll brain you with my cant hook, right after I brain Violet!"

"You and whose army?" giggled Rose, tucking her arm into Maisie's. "And you mustn't let Violet get to you. That's what she wants."

Maisie watched John and Violet walk away, hoping that John might turn and wave. He didn't, and as they disappeared around the bend, it struck Maisie that perhaps John was encouraging Violet and enjoying her fawning attention. And what if he was sharing his poetry with Violet too? Maisie shook that idea away. Some things were too awful to contemplate.

Maisie and Rose had again been paired up with two of the younger lumberjacks, Elliott and Robert. Elliott, it had turned out, was the blond man she'd seen wrestling with John on the day she'd arrived at Auchterblair. The four of them had enjoyed working together yesterday, particularly since Robert and Rose seemed to be getting on especially well. And the assignment for the week hadn't been too hard, thinning out a wide stand of young birches and using the crosscut saw to trim the felled trunks into neat four-foot lengths. Rose commented that she'd heard that the birch would probably end up in Paisley, being turned into cotton reels for J&P Coats, the thread manufacturer.

"Cotton reels?" Robert teased. "Not exactly the vital contribution toward the war effort we thought we were making, eh?"

"Would you rather chop birches to help make parachutes and uniforms?" Maisie asked. "Or oak trees for coffins?"

"Maisie! That's not in terribly good taste, you know," Rose said, jumping to Robert's defense. "What Robbie meant—"

"It's *Robbie* now, is it?" Maisie teased Rose with a smirk. Rose reddened a little, and then a lot, when Robert put his arm around her shoulder and gave her a kiss on the cheek.

"Thank you for defending my honor, Rosie," Robert said, and Rose giggled again.

Watching this sweet, but relentless, flirtation only made Maisie's frustration at not being in a group with John all the sharper, and Maisie had to turn away.

To make her mood worse, it began to rain later that afternoon, and continued almost unabated for whole of the following week. They were all miserable, with the cold rain soaking them as they worked. The air inside in the dormitory huts stayed damp for days, and the small stove never managed to get their clothes and boots even half dry overnight. The weather had also stopped Maisie from meeting John, there being no shelter at the croft. Maisie had been reading John's uncle's poetry every night before lights-out and was desperate to share her thoughts with John.

Finally, the rain disappeared, but, much to Maisie's

chagrin—though satisfyingly, also to Violet's—so did John.

Eventually, Maisie asked Elliott and Robert where John had gone, and had to endure a battery of nudges and winks before Elliott told her that John was on special assignment for a week. Maisie thought about asking one of them to get a note to him, but she knew that would generate even more rude remarks, so she let it go.

But over that weekend, there was some thrilling news that served to distract Maisie from John's absence. Evelyn heard from one of the men that a crew was coming to film the lumberjacks for a Pathé Gazette newsreel. Apparently, their work in the Cairngorms was a positive war story that the nation should hear about. And, since the lumberjills were working alongside the men almost all the time now, Evelyn told everyone, there might even be room in the newsreel for "a few of the prettier girls."

All weekend, excitement ran high. And on Tuesday morning, when the Pathé crew was due to arrive, Maisie and Dot sat together with their cups of tea, watching Violet and her friends battling for the small mirror hanging on the wall.

"This is like Shandford all over again," Maisie said, giggling. "D'you remember them all getting ready to go dancing in Brechin? What a palaver!"

"Are we very immature," Dot suddenly asked, "not to care about how we look?"

"If running around like curly-haired chickens," replied Maisie, "means that you're a mature woman, then I'll keep childhood, thanks. Anyway, you know that Violet won't let you and me anywhere near the camera."

Even so, both girls were wearing their best uniform dress shirts, instead of their usual tired and torn ones, and Dot had even given their work boots an extra rub over with the brush and polish that morning. And while Maisie's hair still wasn't long enough for rolls, she had happily agreed to Rose's suggestion that wearing a pretty head scarf might keep her hair out of her face while she was working. But that was all the sprucing she would do. She wasn't interested in getting too fancy, even for a camera.

Violet led the lumberjills along the road, instead of their usual route through the woods, because no one wanted to risk the mud or low branches ruining their efforts on their clothes and hair. Everyone carried at least one ax, and three pairs carried the long two-handled crosscut saws between them. Maisie and a few others had coils of rope tied around their waists, and hoisted the long shafts of the cant hooks over their shoulders like rifles, to make sure no one else got caught by the sharp metal claws by accident.

There was no sign yet of the Pathé crew when they joined up with the NOFU men. And there was no sign of John either. But thankfully, as they walked up the track to Docharn Craig together, Dot seemed happy to let Maisie sulk about that in silence.

It wasn't until early afternoon, by which time all the work on hair and makeup had been destroyed, that a sleek black car lurched up the uneven forest track and came to a crunching stop, looking more out of place in the woods than the king's golden coronation carriage. Two men jumped out of back seats and pulled a tall wooden tripod from the trunk, then a big black camera, which they set on the top.

On seeing the camera, Violet and her cronies, Claire and Evelyn, immediately laid down their axes, pulled powder compacts from their pockets, and set about repairing some of the damage. Even some of the Newfies pulled combs from their back pockets, smoothing their carefully oiled hair back into place.

Then two other men got out of the car, both dressed in dark-blue suits and hats. One was short and rotund, and the other, who was taller and slimmer, looked rather like . . . wait, it *was* John! Maisie hadn't recognized him dressed so formally. But what was John doing driving a camera crew around? Was there no end to this man's secrets?

John saw Maisie then, and he smiled and lifted his hat in a very gentlemanly greeting. Maisie couldn't help but grin back as John guided the other man over to where Haven was standing and made the introductions. Then John looked back at Maisie and she saw him twitch his finger as if beckoning her forward. Unsure, Maisie hesitated, and in that moment, the space between her and the three men was suddenly filled by Violet, her hand thrust out, greeting the shorter man as if welcoming him into her own home.

"Violet Dunlavy," she squawked, "WTC officer in charge of this motley crew."

Maisie cringed at the way Violet then snorted with amusement at her own joke. And instead of introducing the other lumberjills, Violet kept the man's hand clasped tightly in hers as she went on and on to him about, oh, Maisie didn't care what. What she did care about, however, was that so far, Violet had barely spared a glance at John. Clearly the man from Pathé was far more captivating. So perhaps today wasn't going to be so bad after all.

Eventually, the short man looked pleadingly at John, who stepped in front of Violet, thereby forcing her to let go of the poor man's hand. As they walked to where Haven was gesturing toward a line of Scots pines, Violet went with them, endlessly talking and smiling. John glanced back over his shoulder at Maisie and rolled his eyes.

After another minute or two talking to Haven—and clearly trying to ignore Violet—the visitor suddenly clapped his hands for attention. Violet immediately clapped hers too, and Maisie couldn't miss the annoyed look that passed over the Pathé man's face as she did. He waited patiently for Violet to be quiet, then waved her back toward the group and cleared his throat.

"Ladies and gentlemen," he began, sounding every bit like a BBC wireless announcer, plummy and precise, "I am Sydney Grainger, and I'm here on behalf of Associated British–Pathé. Arthur and Harry here"—he indicated the two men by the camera—"will be working with me to capture, in a few celluloid minutes, the essence of the Newfoundland Overseas Forestry Unit."

Violet's hand shot into the air, waving, but he appeared not to notice.

"And, of course," he continued, "I'm fortunate enough to be getting two for the price of one. We will therefore endeavor to capture some footage of these very attractive ladies also."

Violet's friends congratulated her as if that announcement had been all Violet's doing.

Big Susan leaned toward Maisie and Dot. "And of course, that's why we lug these axes around, after all," she muttered disdainfully, "because it makes us all so damned attractive."

Maisie and Dot laughed in response and immediately got hushed by Violet.

"While we get set up," Mr. Grainger continued, even though Arthur and Harry looked like they were all ready to start filming, "please go back to your work, and if we bring the camera near you, just keep doing what you are doing. Do not look at the camera or at me unless I ask you to."

Violet's hand was up in the air yet again. "And will you be featuring any particular lumberjill in your film?"

"He's here to film us men, not you women!" came a man's voice from the far side of the circle, but Violet paid no attention.

Mr. Grainger simply smiled and nodded indulgently, as if talking to a crowd of schoolchildren. "Let's see how we get on, shall we? Now, if you would all return to your work, we will get on with ours." With that, he ushered them away toward the trees before turning to bark orders at the two cameramen.

For the next while, Maisie saw nothing of John or the camera crew as she worked alongside Big Susan, Wee Susan, and a couple of the men, felling a block of about twenty slender pine trees. Once the trunks were down, they used their cant hooks to roll them to the snedding station where Dot was working alongside Violet, Claire, and Evelyn. Snedding was lighter work than using an ax or saw, unless you were Dot, who energetically swiped her knife back and forth along the bark of a horizontal log to clear off the smaller branches. Meanwhile, the others looked determined not to do anything active enough to risk breaking into a sweat in case the camera found them.

How typical of Violet to assign herself to the less physical task today, thought Maisie, as she and Big Susan manhandled a log into place and returned to their axes and the next tree.

Maisie didn't know how long the camera had been pointing straight at them when she noticed that she and Big Susan were being filmed, but as soon as she looked up, Mr. Grainger signaled for Arthur—or was that Harry?—to cut and to move the camera to get a shot pointing down the length of the logs stacked by the path awaiting removal.

"When did they start filming us?" Maisie asked Big Susan as they rolled the next trunk toward Dot.

"Hmm, a while ago?" Susan shrugged.

"And you couldn't have warned me?"

"But they told us to carry on as if they weren't there," said Big Susan, "so I did."

Maisie let it go but tried to remember if she'd done anything she wouldn't want to see blown up on the big screen. But why worry? It was unlikely any footage of her would be used. He'd said he only needed a couple of minutes of film, yet they'd been shooting all afternoon.

As Maisie hefted her cart hook to roll the next log beside the others, she heard someone say her name. John was walking toward her with that familiar off-kilter step of his.

"Hello." She smiled. "You're keeping some swanky company this week."

John stopped in front of her and grinned back. "Sydney and I met a while back, not long after . . . well, a while back, and we've kept in touch. When he heard where I was, he decided to come for a look, and requested me as their guide for the whole visit. Haven wasn't too pleased about losing a man, but eventually he agreed. This week's work has been quite light, but apparently we've a big job coming up next, and he knows he'll have me back for that."

"So, you haven't found a new career as a roving reporter for the Pathé Gazette?"

"No, I don't think I'm cut out for the movies," John replied. "Anyway, there's more to keep me here than you might expect." Something in John's tone made Maisie blush, but he continued so quickly, she thought that perhaps she'd misunderstood. "Look, the tea break's about to be called, and Sydney wants one more shot before we finish up."

Before John could turn away, Maisie took her chance. "Does that mean you're free this evening? I still have your book, and . . ."

"I'm sorry, no. Once we're done here, I'm driving Sydney and the boys back into Inverness to meet the Lord Provost, and to get their film from today onto the night-mail express to London." John looked genuinely sorry. "And then we're heading onto the Black Isle for a couple of days."

"Oh. Not to worry then." Maisie tried not to look disappointed.

"I'll be back by Friday, though, and there's the dance in Inverness that evening, so perhaps we can see each other then?"

"There's a dance on Friday?"

"That's what Violet said."

"What? Violet asked you to a dance?" Maisie blurted out before she could stop herself.

"No, of course she didn't." John looked amused at the very idea. "She was asking Sydney if he'd still be in the Highlands that night."

"Why on earth would Violet—" began Maisie, but John waved her to silence and nodded significantly to behind her, and Maisie realized that Violet must be within earshot.

John leaned forward to whisper, "Something about having a Highland Fling, I think."

Maisie burst out laughing, which seemed to delight John.

"So, about Friday," he continued, his voice normal again, "there's a band playing at the Caledonian Hotel Ballroom, and I thought we might go."

John was asking *her* to the dance? Maisie couldn't believe it. *Her*, and not Violet!

"Although, I'd understand if you'd rather not." he continued. "You know, after the last time. I'm not much of a dancer, after all. But still, if you'd like to come with me . . ."

"No!" said Maisie. "I mean, yes! Or rather, I love dancing,

and you're not so bad a dancer, really. But, wait. Do you mean, we would all go as a group? Or are you asking . . ."

"Well, obviously"—it was John's turn to stumble on his words—"it won't be a limousine and dinner at the Ritz. We'll have to go along with everyone else. But, if you'd like me to ask you to go with me to the dance, well . . ."

Maisie waited for him to finish his sentence, but his words seemed to have dried up. "Well?" she prompted.

John smiled as it dawned on him that she wanted him to say it. "Maisie," he began again, "would you like to go to the dance in Inverness on Friday with me, even though I'm not a very good dancer, and maybe you'd rather not—"

"Yes please." Maisie interrupted him before he could talk himself out of the invitation. "I'd love to go with you. And we'll see how the dancing goes, shall we?"

John looked pleased. "That would be fine. Thank you."

"It's my pleasure," replied Maisie, bobbing a mock curtsey, which made John laugh aloud.

Then he became suddenly serious again. "Maisie," he began, "about the dance, though, there's something I should probably explain to you first—"

At that moment, a loud whistle blew across the site and someone bellowed, "Tea's up!"

John looked startled at the interruption, and then oddly relieved.

"What is it, John?" Maisie asked with concern, but his mood had clearly changed yet again.

"I'd better get back," he said brightly, letting whatever

he'd been about to say disappear with a wave toward the camera, "before Sydney says something to upset Haven. But I'll definitely see you on Friday."

And then John winked at her. A quick, cheeky wink that brought one side of his mouth up into a quick smile and made the wrinkles around his eyes crease even deeper. And Maisie felt like she was floating right there. How could a single fleeting wink make her feel like she had already reached heaven?

"Come on, let's get some tea," said Big Susan, coming up behind Maisie and prodding her in the arm. "I could drink from a horse trough, I'm that thirsty."

Wee Susan cackled at her friend's joke as she passed Maisie, but Maisie had to wait a second or two to make sure her feet were firmly planted back on the ground before she followed.

Arthur and Harry continued to film all during the tea break, as everyone sat on the stumps and logs near the fire, over which the big teakettle had been brought to the boil. Sydney Grainger kept making funny comments to the girls to make them smile, then told them to lift their teacups to the camera as if raising a glass in a toast, and they all obliged. But as it became clear that even Violet was struggling to keep a smile on her lipsticked mouth, he told the cameramen to cut and set up the last shot.

Once the tin cups had been gathered into the big basket for transporting back to camp, Sydney Grainger clapped his hands once again.

"Thank you all, ladies and gentlemen. It has been a marvelous afternoon, and before long, the lads and I will be hotfooting it back to Inverness to see how soon we can get these tapes down to London and into the hands of the fine editors at Pathé."

Around him, there was a smattering of applause.

"But before we go, I have one last request. I would like to give you strong men of the Newfoundland Overseas Forestry Unit, and you beautiful ladies of the Women's Timber Corps, a chance to send out your very own greeting to the world. I want you all together to give one big shout of 'Timber!' and a wave to the camera. Can you do that for me?"

"Yes, Sydney, yes, of course we can!" cried Violet from in front, clapping her hands. "Come on, everyone, gather around behind me!"

To Maisie's astonishment, everyone—even the men—did as they were told and formed a circle behind where Violet sat perched on a stump.

Maisie instinctively moved to the back of the group, almost hidden from the camera, as Sydney Grainger shouted, "On my count, everyone. I'll say 'one, two, three,' and you all shout 'Timber!' then wave like the blazes. Is that understood?"

There were cries of "Yes!" and "Get on with it!" and Grainger nodded to the cameraman.

"And we're rolling. So it's ONE." He lifted his arms into the air as if he were conducting an orchestra. "TWO. And THREE!"

A deafening cry of "TIMBER!" rang around the woods as everyone, including Maisie, bellowed at the tops of their voices.

As she lifted her arm to wave, Maisie felt someone's arm slip around her waist. She looked up to find that it was John's. He was back in his shirt sleeves, as he usually was when he was working, and since he was standing so close, Maisie saw for the first time that his chest had a fine covering of dark hair where his shirt lay open. She felt a sudden urge to reach out and touch it, and perhaps undo the next button down . . . and the next . . .

And suddenly, John's mouth was right by her ear and she could feel his warm breath on her face.

"I think we'd better start waving to nice Mr. Grainger, or he'll think we don't like him."

John lifted his head and raised his arm, smiling widely toward the camera. But as Maisie too lifted her hand, she knew that John's grin was for her alone.

Ten

Violet spent the rest of the week trying to convince every-one else that Sydney Grainger had made a play for her. Maisie and Dot rolled their eyes at each other every time Violet brought it up, and Maisie had even seen Evelyn and Claire do the same when Violet told them that Grainger had invited her to London so that he could introduce her to a few people "high up in the movie business."

"But he works for a newsreel company," said Dot on Thursday evening as she and Maisie were taking their turn on kitchen patrol, washing and drying the camp's dinner dishes. "I know Pathé makes the newsreels they show at the pictures before the movies, but I've never seen a proper pic-ture made by Pathé, have you?"

"No, of course not," replied Maisie. "It's all a load of

bunkum. Sydney Grainger couldn't get away from Violet fast enough. You know she tried to invite him to go to tomorrow's dance with her?"

"No, she didn't!" cried Dot with glee.

"Now, now!" said Agnes, the camp cook, from behind them as she wiped down the countertop. "You know I don't like nasty talk in my kitchen." Agnes was the oldest woman in the camp, and as the cook, she was also the only one of them not required to work out in the forests every day. Though her cooking left a lot to be desired in terms of both taste and variety, she made up for it in quantity. No one quite knew how she made their restricted rations go quite so far. "As my granny always said, if you don't have something nice to say . . ."

"Yes, I know, don't say anything at all," replied Maisie. "But really, you don't think there's any truth in it, do you? I know Violet fancies herself as something special, but—"

"She really does," continued Dot. "Big Susan was telling me the other day that when Violet arrived at Shandford for training, she was wearing four-inch-high heels and a fox fur coat, as if she were going shopping in Edinburgh, not learning to chop down trees. And then she offered to pay the other girls to carry her suitcases to the hut, as if they were station porters!"

Dot and Maisie hooted until Agnes slapped a wet rag down on the counter, splashing both of them.

"Enough!" said Agnes sharply, glowering at them until Maisie put a soapy finger to her lips. "Now, I hope you two are remembering that I'm getting away early in the morning, straight after breakfast, to go to visit my sister. She's been a bit poorly this last year or so since my nephew died at Dunkirk."

"Oh, I'm so sorry," said Maisie immediately, "I didn't realize that you'd lost someone. But I'm sure your sister will be comforted by having you there for a while."

"Aye, well, he was only twenty, the youngest of her three boys. But the other two are still safe out there somewhere. As far as we know, anyway." Agnes dipped into the pocket of her apron and brought out a large handkerchief. She blew her nose loudly before continuing. "Anyway, I'll be away all week, and young Nancy will take my place. She's not from a large family, so I don't know how she'll get on feeding the masses, but I'm sure she'll appreciate having all the help you can give her, especially tomorrow when you've all got to have your dinner early before you head to Inverness for the dance."

Maisie and Dot promised that they would help Nancy, and make sure that everyone else took a turn too, and once the dishes were finished, they wished Agnes a nice week away and went to get ready for bed. But it was a while before Maisie could fall asleep. Tomorrow was the dance, and she hadn't set eyes on John since he'd asked her to go with him. What would happen if he didn't show up tomorrow? But even more, what might happen if he did?

Peering at herself in the small round mirror of her powder compact one last time, Maisie acknowledged she was a hypocrite. She'd been so scathing about the other women dolling themselves up for the camera, yet here she was trying to make herself look pretty for the dance. If she'd been going only as part of the group, she might not have worried too much, but since John had asked her to go with him, she wanted to show him that she wasn't the plain schoolgirl she generally thought herself to be. She was excited to see John, but also a bit nervous. She only wished Dot would be coming to the dance tonight.

That morning over breakfast, Violet had announced that the NOFU lumberjacks would be picking them all up at six o'clock that evening for the ride to Inverness.

"But, I need a volunteer to stay here," she'd said. "We'll be away for several hours, and we can't leave the camp unmanned."

"Don't you mean 'unwomanned'?" Rose had shouted from beside Maisie and Dot, causing much laughter around the mess hut.

"Yes, yes, very funny. But I still need a volunteer. Anyone?"

"I'll stay." The voice had come from the kitchen, and as everyone had looked that way, Nancy had appeared at the server window with one hand raised. "Quite happy to hold the fort here."

Violet had looked almost annoyed as she said, "Well, thank you, Nancy, that's very . . . public spirited of you. But then, I suppose some people weren't born to dance, were they?"

Maisie had expected Nancy to retaliate with a barbed comment of her own, but instead she'd waved Violet's comment away before disappearing back into the kitchen.

"So, everyone else, ready by six. All right?"

As Maisie cleared up her plate, knife, and cup, Dot caught her elbow.

"Would you . . . ," Dot began, her tone uncertain. "Would you mind if I didn't come tonight either? You know I'm not big on crowds—"

"But you had fun at the dance in Brechin," Maisie interrupted, surprised that Dot was not looking forward to the dance as much as she was.

"Well, yes, but that was . . . well, I think I'll stay here tonight and keep Nancy company, so she's not on her own. If you don't mind, that is?"

"Mind? Of course I don't mind," replied Maisie, though she felt she was speaking a little too brightly. She had been looking forward to having Dot and Nancy with the group tonight, in case things didn't go well with John, or worse, if he didn't show up at all. But that was unfair. She couldn't expect Dot to be as excited as she was, since Maisie's anticipation was less about the dance and more about being with John.

"Well, if you're sure," Dot had said, patting Maisie's arm. "And anyway, I'm feeling that tired, I'll probably be in my bed by nine o'clock anyway."

Now, shortly before six, Maisie put the compact away in her handbag and wished more than ever that Dot would be coming, if only for moral support. She'd managed to brush out the knots in her hair, and Heather, a quiet woman who slept two beds down, had helped her pin it up at the sides. Heather had even offered Maisie some pink lipstick, but Maisie had said no. Instead, she'd dabbed a little Vaseline—from the pot that hadn't yet been mixed with Mrs. McRobbie's lard—onto her lips to make them shine. Maisie had chosen her pretty cream cotton dress with the pink and purple roses and the mother-of-pearl buttons, the one she hadn't worn to the dance in Brechin. The waist was a bit loose these days, but Rose had lent her a pretty pink belt to cinch it in.

With a last check of the mirror, Maisie decided she was very pleased with the way she looked, whether John liked it or not. If nothing else, she was out of uniform for the first time in weeks. Of course, they had to hope now that no one from Timber Corps headquarters caught them, since according to the WTC rules, lumberjills should stay in uniform the whole time. And she'd decided that her fine-knit cardigan over the top of her dress would be enough to keep her warm on the ride, although the air had become colder since last week's rain. Her only warmer options, however, had been her ugly WTC sweater and even uglier greatcoat, so Maisie had decided she would grin and bear it.

Over by the door, the Susans were excitedly discussing a rumor that sailors from a Royal Navy ship just docked in Inverness might be at the dance too, when from outside came the sound of cheers and laughter. Maisie and Heather dashed to the window to see what was happening.

The Bedford truck they used for the logs was reversing precariously up the narrow track toward the women's camp, and on its flatbed there appeared to be makeshift seating made of logs padded with hay. It didn't look entirely safe, to Maisie's eyes anyway, but there would certainly be no shortage of space to carry everyone.

Heading outside with Heather, Maisie waved good-bye to Dot and Nancy, who had just come in through the door from the mess hut.

As she approached the truck, some of the men had jumped down off the flatbed and began to arrange beer crates to form an impromptu staircase up onto the trailer. John was stationed at the top of the stairs and waved when he saw Maisie. As each woman climbed up, he offered her his hand until she was safely on top and could find somewhere to sit down.

When it was Maisie's turn to clamber up the steep crate stairs, John not only held out a hand to help her, but he also slid his other hand around her waist to steady her at the top.

"I thought we could sit together," John murmured, bending low so only she could hear. "I've put a blanket over there on the left, next to Robert, if you want to go sit down. I'll join you once everyone's aboard."

"Thank you," Maisie said, and made her way over to where a gray standard-issue blanket had been draped over a thick layer of hay on the floor, and then up over a log. Perching on top of the log, beside where Robert was fussing over making Rose comfortable, she saw that John was now assisting Violet, who was wobbling precariously up the crate stairs on what must be her infamous four-inch heels. At the top, Violet tucked her arm into John's and seemed to want to lead him to the far side of the seating structure, but John stayed where he was. Whatever he said then made Violet scan the gathered faces until she found Maisie's. Violet positively glared, for what felt like minutes, though it was probably only a couple of seconds. Then she snatched her arm away from John's hand and tottered over to where Claire and Evelyn were already sitting.

With everyone on board and the crate stairs stored, John came and sat down beside Maisie on top of the log seat. She almost asked him whether Violet was all right, but realized immediately that she should not be reminding John that Violet even existed, when he had clearly chosen to sit with her instead.

John leaned toward Maisie, pressing his shoulder against hers. "Once we get moving," he said, as he then eased himself down to sit on the floor, with his back leaning against the log, "you might want to sit down here. After all, you can't easily fall off a flat floor. Well, not unless you . . ." He used two fingers to mime a fall off the side.

Maisie glanced around as the truck lurched forward, almost throwing her on top of John.

"I see what you mean!" she said, laughing, and dropped herself down to sit beside John, stretching her legs out in front of her, parallel to his, silently thanking the Lord that she wasn't wearing silk stockings—although, had anyone been able to buy any stockings at all since the war began?—since the sharp stalks skewering the blanket would have instantly torn ladders in them.

As the truck began to trundle down the track toward Carrbridge and the main road to Inverness, the cool breeze fluttered the hem of her dress and brought goose bumps to her bare legs. Once the truck reached the road and picked up speed, Maisie began to regret leaving her big coat at camp, and within a mile, she could not contain her shivers.

"Are you cold?" John suddenly asked, already shrugging out of his thick green tweed jacket and holding it out to her. "Here, have this."

"No, really, I'm fine," said Maisie, even though her teeth were already chattering, making it hard to get the words out—when had the temperature dropped so low? "You'll be needing it yourself. But thank you."

"Come on now," John said, and lifted the front of the jacket wide, making to pass it around her shoulders. "You forget, I come from a place with eleven months of snow every year, so this feels almost like summer."

"Eleven months of snow? Are you serious?"

"No, not really, but you can still have my jacket."

"Well, if you're sure, then thank you," she said, smiling up at him before leaning forward so John could slip the jacket around her shoulders. At that moment, the truck hit a pothole and Maisie was thrown against John again. Since his left arm was already behind her and his right hand pulling at the front panel of the jacket, Maisie found herself in a sudden and very secure embrace.

Instinctively she made to pull away, embarrassed, but even as she did, John's arms tightened around her to steady her as they were bumped yet again.

"Or this is the other option," John said quietly, his mouth now unnervingly close to her cheek. "We might both be a little warmer and safer sitting this way."

Maisie knew he was right but didn't quite trust her voice not to squeak. So she only nodded, and let herself lean against John a little, and then a bit more. After a few minutes, she felt John relax against her too.

As Maisie's shivering subsided, she wondered what she ought to say. She could tell him she was grateful, or that she was happy to be there. But John seemed content to sit quietly, watching the fields pass by, so Maisie decided that saying nothing would work fine too.

Then she recalled that he had said there was something he should explain to her, about the dancing. "What was it you wanted to tell me?" she asked.

"Tell you?"

"When you invited me to the dance, you said there was something you ought to explain first." Maisie felt John's arm stiffen around her shoulder, though he didn't immediately reply. "I just thought, well, since we're sitting here for the next little while . . ."

John cleared his throat, once, and then again, and Maisie looked up at his face, trying to gauge what she saw there. Uncertainty? Guilt?

"There is . . . something . . . ," John said quietly, turning his shoulder slightly, as if to shield their conversation from Robert and Rose, who were sitting on the other side of him.

"But I'm not sure . . . I think I'd rather . . . at least, I think we need a more private—"

"But that's the truth, Rose, I swear!" Robert's loud and delighted cry made John start. "Johnny, you'll vouch for me, won't you? Tell Rose I'm not lying about that enormous wildcat that attacked us that day. Remember? When we were working along the road from that little village? The one with the pub? You know the one, don't you? That wildcat was the size of a guard dog, I swear, and twice as vicious. Come on, help me out here. She thinks I'm making it up."

John held Maisie's gaze for a split second longer, and then he looked up at their friends with an almost believable smile. "Rose, don't believe anything that man tells you. The cat was nothing more than someone's pet ginger tom on the scrounge for Rob's meat-paste sandwich."

"No-no-no! Don't tell her that, you traitor!" Robert made is if to punch John's arm in protest, but John deflected the pretend blow with an easy swipe. "How's she going to believe that I'm the hero if you keep denying all my stories, eh? Next thing, you'll be telling her I didn't grow up wrestling grizzly bears for fun."

The banter between the two men carried on, and so did Maisie's and Rose's laughter, as they watched John and Robert compete to tell the tallest tale all the way to Inverness. By the time they crossed the bridge over the River Ness, the sky to the west had turned orange, then pink, and Maisie's sides ached from laughing so hard. Seeing John so light-hearted and funny, it was easy to dismiss those moments of seriousness earlier on.

When the truck drew up in front of the La Scala Cinema, however, Maisie's delight turned to confusion. John had said they were going to a dance at the Caledonian Hotel Ballroom, not at La Scala.

"Is this the right place?" she asked John, pulling out of her warm nest in his arms. "I thought—"

"We're taking a little detour before we walk over to the dance hall. Something we all want to see." John grinned, then glanced at his watch. "Come on, though, or we'll miss it."

John pushed himself up to sit on top of the log behind them. He seemed to hesitate for a moment before he heaved himself up to standing, the movement apparently requiring some effort. Embarrassed to think that he had got pins and needles in his legs because she'd been pressed so tight against him and he'd been too polite to move, Maisie quickly slipped the jacket off her shoulders and held it out to him.

"Thank you for the loan," she said. "I'll remember to bring my own coat next time."

"Next time?" John replied, and she heard the smile in his voice.

"Yes, next time," she said, and let herself smile too, "though perhaps I should handle the transportation arrangements, so that we can travel in something a little more stylish."

"What? You mean a hay truck?" John said, chuckling.

"Oh, at the very least." Maisie grinned back. "Or I might even splash out on hiring us a potato wagon."

"You certainly know how to look after a chap, don't you?"

said John, giving her a little bow, and Maisie was suddenly sure that tonight was going to be fun.

"If we're going into the cinema," she began, "are we seeing what I think we're seeing?"

John smiled. "You'll have to wait to find out, won't you?"

Once everyone was down off the truck, John whistled for attention, then gestured for everyone to gather around. "We need to keep a lid on the noise, all right? We won't be staying long, but we don't want to get thrown out. Otherwise my friend over there"—he waved to an older, gray-haired woman who had just come out of the main doors—"might get into trouble. Everything set, Janet?"

The woman nodded and put one finger to her lips, then disappeared back inside. As the group started to move toward the door, John whistled again.

"Wait! It's *this* way." He pointed down a cobbled lane at the side of the building. "And remember, keep it quiet, for God's sake!"

John led them down the alley, and Maisie could hear Violet complaining from behind about how John was expecting her to walk in high heels on cobblestones and that was "verging on cruelty."

On their right, Janet reappeared through a narrow door, waving them in with one hand while the single finger remained clamped to her smudged red lips. Amid much jostling and giggling, the group entered one by one. Maisie waited with John until the last person was inside, and as she followed, she felt a sudden and delightful warmth in the small of her back as John's hand guided her through the door.

"Thanks, Janet," John whispered as they passed the woman. "You're a saint. We'll be gone before you know it. Promise."

Once inside the doorway, Maisie found herself in a small pitch-black space, stuffy and claustrophobic. Then someone lifted aside the blackout curtains and she walked into the dark airiness of the cinema. Suddenly, a sharp blade of light cut across the auditorium from projector to screen, and in the reflected light, Maisie could see that the cinema was almost full. Their group was now strung out along the aisle across the back of the theater, and in front of them, row upon row of seats were full of people waiting expectantly for the picture to begin after the usual newsreel.

The Pathé Gazette newsreel! Maisie felt herself bursting with excitement. It had only been a few days since the camera had been filming them, so could Mr. Grainger really have turned it around so quickly? Maisie looked up at John to find that he was grinning down at her.

"It's us, isn't it?" she whispered.

"Wait and see," John whispered back, and Maisie couldn't help but giggle, prompting the woman wearing a large hat in front of them to turn and shush them even more loudly than Maisie's giggle had been. Maisie felt even more laughter bubbling up and put her hand over her mouth to stop it from coming out, pressing her face into John's shoulder to smother the sound. John was laughing too, though silently, his chest rumbling under her forehead. Maisie thought she might explode with delight.

But then John's fingers were under her chin, lifting it up so Maisie could see into his face, his eyes sparkling even in the dim light. All her laughter was frozen in that breathless moment of anticipation as John, ever so gently, turned her face toward the big screen.

"You might want to be facing that way," he breathed, as the familiar Pathé cockerel appeared on the screen.

Eleven

The newsreel began with film of the king and queen visiting a factory and then a primary school. As they climbed into the waiting car, they waved to the assembled group of children and then the screen faded to black. It opened again on a woodland scene with two men, shirt sleeves rolled to the elbow, swinging their axes in turn against a tree trunk.

"It's Haven and Alfie!" someone called out from farther up the row, causing an eruption of laughter and clapping all around. Maisie glanced up at John to see if he was worried by the noise, but he was still watching the screen, grinning widely.

And there on the screen were Elliott, Malcolm, and Robert, and the other Newfoundlanders, as a narrator with a very posh English accent talked about the "fine men" who'd "come over from the New World to do their wood-chopping duty in the name of His Majesty, King George." As the camera panned along a line of trees, each one being assaulted by a man with an ax—Mr. Grainger must have set up that shot solely for the camera, because Maisie could see that the men were all working too closely together for safety—the narrator declared, "You couldn't find a finer bunch of jolly good fellers."

"*Fellers*," she heard John say, "that's funny."

Then there was a close-up of Malcolm grinning rather manically into the camera lens, and a muffled cheer went up from the other end of the group as the film cut to a shot of a tall Scots pine dropping to the ground.

"And these girls are jolly good fellers too," the narrator continued, as the image changed to a line of perhaps a dozen women walking single file across a field.

"That's us!" It was Violet's voice this time. "No, wait, I'm not there. Why am I not there?"

"Shhhhhhhh!"

"If that seems strange, take a look at these sturdy lumberjills on their way to fell a forest giant or two somewhere in Scotland. Chopping down trees may harden the muscles, but see what it does for the dimples."

And there was Heather, smiling bashfully at the camera, her dimples on full display. Then there was a close-up of a whetstone being rubbed across an ax blade.

"Setting the ax-head keeps it as keen as the girls are

themselves." And there was Rose spitting on her whetstone. "And that's for luck."

"That's disgusting!" declared the woman in front of them.

"Shhhhh!" hissed John at the woman, and Maisie couldn't stop herself from giggling again.

On-screen, three lumberjills were swinging their axes at some Scots pines. Maisie was excited to recognize the two Susans at once, but it took her a moment more, and a soft nudge from John's elbow, to recognize herself. That slender and strong-looking girl—no, that *woman*—who was swinging her ax so smoothly and naturally, almost gracefully? Was that really *her*?

John whispered, "Nice swing!" and Maisie was glad it was dark so John wouldn't see her blush. Maisie did feel rather proud of herself as the shot closed in on her ax blade cleanly cutting into the base of a tree.

"There's a great deal of effort in swinging an ax, especially for a girl who has never swung anything heavier than a handbag."

"Bloody cheek!" Maisie muttered.

Beside her, John chuckled, and even though she wasn't sure if he was laughing at the narrator's comment or her own, she dug him hard in the ribs with her elbow, to make sure he knew it wasn't funny. Her indignation seemed to amuse John even more, however, because he laughed out loud now and neatly dodged away from her elbow as it headed for his ribs again. And as he stepped back beside her, Maisie felt his arm wrap around her back and squeeze her into his side for a moment, and somehow, it felt quite natural for them to stay like that, his hand resting on her waist, her head against his shoulder.

The film continued with more shots of the two Susans, this time on their knees using the long crosscut saw, and of Evelyn and Claire lounging against a pine tree, chatting. And there was Dot, her red-cross patch on her sleeve, using her knife at the snedding station. Maisie was surprised to see that Dot's action, like hers, looked very natural and efficient, almost graceful, and she suddenly wished that Dot were here to see how wonderful she looked on the big screen. Why hadn't she pushed Dot and Nancy to come along with them on the trip?

And then it was Nancy's turn to be featured, along with Clyde, as she wrapped the towing chain around a log and walked him out of the range of the camera, all the while trying to look like she wasn't being filmed and wasn't wanting to grin, but failing miserably at both.

"See how the lumberjill and the Clydesdale are the best of pals?" said the narrator.

"But where am *I*?" whined Violet, making no attempt to keep her voice down. "Why haven't they shown *me* yet?"

But only a second or two later, she cried out, "There I am!" A close-up of her face—uncomfortably close—filled the whole screen, showing Violet lifting her powder compact mirror up and applying a thick layer of lipstick.

"And even in the wilds of the Scottish mountains, some

of these lovely ladies simply can't live without their lipstick."

Violet applauded herself, amid another chorus of shushes from those around her, and Maisie could only assume that Violet had completely missed the unmissable sarcasm laced through the narrator's tone. Or perhaps that was only what Maisie's imagination wished to hear.

The final piece of the film showed the entire gang of lumberjacks and lumberjills all silently mouthing "Timber!" before laughing and waving at the camera.

"With these strapping lumberjacks and lovely lumberjills working side by side," the narrator declared, "it's a mixed company to be sure. But take my word for it, they all make up a bunch of jolly good fellers."

Searching the screen, Maisie could see herself at the back, laughing and waving, as John leaned down to kiss her cheek. Or at least, that's what it looked like, and she had to remind herself that he had only been whispering in her ear. Even so, watching it happen up there on the screen, as if to some other girl, she imagined she could feel his lips on her skin.

When the screen went black, the large group of lumberjills and lumberjacks along the aisle started cheering themselves—so much for sneaking in and out quietly—and to Maisie's astonishment, the rest of the audience started applauding too, many of them turning around in their seats as the lights went up to acknowledge the movie stars in their midst. Soon the whole line was bowing, at least until the double doors at the back of the auditorium opened and a grumpy-looking man appeared. He stood, hands on hips, clearly trying to work out who these people were, cluttering up his aisle.

Maisie felt John tugging at her elbow, pulling her toward the side door, and Maisie realized their moment of celebrity was over. Time for a hasty exit. She passed on the signal to Heather, who was standing beside her, with a tug on her sleeve, and they headed for the door at the side through which they'd entered. John held the door for everyone else as they piled out into the alleyway, clapping one another on the back and cheering even louder than they had done inside.

"Right, everyone, who's ready to dance?" John said, once the door was shut. "Follow me then, the Caley Ballroom is thisaway!"

His words were met with a cheer, and before Maisie knew what was happening, John had taken her by the hand and was leading her at the front of the merry band, back up the alleyway and along Kessock Street toward the Ness Bridge. Having his large hand wrapped around hers, calluses to calluses, felt so nice and rather thrilling, given that everyone behind them must be able to see, Violet included. There was a lightness in Maisie's step and only a little burning in her cheeks.

By ten o'clock, Violet was drunk. And obnoxious.

Maisie had been enjoying herself, chatting with John and Elliott and listening to the band. Rose and Robert, clearly sweet on each other, had also joined them between dances and during the break, where sandwiches and cups of tea were served in what would have been the hotel's bar in prewar days.

Maisie hadn't given up hope that she and John might dance, but she wasn't going to push him. Perhaps later. The other lumberjills had certainly been having fun too, especially once the rumors had proved true and His Majesty's Navy had arrived. As she'd watched her friends dancing with the sailors, Maisie had realized that one of the sailors was watching her. He'd smiled, and for a moment she'd thought he might approach her, but then John had said something to bring her back into the conversation, and when she looked again, the sailor had gone back to studying his fingernails.

But now Violet was becoming a problem. Her strident voice had been dominating even the band's music, and once the band was on a break and there was only gramophone music playing, she proved impossible to ignore. Maisie had heard her earlier on bragging to a handful of local women that she had been the star of the latest Pathé newsreel, and that it was only a matter of days until Sydney Grainger's letter arrived, inviting her to join him in London. Now she was weaving through a group of sailors insisting that that no one else within a hundred miles had her star quality and waving a dismissive finger at her fellow lumberjills, admonishing them for being "simply pathetic" for choosing to be stuck in the middle of nowhere instead of looking toward the bright lights of the capital as she was.

"I mean, look at them." Violet swept an imperious arm to take in the whole group. "It's pitiful really."

Rose turned to Maisie and asked, "Where did she get the booze? It's a dry dance, after all. Mind you, I wouldn't turn down some of whatever tea she's been drinking." Rose lifted up her teacup as if toasting Maisie.

"Me neither," laughed Maisie, clinking the rim of her cup against Rose's. "But I'm fairly sure the Royal Navy has been subsidizing every one of her dances with a shot of rum from one hip flask or another."

"Well, she's being downright horrid now"—Rose frowned—"so should we be getting her home before she says something really offensive?"

Even before Maisie could respond, she knew it was too late. Robert had already left their group and walked over to Violet.

"That's enough, Violet," he said, calmly but sternly. "You need to pipe down now."

"Pipe down?" Violet slurred. "Pipe down? I'm only stating the truth of it, Robert dear. And anyway, what would you know? The only thing your girlfriend did on the film was spit. I mean, it was simply disgusting!"

"Maybe she did spit," replied Robert, "but that just proved she was working hard to set her blade. She wasn't up there looking ridiculous by putting all that muck on her face in the middle of a working forest. And the other girls were on the film five times as long as you. So, like I said, why don't you pipe down, Violet, because you're embarrassing yourself, and us, and at this rate you'll be lucky to make it back to

Auchterblair in one piece, let alone London."

"Are you threatening me?" Violet started forward, pointing a bony finger into Robert's face.

Rose dashed to Robert's side, grabbing his arm and pulling him away. "Leave it, Robert, please."

"She's not worth it," Maisie agreed quietly, but not quietly enough.

"Not worth it, am I?" Violet now pointed unsteadily at Maisie. "And you're worth more? God! Is that why you can't even get your pretty boy Johnny to dance with you?"

"Violet, don't!" Maisie did not want to have a fight with Violet, not tonight. Not any night.

"But I bet he'll dance with *me*," Violet slurred as she lurched toward John, grasping his hand, "won't you, Johnny?"

Violet pulled John toward the dance floor, and to Maisie's horror, John went with her.

Maisie was stunned. What was John doing?

Maisie had been shuffling her feet and swaying to the music all night, hoping that John would get the hint, but all they'd done was chat. Then, a little while ago, John had gone to get them some more tea—Maisie wondered how much more tea she could drink in one night—and Elliott had asked Maisie to dance. She'd said thank you, but no, she'd wait to dance with John. Elliott had shrugged and Maisie had thought she'd heard him say, "Good luck!" before he asked Heather to dance instead. When John had come back, Maisie had asked him straight out if they might dance, but John had only said, "Maybe, in a little while." Then he'd checked his watch, as if he was simply marking time with her until he could leave.

And now? *Now* he was going to dance with bloody *Violet*, of all people? It was all Maisie could do not to grab his hand out of Violet's and force him to dance with her.

But wait, maybe she was wrong. John seemed to be unsteadily pulling back against Violet's grip, but she was not letting go. Finally, his fingers unlocked hers and Violet's drunken momentum suddenly had no resistance, so she went sprawling. One high heel spun across the floor, and her cotton dress flew up, barely covering her thighs. Other dancers had to dodge out of the way to avoid tripping over her.

People around started laughing, and despite her annoyance, Maisie tried to help Violet to her feet. Holding her by the elbow, she swiped her hand down Violet's skirt as someone else retrieved the errant shoe.

"Get off me!" Violet snapped, slapping Maisie's hand away and then rounding on John. "What the hell was that? You shoved me! Why the hell did you shove me?"

"No, that's not—" began John.

"Yes, you did. Didn't he?" Violet turned to shout at the crowd of people now forming a circle around them, her volume rising with each indignant declaration. "Didn't he shove me? You saw him! Pushed me right onto the floor! He asked me to dance and then pushed me and made me fall. Stupid oaf, you could have hurt me!"

There was laughter again—clearly no one believed Violet's

accusations. Maisie glanced around to get one of Violet's cronies to help, but the last she'd seen of Claire and Evelyn, they were wrapped around the necks of two members of His Majesty's Navy in the darkest corners of the hall. So, it was up to Maisie to try again to stop Violet from making a fool not only of herself but of all the lumberjills too. If the WTC head office got to hear about this . . .

"Violet, calm down." Maisie tried to take Violet's arm again, only to have it snatched away. "There's no need for any of this. John didn't push you, he only—"

"Oh, what would you know?" Violet snapped back, stabbing her finger into Maisie's chest. The sharp movement made Violet reel forward and then back, as if the floor were tilting under her feet. "Pathetic little girl, trying to act as if she's a grown-up. You wouldn't know what to do with a man if he was presented to you naked on a silver platter."

"Violet, stop!" Maisie cried, as the laughter around them grew, especially from the rest of the sailors, who had now walked over to watch the fun.

"Not that any of these bloody useless NOFUs could call themselves men." Violet turned to resume her rant at John. "Christ! You lot aren't even worth a uniform. What bloody waste of a man can't get himself into a bloody uniform in the middle of a bloody war? Answer me that, you bloody useless bastard!"

John remained still, saying nothing, though the tension in his jaw made it obvious to Maisie that he was having to work hard to keep silent.

"Load of cowards, the lot of you." Violet was waving her arms wildly now, including all the NOFU men into this slur, not only John.

"Violet, be quiet!" Maisie snapped. "That's enough!"

But Violet was on a roll. "You come over here and you have the gall to breathe in the same air as these *heroes*." Violet threw herself against the chest of a gangly-limbed sailor standing nearby. She wrapped her arms around him, much to his apparent surprise, yet she continued to harangue John. "*These* are real men, you know, *these* are the heroes. They're not afraid to do their bit for king and country. And they know how to treat a woman properly. You do, don't you, Bill?"

"Tom, actually," mumbled the young sailor, looking both aghast at being picked out and delighted at having this bux-omly beautiful woman wrap herself around him in front of all his shipmates, all at the same time. "I'm Tom, not Bill."

"That's what I said, Bill." Violet now looked like she was having to hold on to him to stop herself from falling, not out of any lustful intentions. "That's what I said. All you navy boys know how to satisfy a woman. Not like these bloody NOFU cowards. You'll dance with me, won't you, Bill? C'mon, we can dance together right now."

"Tom," the sailor said again. He looked embarrassed, and tried to extricate himself from Violet's arms. But all his pals jeered and shoved him toward her again.

The wider circle was breaking up, people no longer as interested in Violet's drunken ramblings now she had moved on from confrontation to whining. After some prodding from the men behind him, the sailor seemed to change his mind about walking away. Instead, he wrapped his arms around Violet and almost lifted her bodily onto the dance floor, where he proceeded to stick his tongue into her mouth.

Maisie didn't have any desire to watch that, so she turned to find John, who was still standing rigid, his hands thrust into his pockets. His face was pale, and his lips, usually so full, were thin and squeezed tight.

"John," she began, though he didn't seem to hear. "John, don't listen to her. She's always been a real piece of work, you know that, and she's obviously been drinking. Ignore her. Please? We could dance, you and me. What do you think? Yes?"

At that moment, Maisie heard a cough behind her and turned to find a sailor, the one who'd been watching her earlier, standing there, looking awkward. Not much older than her, his hairline was already receding, but he had a pleasant, if nervous, smile. He glanced up at John and then back to Maisie.

"I wondered"—he hesitated, looking again at John—"I wondered if perhaps you'd like to dance, miss, if you're not already . . ."

Again, his eyes shifted to John, and his voice trailed away to nothing.

Maisie didn't know what to say. Of course she wanted to dance, though like she'd told Elliott earlier, she wanted to dance with John. But he was obviously upset by what happened with Violet, so it wouldn't be right to leave him now.

"Thank you so much, that's very kind of you, but I was about to dance with . . ." She turned to take John's arm, but he had walked away from her in the direction of the bar. "Oh."

Where was he going?

"John!" she called, "hold on."

John kept walking.

"I'm so sorry," she said to the sailor, "I'm not sure . . . I mean, the answer's no. But thank you for asking."

"But it doesn't look like he's interested," the sailor replied, with a slight pout.

"I said *no*," snapped Maisie, annoyed that he was pointing out the obvious. Then she went after John, catching up with him as he reached the bar, where only the remnants of the sandwiches remained scattered across huge china platters.

"John, what are you doing?" Her attempt not to whine was not successful.

"I thought you were dancing," John said without turning around, his neck and shoulders stiff. He leaned on the bar and waved one finger in the air to catch a waitress's attention. "You've had an invitation, so go and dance. That's why you came, isn't it?"

"I don't want to dance with any old sailor."

"Is that right? You've been bouncing about all night as if your feet are on fire. But there's no point in waiting for me, because like I told you before, I don't dance." At that moment, one of the waitresses noticed John's signal and came down the bar to stand in front of them, wiping up crumbs into a cloth as she came.

"I'll have a whisky," John said. "Malt if you have it."

"There's no whisky, dear—there's a war on, in case you hadn't noticed," said the waitress tartly, as she lifted one of the empty sandwich platters. "I can get you tea, or tea."

John pulled out a packet of cigarettes from his pocket, followed by a handful of coins, which he slammed onto the wood under his flat hand.

"I think we both know there's whisky somewhere behind this bar, don't we?" He removed his hand, leaving the coins where they were.

The barmaid looked at the coins, then back to John. Then she scooped the money into the pocket of her apron. "Well, since you put it that way . . ." She disappeared through the door and appeared thirty seconds later carry a chipped china mug. It looked much more workmanlike than all the other delicate china cups in the room.

"Tea, you said." The waitress placed it down very deliberately in front of John.

"Not tea," he muttered bitterly. "I wanted—"

"I know what you wanted, *sir*. And I'm giving it to you."

In the mug, Maisie could see clear golden-brown liquid almost glowing against the white ceramic.

"As I said, here's your *tea*, sir." The waitress shoved the mug toward John and walked back down the bar.

Almost before Maisie understood it wasn't anything as innocent as tea, John had lifted the mug to his lips and drained it in two or three quick swallows.

"John! What are you doing? Why are you being like this?"

"Jack Tar's waiting for you." He nodded in the direction of Maisie's sailor, voice crackling through the whisky's burn. He put a cigarette between his teeth and struck a match, drawing in a breath until the tip caught and flared red. "Go and dance. Get what you need from *him*, because you won't be getting it from me."

Maisie stared at John through a curtain of cigarette smoke. What had happened? Yes, Violet had been vile to him, and he had every right to be angry about it, but why was he taking it out on Maisie?

Well, damn him! She *would* go and dance with the sailor. And John could go to hell.

Twelve

Without even giving John time to stop her, Maisie walked back to the sailor, who was clearly wishing he'd never asked her anything in the first place. "If you would still like to dance with me, I'd be delighted."

Maisie didn't wait for him to respond but grabbed his hand, which was softer and moister than she'd have liked, and led him to the dance floor. She could see the other lumberjills giving her some very strange and questioning looks, but Maisie didn't care. She'd come here to dance, and so she was damn well going to dance.

For the first few minutes, she made a conscious effort not to look to see if John was watching them, to check if he was looking angry or jealous, but eventually she had to look.

But John wasn't there. Not by the bar, nor with Elliott and

his other friends by the door. Without making it obvious to her dance partner—had the sailor ever told her his name?—Maisie scanned the rest of the room, but could still find no sign of John. Oh well, if he'd gotten jealous, then that was his problem. Anyway, he'd probably only gone to the gents'.

But when John still hadn't returned a few minutes later, she started to worry. He hadn't only looked angry. He'd also looked . . . jealous? Disappointed? She wasn't quite sure, but he'd knocked back that whisky in three gulps, and it had been easily a double measure or even a triple, so what if he'd made himself sick? How many men could handle that much neat whisky in one go?

Maisie grew concerned. Should she go check on him? What if he'd wandered off and fallen in the River Ness?

She stopped dancing so suddenly, the sailor almost pulled her off her feet.

"I'm sorry," she said, as she found her balance again. "Thank you, but I do need to go."

If he replied, Maisie didn't hear it because she was already across the room, tapping Elliott's arm.

"Have you seen John? Is he all right?"

Elliott gave her a shake of his head—no, he hadn't seen John—and a shrug, and she knew she couldn't count on Elliott for help.

She was too embarrassed to peer into the gents' bathrooms, so she waited a little farther down the hallway for a while before lifting aside the blackout curtains and heading out the front door.

The moon was low in the sky, but bright, so although half of the street lay in deep shadow, it took Maisie only a second to see John sitting on the front wall of the building next door to the hotel. She walked along to stand in front of him.

He was sitting forward, his elbows on his knees and his head in his hands, so she had to get quite close before she was sure he knew she was there. Even so, he still didn't move.

"John?"

Nothing.

"John, are you all right?"

He didn't look up, but he slowly let his hands drop away from where they had been cradling each side of his head, leaving his dark hair messy. Maisie had to fight the urge to run her hand through the rumpled hair to smooth it down. Even in the semidarkness, she could see that he looked more tired than drunk.

"I thought you were dancing." John didn't sound angry or accusatory—it was a simple statement of fact.

"I came to find you instead. I was worried."

John sighed. "I'm fine. Please go back and dance. You deserve to enjoy tonight."

"I *was* enjoying tonight," replied Maisie, "at least until Violet got so out of hand, and you reacted the way you did."

"But you wanted to dance."

"I wanted to dance with *you*."

"You know full well that I can't dance."

"That's not true. Not exactly, and anyway, you did dance with me once—"

"And what a triumph that was!" The bitter edge had returned.

"I don't need to dance to have a good time," Maisie said, making sure no hint of the white lie tinged her voice.

"But you should be able to dance if you want to."

Maisie sat down beside him on the wall. "I *did* dance, but it wasn't the same. And I would rather spend this evening not dancing with you than dancing with someone else."

John sighed, and his voice became quiet. "You're not being honest."

"I am. Mostly." She nudged her shoulder against his. "What's wrong? Please tell me you didn't pay attention to any of the rubbish that Violet was spouting. She was drunk, and therefore she was spitting out even more venom than usual."

"But that doesn't mean she was wrong." John turned to look at Maisie for the first time since she had approached him. "A girl like you wants a hero, someone who can give her everything she deserves, everything she needs. You don't want someone . . ."

His words trailed away and he dropped his gaze back to his feet.

"I don't want someone *what*?" Maisie was getting annoyed by all this self-pity. "I don't want someone who volunteers to come thousands of miles from home for the sake of another country's war? Or someone who's making a bigger contribution to the war effort every day than half the army sitting on their bums in the canteen? Do tell me more about the kind of man you think I don't want."

When John didn't reply, she shifted sideways so she was facing him. She reached to place her palm against his cheek and drew his face around until he had to look her in the eye. The moonlight flecked his dark irises with silver.

"You can't tell me, can you?"

"Yes I can." John said quietly. "You want a man who still has both his legs."

For a moment, Maisie thought she'd misheard him. Of course John still had both his legs.

But even as she reassured herself, the puzzle she didn't even realize she'd been piecing together began to slot into place, and a new picture was revealed. The lopsided gait, the way he always paused for a second to find his balance when he stood up, and the fact that he was such a reluctant and, frankly, rotten dancer. It was obvious now. John was missing a leg.

Maisie was stunned. Not about his leg, but about her own stupidity. How could she have known him all these weeks and never suspected he was missing a leg? The clues had all been there, yet she still hadn't guessed the truth. And why had he not told her before? Did he really think it would change the way she looked at him, or the way she felt about him?

"I didn't tell you before," John said, "because I haven't told anyone. Haven and a couple of the others know I use a prosthetic leg—a false one—but that's all. And I've *wanted* to tell you, ever since that day up by the croft, but I knew I wouldn't be able to bear how differently you would look at me if you knew. I've seen how people react, most people anyway. They immediately assume that you can't do anything for yourself, that they need to help you with the smallest task, that you need to be looked after. And they pity you. And from my experience, pity is not a great basis for a friendship, or for anything more."

John closed his eyes and gave a tired sigh. "Now do you see why I know I'm not the man you thought you wanted?"

Maisie bridled at that. How little he understood her.

She opened her mouth to speak but found her throat was so tight she had to swallow hard first to make sure her voice could carry the weight of what she had to make him hear. "No, I don't see that at all. I don't want a man in a uniform, and I don't want a man who can dance. And while it might surprise you, I'm not generally in the habit of counting the limbs of a man I'm falling in love with. But I do know the man I want is you."

As it came out of her mouth, she knew it was true. But she also knew John did not believe her. In fact, she didn't think he was even listening. Somehow, he was looking into her eyes, yet he'd withdrawn into himself during his little speech about pity, and now he seemed to be looking beyond her.

Well, perhaps *this* would help him get the message.

Maisie leaned forward and, with no hesitation at all, she placed her lips against his.

She held the kiss for a couple of seconds, and while she wasn't sure exactly what was supposed to happen, she was sure it should be more than . . . nothing. John didn't move, didn't react, didn't respond in any way. He sat there frozen.

It was like kissing marble.

Maisie drew back far enough to look into John's dark eyes again, and she realized that he had moved. His focus was back on her, not past her, and it was as if he were seeing her for the first time. His eyes searched hers for something, as if he had to find whatever it was to release him from his immobility. She had no idea what he needed, but perhaps it was as simple as reassurance that she wasn't going anywhere.

So, Maisie smiled. And then she kissed him again. And this time his mouth was soft and warm, and she felt it move under hers, so she pressed a little harder.

Then John was kissing her back, his lips responding at last. His hand slipped under her hair to cradle her neck, and he pulled her mouth even tighter onto his.

But it felt *too* tight, *too* desperate, so Maisie pushed her hand against his chest until his mouth left hers and she felt John relax his hold. But she sensed his disappointment at the loss of her touch, so she laid her hand against his face.

"Softly," she whispered.

And this time when she kissed him, his touch was gentle, but soon it was her lips and tongue searching for his. There was a sweet tang of whisky on his breath, and it sent a thrill through Maisie, tightening every muscle, making her want more.

She moved her hand into his hair, but it was awkward, sitting sideways on the wall as they were, and she knew how she could make it easier for them. She'd never been so forward with a boy before—in fact, she'd never done much of any of this before—but there was a first time for everything. And anyway, John wasn't a boy, and Maisie was certainly no shy little girl these days, so she decided to be brave. She lifted herself off the wall a little, without letting her lips leave his, and turned until she could feel the sturdy, warm muscles of John's thighs under her own. Letting her arms wind all the way around his broad shoulders, she sat down onto his lap, and . . .

John stopped her before she had even let her weight settle. His hands grasped her upper arms and lifted her off him forcefully, though not roughly, and placed her back onto the wall.

"No, Maisie, you can't, I mean, *I* can't . . ." John pushed himself up onto his feet, breathing hard. "I'm sorry, Maisie, I really can't—"

Maisie's face burned with humiliation as she realized what she'd just done. Of course he couldn't let her sit on his lap. Hadn't he just told her about his leg? And yet she'd been so caught up in her . . . her yearning to be closer to him that she'd tried to . . . she'd tried to . . .

She covered her face with her hands, unable even to look at him. "I'm so sorry, that was so stupid of me. I didn't mean to . . . oh, my God, I hurt you, didn't I? Landing on you like that with all my weight, right on your—"

"Maisie, stop." John sounded unreasonably calm. "You didn't hurt me. Not at all. It's only that my right leg—"

She felt his hand on her shoulder, but she wriggled away from his touch and jumped to her feet, furious with herself.

"Exactly! Your leg! And yet I still try to sit on your lap. I can't believe I did that. Of course, you wouldn't want me to—"

"Maisie, please." John was standing now, and he took her by the wrists and gently pulled her hands down from her face. "Right now, I'd like nothing more than to sit here with you in my lap and to kiss you And to keep kissing you, till midnight and beyond, if you'd let me. But, well, when you're missing a leg, you have to make, erm, let's call them *adjustments*."

Still Maisie was too embarrassed to look up at him, until she felt his finger under her chin, lifting her face up toward his.

"So while it might not be the best thing for you to sit on my lap, there's nothing to stop me from kissing you right here, standing up, is there?" He wiped his thumbs delicately across her cheeks to catch the tears of humiliation as they escaped her lashes. "Is there?"

Maisie shook her head, and John lowered his lips toward hers once again. At that moment the door from the hotel ballroom flew open and a mass of uniformed men came bundling out. The one at the front—Maisie had only a split second to recognize him as one of the sailors who had pushed his friend Tom—or Bill?—into dancing with Violet—crashed into Maisie and made a grab at her dress to stop himself from falling.

"Get off!" John shouted over her head, and Maisie felt herself suddenly released from the sailor's weight as John pushed him roughly away from her. "Watch what you're doing, for God's sake!"

The sailor staggered back from John's shove, but even before Maisie could right her balance, he was hurtling back toward John, fist raised.

"No! Don't hurt him!" Maisie cried, but the sailor didn't hear her, or perhaps he didn't *want* to hear her.

Suddenly, the doors burst open again and out came Elliott, closely followed by Haven and Robert. Within two seconds, they were charging at the sailor, only to find their way blocked by his hulking friends.

Maisie couldn't believe it. There was going to be a huge rammy, in the street, and all over an accidental collision. The sailor hadn't hurt her when he'd bumped into her, so there was no need for any of this. God! Why did men have to be so stupid?

Maisie didn't see who threw the first punch, but she did see John tumble backward onto the ground, and the sailor immediately fell on top of him, as if the momentum of his own punch had unbalanced him. She'd never seen men in a fight before, but had always imagined it would be like the photos she'd seen in the newspaper of a boxing match, upright and controlled. But looking in horror at all the men around her, this was more like wrestling—they had their arms wrapped around each other, pulling and shoving, back and forth. And even in the bright moonlight, it was almost impossible to tell the navy blue of a sailor's uniform from the dark wool of a Newfoundlander's suit.

Perversely, Elliott and the others looked like they were rather enjoying themselves, so she left them to it. She had to help John. He was lying on the ground, his hands up to protect his face from the fist of the man crouching over him. What kind of a man was that sailor, punching a man when he was on the ground? And what defense could John put up when he was being pinned down, about to be pummeled, and when he had only one leg?

Before she had time to think what she was doing, Maisie was screaming, "Leave him alone!" and her fist was flying up into the sailor's jaw.

Thirteen

The sailor was caught so unawares, he tumbled backward off John and lay dazed on the cobbles. Maisie was as surprised as he was by what she'd just done, and even more by the agony lancing across her knuckles.

Bloody hell! How could one punch hurt so much?

She thrust her throbbing hand under her other arm and pressed down hard, trying to squeeze away the pain, as John scrambled to his feet.

"What did you think you were doing?" he shouted at her.

Maisie was taken aback by his tone—what did he think she had been doing, for God's sake?—but her blood was still pumping and she was not going to take a telling off from John, not when she'd just saved him from a beating.

"I was protecting you from that bloke's fist," she shouted back, right into his face. "That's what I was doing."

"I don't need you to protect me." John was towering over her now, apparently oblivious of the battle going on around them between the other lumberjacks and sailors. "I was handling it myself."

"But he had you down on the ground, and he was about to punch you. And I knew you wouldn't be able to get up, not with your—"

"Don't say it!" Suddenly, John was not shouting any longer, but the lack of volume made his fury all the more chilling. "Do *not* say what you were about to! This is *exactly* why I didn't tell you before—because I knew you would see me differently. I knew you would pity me, just like all the others did."

"That's not true," Maisie replied, though her throat was tightening as she spoke, knowing that John was not entirely wrong. "I was only trying to—"

"You were only trying to *protect* me. Yes, you said that already. But I don't need you to protect me, Maisie." John turned and stalked toward the entrance to the hotel, stepping around the sailor Maisie had punched, who was now struggling to get to his feet. "No matter what has happened to me, I will never need a woman to protect me."

Maisie felt her own anger build in an instant, and as he slammed open the door and disappeared inside, she yelled after him, "I am *not* a woman. I am a *lumberjill*!"

* * *

Maisie sat in the cab of the Bedford and stewed. She was furious, mostly with John, but also with herself. Actually, quite a lot with herself.

Seconds after John had gone into the hotel, she'd heard a whistle blowing, then another, and someone nearby had shouted, "Coppers!" The fights around her had broken up instantly as half the men—the Navy half, she noticed—took off running up the street, leaving the Newfoundlanders, and Maisie, to nurse their bruises and face the music.

Even though Elliott's diplomacy and charm had persuaded the constables that there was no need to take names, or to ban them from Inverness as the policemen had threatened, it had still taken a long while to sort out. By the time Elliott and Haven had exchanged friendly handshakes and backslaps with the constables, the rumbling engine of the truck had been echoing off the cold gray walls down Castle Street, signaling that it was time to return to camp. As the truck had drawn up beside them, John had reappeared, holding Violet upright by one arm, while Malcolm propped her up under the other. She had looked virtually comatose, and it had taken four of the men to heave her up onto the flatbed so that Rose and Heather could make her comfortable with blankets for the ride home.

As if Violet deserved that kind of care and attention after what she'd done and said earlier.

Once he'd handed Violet into Rose's care, John had walked toward Maisie, and in the glow from the shaded headlights of the truck, she'd been able to see clearly the bloody results of the beating he'd taken before she'd reached him. Cautiously, John had stretched his hand toward her, callused palm up as if expecting her to put her hand into his.

"Maisie," he'd said, "I shouldn't have shouted."

Maisie had stared at his hand. Whatever she'd done to defend John, it had been in the heat of the fight, and it had been nothing to do with pity, or with thinking less of his ability to look after himself. How could he even think that? Then Maisie realized that he hadn't actually apologized for shouting at her. He'd just said that he shouldn't have. And he also hadn't apologized for accusing her of pitying him either. And that set her fury at the unjustness of their argument ablaze all over again.

So she'd called to Clarke, the driver, pointing at the cab door, then at herself. Clarke was helping the last of the group onto the back of the truck, but he'd given Maisie a shrug, which she took as permission, and she'd hauled herself up into the cab.

Holding the door open, she'd looked back down at John with a sneer worthy of Violet. "No, you shouldn't have shouted. And if you really think that I helped you because I pity you, rather than because I care whether you get hurt or not, then you don't need to worry, because next time, I won't bother."

Before John could respond, she'd slammed the door closed and leaned her back against it. Two could play at that sulking game.

But now that they were on their way back toward Carrbridge, she had nothing to do for an hour but brood. Thankfully, Clarke was not chatty, so Maisie could keep her face turned away, her head resting against the grimy glass of the window. She could wipe her tears, blow soothing breaths onto her stinging knuckles, and wish she'd stayed at camp with Dot and Nancy.

How could John have thought she pitied him? Finding out about his leg had certainly caught her by surprise, but strangely it hadn't shocked her, and it certainly hadn't changed the way she thought about him. And hadn't she shown that when she'd kissed him? And it wasn't like John hadn't responded to her kisses. He had responded, and she had responded, and there had been so much responding going on, she'd simply wanted to be closer to him. And anyway, if his kisses hadn't been driving her senseless, she would have realized sooner that trying to sit on his lap was a dreadful mistake, so really it was more his fault than hers. And she'd only punched the sailor because he was a sniveling cowardly excuse for a man, punching a man on the ground, and not because she thought John couldn't take care of himself.

Oh! It was so infuriating that such a thrilling evening, with the snug hayride and the newsreel, and even the dance, had gone so horribly wrong. The evening had been completely ruined by Violet's bile and John's ridiculous reaction to her punching a sailor on his behalf, and now her bruised and bloody hand. Well, thank God it was almost midnight and she could rest her head against the glass, knowing this awful evening was almost over. What else could possibly go wrong today? She would deal with tomorrow when it came, but she was so glad to be done with tonight.

When they reached Auchterblair camp, Clarke called good night as Maisie clambered down out of the cab. She didn't wait for anyone else, and kept her eyes lowered in case John was looking down at her from the flatbed. She pulled her cardigan tight around her and hurried into the sanctuary of the dormitory hut.

It was late, yet to Maisie's surprise, all the lamps were still lit. Dot and Nancy should have put out all but one when they went to their beds, to save on fuel, but strangely, the hut was as bright as it would have been midevening. And then the answer to her earlier question hit Maisie straight in the face like a wet slap.

She'd asked herself what else could possibly go wrong today?

Well, the answer was sitting on Maisie's bed, happily waving and smiling.

Fourteen

"Beth!" Maisie exclaimed. "What are you doing here?"

Maisie struggled to understand as a flash of uncertainty replaced the grin on her younger sister's face. But what reaction had Beth expected? That Maisie would welcome her in with open arms?

"I mean, why are you—? How did you—? Does Mother know you—? What the hell, Beth?"

Maisie could not process this. It was midnight in a hut in the middle of the mountains, in *her* hut in the middle of *her* mountains, and Beth was here.

Beth opened her mouth and then closed it again, looking instead to the other side of the hut, where Dot and Nancy were sitting on their own beds, their smiles slipping as they saw Maisie's furious reaction.

"Don't look at them." Maisie could hear her voice was getting shriller by the word, more like her mother's, but she couldn't help that. "I'm not asking them, I'm asking you. Why are you here?"

She'd been about to say, *This is my place, not yours*, but even in her confusion, she knew that would sound childish and petty, and she knew she needed to be the mature one here.

"Maisie, don't be like that." Dot came over to sit beside Beth, and Maisie's stomach tightened. Why was Dot standing up for Beth, and not Maisie? "I think it's lovely that your sister's come all this way to see you. Shouldn't you be thanking her, not—"

"Thanking her?" Maisie was screeching now. "Thanking her? What for? I didn't invite her. Beth, you should be at home. And did you even tell Mother and Dad you were leaving? God! They're going to you kill you for this. No, wait, they're going to kill *me* for this. You're only fifteen. What were you thinking?"

Again, Beth opened her mouth to speak, but as she did, Maisie saw a big, fat tear well in Beth's eye and then shimmer down her cheek.

"Oh, Beth, don't cry," said Dot, putting her arm around Beth's shoulder. "She doesn't mean to be crabby. You gave Maisie a surprise, that's all."

"I *do* bloody mean to be crabby," Maisie retorted. "Seriously, Beth. Mother will be going out of her mind with worry."

Finally, Beth found her voice amid the chokes and sniffles. "I left her a note telling her I'd be with you, so she won't be worried."

"Of course she'll be—"

"No, she won't. I know she won't. Neither will Dad." Beth dug into the pocket of her skirt and brought out a crumpled handkerchief to wipe her runny nose. "They won't even notice I'm not there. They've barely even spoken to me since you left, or to each other. Dad stays in his study whenever he's home, and Mother spends more time polishing the silver or washing the curtains than talking to me. And she keeps crying. She thinks I don't notice, but I do. Every time I come into the room, her eyes are all red. It's because you went away and she's been stuck with me."

"Beth, that's not true."

"It is, and you know it. She doesn't even bother to cook anymore. It's cold meat and potatoes every night, or a pie from the butcher. She can't bring herself to make the effort when it's only me and Dad. Then Judith and I went to the pictures last night, and we saw you on the newsreel, and you looked so happy, and I wanted to see you so much. It's been miserable at home, Piggly, it really has, and—"

"Don't call me that here!" Maisie snapped, though she was struggling to maintain the fury in the face of her sister's tears. "I hate—"

"Yes, I know you hate me, you always have, but I only wanted to—" The rest was lost as Beth buried her face in her handkerchief.

Maisie was stunned. Beth thought Maisie hated her? But really, why should that be a surprise? Hadn't she always been horrid to Beth to make herself feel better? Suddenly, Maisie realized how much she'd missed her sister, how much she loved her. And yet, here she was again, true to form, making Beth cry because the rest of her own evening had gone so wrong? Beth was looking wretched, and Maisie knew she had to make this right. She drew in a deep breath and forced a smile onto her face.

"I was about to say, 'I hate you *calling me that*,' not that I hate *you*." Maisie lowered her voice. "I don't hate you, Beth. How could I hate you? For goodness' sake, you've trekked halfway across Scotland, alone, into the back of beyond to see me. How could I hate—"

Then the most obvious question occurred to Maisie. "By the way, how *did* you get here?" She looked at Dot, as if she might already know, and found Dot frowning at her as if to say *be nice*. "I mean, I don't remember seeing a bus with Back of Beyond on the sign, do you, Dot?"

Dot smiled then, and took her arm from Beth's shoulder. "No, I don't think I have either. There's certainly one that goes from Inverness to the Middle of Nowhere—"

"And the number seventy-six runs every day from Forres to Braemar via the Arse-end of Anywhere, but . . ."

Beth started to laugh with them, or at least, she was snuffling into her hankie. Maisie held out her hand and folded Beth into the hug that she found she was now desperate to give her. Maisie hadn't meant to be a cow, it was . . . well, it had been a shock, especially after everything else tonight.

"Seriously, though," Maisie said, "we need to let Mother and Dad know that you're safe." Maisie felt Beth nod wetly against her shoulder. "In the morning, we'll take the bikes and ride down to Carrbridge so we can telephone home. And then we have to work out how to get you back there again."

"No! Please let me stay." Beth pulled back a little and Maisie could see her torn face. "They don't want me there."

"They do want you there, you know they do." Suddenly Maisie felt very tired, so she gathered Beth in again. "But right now, let's find you somewhere to sleep. And we can talk about all this in the morning over a bowl of Nancy's best porridge."

Beth nodded against Maisie's shoulder. "Thanks, Piggly. And over breakfast, will you also tell me why your knuckles are all bloody?"

In spite of her initial annoyance at Beth's sudden appearance, by Thursday of that week, Maisie was glad she'd decided to let her sister stay for a few more days. Beth had been exactly what Maisie had needed to distract her from thinking about John, and about what had happened on Friday evening.

Originally, Maisie had been determined to send Beth home the next morning, and neither Beth's pleading nor Dot's reassurance that the WTC head office would never find out had swayed her. However, she'd decided to let Beth stay the moment she'd called home, from the public telephone in the Carrbridge post office, and had heard the cold detachment in her father's voice when she'd told him that Beth was safely with her. He'd sounded like he hadn't even noticed Beth was gone, and wasn't much bothered when she would come back again. Then, when Maisie had asked to speak to Mother, he'd said that she was out at the hairdresser's and wouldn't be back until lunchtime.

Maisie had been appalled. A fifteen-year-old girl had run away from home, and yet her mother had still gone out to get her hair done? It would have been unbelievable, if it wasn't so entirely believable. Beth was right—they obviously didn't care.

Of course, persuading Violet to let Beth stay had been easy. Violet had been feeling so awful all day after the dance, she would have agreed to anything just to get Maisie to leave her in peace. Once the hangover had abated, however, Violet reverted to her usual snappy self, and worse. Even Claire and Evelyn had been keeping their distance. Violet was clearly embarrassed by what had happened, or rather, by what everyone else *told her* had happened, since she apparently still had almost no memory of what she had done and said after about nine o'clock.

When Maisie finally told Beth she could stay, she also set some ground rules.

"If you are going to be here for the rest of this week," Maisie had told her sister, "there are three rules you must abide by. Don't interfere with our work, don't be a pain in the neck, and, for God's sake, keep out of Violet's way. Understand?"

Beth had leaped to her feet and saluted Maisie as if she were in the army. "Understood, *sir*!" Then she'd thrown her arms around Maisie's neck and squeezed until Maisie'd had little choice but to hug her back.

And so far, Beth had stuck to all three rules, which was three more than Maisie had expected. Even more surprising, she'd made herself useful too, particularly since Nancy was still covering Agnes's work in the kitchen. To Maisie's astonishment, Beth had been up at half past five each morning to help Nancy get the enormous pot of porridge oats on to cook. She also made piles of sandwiches and packed them into the lunch tins, which she stacked next to a basket of apples, before filling the water canteens for the lumberjills to pick up as they finished breakfast. Beth even helped Nancy clear up, and make a start on dinner before she went out to assist Wee Susan, who had agreed to cover most of Nancy's stable duties once Maisie had explained that although she liked Clyde, she still didn't feel very confident about being solely responsible for him.

"Beth's been marvelous," Nancy said one evening. "Agnes makes all this cooking and clearing up look like it's nothing, but it's such a lot of work, I don't know how I would have got it all done without Beth to help me. And she's great company too, with so many funny stories—most of them about you, of course."

"Of course," laughed Maisie.

"Can you not work out how we can keep her for another week?" asked Nancy with a grin. "Or another month?"

Maisie knew Nancy was joking, but actually, she rather agreed—it had been nice to have Beth here. Having said that, the Auchterblair version of Beth was a lot more likeable than any Beth Maisie had known at home. But then, perhaps the Auchterblair version of Maisie was not the same person Beth had grown up with either. There seemed to be nothing here to cause the usual resentment and petty squabbling they went in for at home.

But had they always fought like that? Maisie knew they hadn't. One evening, as they were settling into their cots at bedtime, the two of them had reminisced about a trip they had when they were little, long before the war, before Beth started school. The family had taken the train from Glasgow Central down the coast, to a sweet little boarding house in Ardrossan, near the harbor. It had rained almost every day that week, but it hadn't mattered. They'd still had so much fun together as a family, with wet walks along the beach, and fishing for crabs from the harbor wall, and instead of ice creams, they'd had tea and warm scones at the café every afternoon. Of course, those were the days when Dad would tell them funny stories and make up games for them all to play, and he would hold their hands as they walked. And those were the days when Mother would smile.

Neither Maisie or Beth had been aware of the exact moment their parents began to change, though thinking back, Maisie was sure it started around the time of their grandmother's death. They were told they were too young to go to the funeral, and had been shut out of many grown-up conversations for weeks after. But from then on, Maisie had been aware that Dad seemed to be working most of the time, and their mother had become short-tempered and too tired to play or read them books. Maisie remembered noticing that she and Beth didn't get as many new toys or clothes as before, and there were certainly no more holidays in Ardrossan either. And then, when the war broke out across Europe, their dad had disappeared completely. But unlike some of her friends' fathers, Dad wasn't sent away to fight. Instead, he shut himself away in his study, and it was as if she and Beth didn't exist.

With their father's silence, and their mother's dark moods, the girls couldn't help but bicker with each other. Sometimes it had felt as if war had broken out inside the McCall home too.

But here at Auchterblair, she'd found the old Beth again. And perhaps she'd found the old Maisie too.

But in spite of the welcome distraction, there was still the problem of John.

Somehow, she'd managed to avoid seeing him so far this week by volunteering to take on a small job clearing saplings down by the river, along with Dot and, rather strangely, Violet's crony Claire. Maisie had enjoyed getting to know Claire better, because away from Violet, she had turned out to be a far nicer person than Maisie had expected. All in all, these four days by the water had been a refreshing break, not only from the heavy work of felling the pine trees up the hill, but also from the anxiety of bumping into John, or worse, having to work alongside him.

There was another anxiety though, a niggling thought that Maisie couldn't quite shake from her mind, irrational though it was. It was the idea that perhaps John was avoiding her too.

She'd find out soon enough, because tomorrow, Friday, their trio would be back with the main group again for a new job on a big estate near Nethybridge, and chances were, Maisie'd see John; and that thought made her insides squirm. At dinner, Maisie had no appetite and was obviously looking so awful that Dot asked three times if she was feeling unwell.

But Maisie was not feeling poorly—she was just torn. On the one hand, she really wanted to see John and apologize for sulking all the way home from the dance. He had tried, in his own way, to apologize, and she'd ignored him. But on the other hand, she still felt so furious and hurt that he'd shouted at her at all. He should have known she'd only been trying to help him. But on the other hand—was this back on the first hand again, or did she have to find a third from somewhere to work out this conundrum?—why had she jumped into a fistfight between two men much bigger and stronger than herself if not because she thought that John was somehow incapable of protecting himself?

Had he been right when he'd said that pity had driven her actions? Did she really think him less manly, or at least, less of a man—she thought those two things might be different— because of what he had told her about his leg? She had promised him that it wouldn't change the way she saw him, but perhaps it had. Maybe he'd never forgive her for letting that happen, and perhaps those delicious kisses they'd shared on Friday night would mean nothing to him anymore.

Either way, she would certainly find out tomorrow morning if he would even speak to her again. And if he wouldn't? Well, everyone would notice that he was ignoring her, and her public humiliation would be complete.

To make matters worse, that morning when she'd been looking for her spare sweater to lend to Beth, she'd found the red book—John's uncle's poetry—deep in her suitcase where she'd stuffed it after the dance.

As she pushed her uneaten stew around her plate with her fork, Maisie decided that she had no choice but to return the book to John as soon as possible. The book was so precious to him, after all, and she owed him that much, however he felt about her now. She supposed that she could send someone else to return it for her, but that would be the coward's way out, and anyway, by seeing him, she would find out in private whether what they'd had together was gone. She could get all the anxiety and embarrassment out of the way before work tomorrow, clear the question mark hovering between them, and allow Maisie to get on with her life as a lumberjill.

Maisie laid down her fork and pushed away her plate with a determined shove.

Yes. Definitely. That's what she'd do. She would go to see him straight after dinner.

Thankfully, Beth was already involved in a card game with the Susans, so no one questioned Maisie as she left the hut, the red poetry book tucked into her trouser pocket.

She took the quicker shortcut through the trees, since she wanted to be back before dark, and it wasn't long before the lights of the men's camp were sparkling through the gloaming.

Their campsite layout was not so different from the women's, but their huts looked like they were of far sounder construction. Elliott had once told her that they'd lived in old canvas army tents for their first few weeks in Scotland, until they had built their own huts. That was presumably why these huts looked like they would be much warmer than those at Auchterblair, which were already uncomfortably cold at night, even though the weather outside was still relatively mild for the time of year.

A handful of men sat outside, smoking and talking, and as she walked toward them, one of them jumped to his feet. Maisie recognized him—he was much older than her, and huge, with a full red beard—though she couldn't recall his name.

Grinning widely, the man put up his fists. "Watch your-selves, boys," he warned. "This one flattened a six-foot sailor with a single right hook." He danced around on his toes like a boxer, fists punching the air.

Maisie was mortified, and although she hated the blush that had crept into her cheeks, she was relieved that her scabbed knuckles were in her pocket, out of sight. "I'm look-ing for John, actually. John Lindsay?" she managed to choke out, fighting both her annoyance and the urge to flee.

The older man was still grinning. "Are you now?"

"I'm returning a book I borrowed," Maisie continued, "so if you could go and get him instead of playing the comedian."

Just then, the hut door thumped open and Haven appeared on the threshold. His left eye was sunk deep in a purple and yellow bruise, clearly his own souvenir from Friday's dance. Seeing Maisie's blushing face, Haven glowered at the other man.

"If you've been less than polite to this young lady, Eric, you'll be emptying the latrines for a month. You get me?"

Eric dropped his hands and mumbled something about him only having a laugh.

Maisie smiled at Haven as an unspoken thank-you and said, "I was looking for John Lindsay. I have a book to return to him."

"Lindsay's not here," Haven replied, "and he won't be back tonight."

"Oh, right," said Maisie, at a loss now for what do to.

Haven held out his hand. "But I can throw it on his bunk if you leave it with me."

Maisie pulled the book from her pocket, being careful to keep her purple knuckles where Eric couldn't see them. But before she handed it to Haven, she faltered. If she gave Haven the book, she wouldn't get to see John. And if she didn't see John, she wouldn't find out where they stood. Of course, she might leave him a note, but if he wasn't back tonight, she might see him at work before he'd read it, and that would be awkward. And anyway, she didn't want to write to him. She wanted to tell him in person, and privately. She wanted to sit down next to John and talk.

And Maisie suddenly knew that this was why she had come. Not to return the book at all, and not to see if he would ignore her. Quite the opposite. She'd come because she wanted to make sure that John would talk to her, and that he'd let her talk to him. Because she needed to tell him again that what he'd told her about his leg really hadn't changed anything between them. And she needed to tell him how much she wanted to kiss him again, and to feel him kiss her back.

Hoping desperately that Haven was not some sort of mind reader, and that the rosy light of the sunset was disguising her blushing cheeks, she pulled the book away from Haven's hand and put it back in her pocket.

"That's all right," she said. "It can wait. I think I'd rather give it to him myself."

Haven shrugged. "As you like."

Giving Haven a wave good-bye, she walked quickly back toward the path. If the light was still good enough, she might stop on the little stone bridge over the burn for a while. Perhaps talking to the water as it tumbled over the rocks and down the hill would help her to think more clearly, because right now there was no one else she wanted to talk to.

Well, perhaps there was one person.

But he wasn't here.

Fifteen

It was almost dark by the time Maisie returned to camp. She stumbled as she went in through the door because she was trying to wipe the burn-bank mud off her boots as she walked. Dot and Nancy were sitting side by side on Dot's bed, a magazine spread across their laps.

"Maisie! You're back," said Dot, and even in its blandness, the statement seemed to carry some strange significance.

"I went out for a walk," Maisie said defensively, "to stretch my legs a bit."

"Oh, right," said Dot, and her glance strayed to Maisie's bed.

Nancy seemed to be staring at Maisie's bed too, which was strange. And when Maisie turned to see what they were looking at, it was as if all the other women in the room suddenly looked away to their books, magazines, and playing cards as if Maisie had caught them staring.

Maisie walked across to her bed, still puzzling, and then stopped short. On her pillow sat an envelope with her name written in ink on the front. She knew the writing. It was the same scattered scrawl she'd seen in a black leather notebook.

John had written her a letter.

Maisie lifted the envelope from the pillow and found that it was simply a piece of paper, folded and tucked into itself to offer some privacy.

"Oh yes," said Dot, clearly trying to sound nonchalant but failing miserably, as she rose to join Maisie. "John was here earlier and left that for you."

"John Lindsay?"

"Yes. John Lindsay. Is there any other John than your John?"

"He's not *my* John, and keep your voice down."

Dot shrugged, again, a little too casually. "Either way, he waited awhile for you, but then he said they had to go."

"They?"

"Elliott was here too."

"And how long since they left?"

"Maybe half an hour?"

John had been here, and Maisie had missed him. Maybe if she'd walked home quicker, if she hadn't stopped on the bridge, they'd have bumped into each other and she'd have had the chance to return his book in person and tell him how much she wanted them to . . .

But wait, what if John had come to end things with her? She turned the note over in her hand. Was this an explanation or an apology? Or a good-bye? As Maisie put her fingernail under the fold of the paper, she realized that Dot was still watching her.

But what did that matter? Dot was her friend, and she'd tell her all that had happened soon enough. Or perhaps not everything. She'd meant to tell Dot that they'd arrived, but John's leg was a secret that Maisie knew was not hers to tell.

Maisie pulled at the edge of the paper and opened it up.

The note was only one line long, aside from the signature.

Perhaps page 35 might help to explain.
Yours,
John

Maisie read it again. And again. He hadn't explained or apologized, but he hadn't ended things either. In fact, he hadn't said anything at all. And page thirty-five of what? But that was a stupid question when she could feel the weight of *In Flanders Fields* in her pocket.

Dot was peering over the top of the letter at what John had written, so Maisie thrust it at her.

"It's nothing," she said, fighting the urge to pull the book out of her pocket and start flicking through the pages to see what he meant. But no, that was something she would do alone.

"So what does that mean?" asked Dot, running her finger along each word, as if that might help her decipher it. "Beth thought it might be an apology, but I said it was a love note."

"What tripe!" Maisie tried not to snap. "Why would John write me a love note, for goodness' sake? Or an apology? He owes me neither."

"Are you sure?" Dot asked. "I mean, the way you've been avoiding him, and yet pining for him too, ever since—"

"I have *not* been pining for him, or avoiding him . . . well, maybe a little, but either way, this isn't about any of that. It's just a reference to a discussion we had about a poem the other day. Nothing more."

"A poem?" Dot sounded so disappointed that Maisie was sorry for being sharp with her.

"Yes, a poem." Maisie took the paper back from Dot, folded it, and tucked it into her pocket. "Look, I'm exhausted, so I think I'm going to turn in early."

"But—"

"Will you tell Beth I've already gone to bed?" Maisie said, but Dot didn't move. "Go on, please. Honestly, it's nothing. Anyway, Nancy's waiting for you."

With apparent reluctance, Dot walked back toward Nancy, and Maisie began to get ready for bed. All the while the note burned in her pocket, demanding to be reread. But she'd make it wait—make John wait—and so it was several minutes more before she was settled into bed with John's note and his uncle's book.

After reading again what he'd written, Maisie flicked through the pages till she found the right pages. On page thirty-four she found the title and first few stanzas of a poem called "Eventide."

> *The day is past and the toilers cease;*
> *The land grows dim 'mid the shadows grey,*
> *And hearts are glad, for the dark brings peace*
> *At the close of day.*

The dark certainly wasn't bringing Maisie any peace tonight. Looking across to the opposite page—page thirty-five—Maisie scanned the text.

> *It speaks of peace that comes after strife,*
> *Of the rest He sends to the hearts He tried,*
> *Of the calm that follows the stormiest life—*
> *God's eventide.*

Peace that comes after strife—the calm that follows the stormiest life . . .

Was one of those the line he was pointing her to? And if so, did he mean her stormy life, or his? Or perhaps the strife between them after last Friday. She wasn't sure.

Oh, this was frustrating! Even more now, she wished she'd been here to see him in person. She wanted to understand what he was trying to tell her, but right now, she was guessing. And what if she guessed wrong?

But then it occurred to her that perhaps there was a positive side to this after all. John had come to see her, and had waited for quite a while, and then he'd left her a note. So perhaps all was not lost. But really, why did he have to be so bloody mysterious about it?

Feeling a little reassured, Maisie read the poem twice more before her eyes began to droop. She tucked John's note inside the cover, closed the book, and slid it under her pillow. She could feel the hard edge of the book below her cheek, but instead of feeling uncomfortable, it was rather reassuring. Whatever John had meant her to understand, perhaps she might find a way to solve the mystery tomorrow.

Sixteen

"Come on, lazybones, look lively!" Dot said, thumping down two lunch tins and two water canteens on the table beside Maisie's breakfast, making Maisie jump. "Have you even woken up yet?"

"Do you have to be so bright and cheery every bloody morning?" Maisie moaned through a mouthful of porridge. She hadn't slept well at all, awakening regularly throughout the night, and she was exhausted.

"Get a move on!" Dot was not giving up. "We've got a long walk ahead of us, you and me. I'm going to have a wash, so you've got five minutes to finish up your breakfast and get your boots on, and then we'll be off!"

"Wait a second. Isn't everyone getting picked up and driven to the new job over . . ." Maisie waved her hand in a vague easterly direction. Even through her foggy brain, Maisie was sure they'd been told to be ready for pickup at seven to drive to the new job site at Nethybridge.

"Everyone else is, except you and me, remember? We're walking back up to Docharn Craig. You know all this. Oh wait, no, maybe you were still out when Violet gave us the orders. Sorry."

"But that job got finished yesterday."

"Apparently not. All that's left are the big logs that need real muscle power." With a grin, Dot lifted her arms up at right angles and flexed her pale and skinny muscles. "And that is, of course, why they're sending me. But *you*? You'll just be there to make me look good."

Maisie picked up a leftover crust of bread and threw it at Dot, who dodged it easily, picked it up, and threw it back again, hitting Maisie on the forehead.

"Apparently," Dot carried on, as if nothing had happened, "Haven's already sent the truck up there, and Wee Susan will bring Clyde to join us once she's got him fed and watered. Nancy might come up too, once breakfast is all done. So stop frowning and start moving! It's going to be a lovely morning, and remember, the wood waits for no man."

Maisie tutted as Dot disappeared out the door, but even so, she pushed herself up from the bench and carried her dirty plates and cup through to where Beth was helping Nancy clear up the kitchen. Beth was too busy chatting to spare Maisie more than a quick and soapy wave, and so Maisie left them to it. By the time Dot returned, Maisie had put her boots on and was strapping on her leather belt, positioning the knife sheath so that it rested comfortably against her hip.

Even though Dot had said they were late, when they walked across the yard to get their tools from the shed, it was clear that full sunrise was still half an hour or so away. There was, however, enough light for them to find their way without a lantern, so they set off, each with a cant hook in one hand and an ax in the other. Maisie had the lunch tins and water bottles in a canvas bag, the strap across her shoulders, and Dot carried, as she always did, her first aid satchel.

The morning was fresh and chilly, and Maisie was glad that Dot had insisted they both wear their greatcoats. The light from the hidden sun outlined the eastern hills in a soft pink glow. Maisie cast a suspicious eye toward the thick gray blanket of cloud to the southwest, on which crimson tinges threatened a change in the weather, even if it didn't appear to be approaching at any speed.

As they crossed the field, Dot frowned up at the sky. "You know what they say, don't you? Red sky at night, shepherd's delight. But red sky in the morning, shepherd's warning."

"No, no, that's not how it goes at all," Maisie replied with a smile. "Red sky at night, your barn's on fire!"

Dot groaned at the old joke, and since they'd reached the path through the trees, which was narrow in places, she fell in step behind Maisie, humming softly to herself.

The scent of the heather enveloped them as they kicked their way between the encroaching shrubs on the winding path. Songbirds called to the dawn from within the thickets of gorse lurking beneath the stretching arms of the Scots pines and larch saplings. It was certainly a glorious morning to be outdoors, and it occurred to Maisie that walking this far, with a heavy coat on and so much equipment, would have exhausted her only a couple of months ago. But now that she was so much fitter and stronger, it felt like she was only warming up for the day's work.

Before too long, they reached one of the wide tracks that crisscrossed the lower slopes, allowing the larger trucks to access the higher reaches of the forests. The road was much smoother, and with no boulders and tree roots in their way, the last part of the climb would be a lot faster. Now that they were walking side by side, however, Maisie became aware that Dot several times took a breath as if to say something, only to change her mind.

"You'll choke on all those unsaid words, you know," Maisie said finally. "Say whatever it is you want to say."

Dot groaned again. "I don't know where to start, that's all."

"Because . . . ?"

"Because . . . I wanted to ask you about John."

"Ah. Well, there's not much to say about John now, is there?"

"Isn't there? I mean, you've said you don't want to tell me what happened on Friday night, but something happened, didn't it? You've been avoiding him since then, and pining for him—"

"Will you stop saying I've been pining for him? It's just not true."

"No, of course it isn't," said Dot with gentle sarcasm.

"And anyway, what makes you think I've been avoiding him?"

"Have you talked to John since the dance in Inverness?"

"No, but—"

"Have you even seen him since then?"

"No, but—"

"See, I told you. Until that night, you seemed to be getting on so well, but then—"

"But then things got . . . complicated, and he made it clear he doesn't like me anymore, and now there's nothing to talk about."

"Doesn't like you? But that's rubbish! I saw the way he looked at you last week when the camera was there. He looked besotted. And you looked back at him like you were . . . I don't know . . . *besotted* too."

"Oh, stop, Dot. Please don't."

"And you always blush when he's around. And so does he. And then—"

"Wait, John blushes?"

"And then," Dot repeated, to silence Maisie's interruptions, "he came all the way over here last night, and waited for ages, and left you that note, and you blushed again when you opened it. So you might as well admit it—you really like him."

Maisie sighed. "It doesn't matter if I like him or not, Dot. He made it clear he doesn't like me."

"But he does, I'm sure of it."

"No, he doesn't, otherwise he wouldn't have . . ."

"Wouldn't have *what?*"

Why wouldn't Dot let it drop? Maisie couldn't bear this. How could she explain to Dot any of what had happened without sharing John's secret, and without sharing the way that she had reacted to it with pity, just the way John had said she would.

"It's all done now, Dot, and I can't explain any of it."

"But you don't need to explain." Dot laid her hand on Maisie's arm as they walked. "I do understand, you know, how it feels to really like someone."

Maisie glanced sideways at Dot. "Is that right?" It came out laden with more sarcasm than Maisie had meant, but really, what could Dot know about how Maisie was feeling right now? "You know how *this* feels?"

"Maybe I do." Dot sounded hurt by Maisie's derision.

The path was steeper now, and Dot said nothing more. Maisie knew she had no right to snap at Dot the way she had. None of this was Dot's fault, after all. To calm her irritation, Maisie tried to match her breaths with her footsteps. After a few more steps, a few more beats, she found some calm again.

"I'm sorry, Dot. That was horrid of me. Please, tell me."

Dot shrugged.

"No, really, tell me. Do you like someone?" Maisie suddenly clicked with what she had just said. Dot *liked* someone! Maisie smiled encouragingly.

But again, Dot shrugged. "It doesn't matter."

"It does matter. If you fancy someone, you have to share. Is it one of the NOFU chaps? Which one?"

"I said it doesn't matter!" Dot was sharp this time. "Anyway, before we reach the site, there's something I need to—"

"But Dot, I was only—"

"Annoying, isn't it? When you offer to help your friend, but she won't talk to you about it?"

"That's not fair."

"I only wanted to talk to you about John because we—"

"You're right." It was Maisie's turn to snap. She would not start talking about John again. "Let's just drop it. You don't want to talk, I don't want to talk. Happy now? The only thing I have to say is that if I never saw John Lindsay again, it would be too soon."

Maisie allowed the sudden blast of annoyance to pour new energy into her legs. But as she powered away from Dot, she knew that what she'd said wasn't at all true. She *did* want to see John again. She *did* like him, a lot. But after what had happened on Friday, his kisses, his anger, and then his cryptic note, which she still hadn't come close to deciphering, she had no idea what feelings he might have for her. If any.

After only a few paces, Maisie began to hear something strange above the noise of the wind in the trees. It sounded like some sort of not-quite-rhythmic percussion. She slowed her steps. What was that?

Dot caught up to her. "Maisie, please, there's something, before we get to the—"

"Shhh!"

"But Haven already sent . . . I mean, up at the site . . . with the truck . . . Maisie, what are you doing?"

"What's that noise?" Maisie slowly turned her head, trying to pinpoint the direction of the sound.

"What noise?"

"Listen!"

And then the sound came again, loud enough that Dot could hear it too, and Maisie realized it had accompanied them up the last stretch as they'd argued. It was erratic, and metallic, definitely not a knock against wood. But it was also not a bell chime, or even a bright clang. This was more a clunk.

Clunk . . . clunk . . . Then nothing for a few seconds, then *clunk-clunk*, two beats close together.

What *was* that?

Maisie turned slowly in a circle, but it was too hard. The sound was bouncing off the trees and the slopes, and it might fool her into walking entirely the wrong way. But after a few more clunks had rung out, she pointed into the trees a little farther up to their right. "Is that where it's coming from?"

"Might be," Dot replied, turning around too. "But what is it?"

Maisie pulled the map out of her pocket and ran one finger up the line of path they were standing on, gauging where exactly they'd got to and how much farther they still had to go to reach the job site. At almost the same time, the thick cloud bank that had been climbing in the sky rolled across the rising orange sun, smothering the woods with a gray cloak. Everything was silent except for that clunking. A shiver climbed Maisie's spine. There was something about that noise . . .

"Is it a signal?" she whispered.

Maisie and Dot listened again. But the clanging had stopped.

Seventeen

They waited.

Nothing.

If it had been a signal, whoever was making it wasn't making it now. Maisie felt dread rise inside her. This couldn't be good.

Dot began to speak, but Maisie held up a hand.

"Come on!" She launched herself up the track.

"Wait for me!" called Dot.

"It can't be far now," Maisie called back, not slowing down at all. Suddenly she stumbled, pitching toward the tree line, and as she righted herself, she felt a twig scrape a stinging slice from her nose to her ear.

She pressed the back of her hand to her cheek. When she pulled it away again, there was a neat smear of blood, but before she could swear, she heard the sound again.

Clunk . . . clunk . . . then nothing.

Whatever it was, they were close now. And then Maisie saw where the tire ruts ran through a gap in the trees up ahead, and she ran faster up and around the corner.

"Maisie!" Dot wasn't far behind her.

Maisie came to a small clearing and caught her breath. There, almost filling the entire clearing, was a logging truck she didn't recognize, even bigger than the Bedford they were used to loading. It looked as though someone had started to load it but had then abandoned the work halfway through. Maisie shivered. Haven wasn't the kind of supervisor to leave a job half finished. Yet no one was around.

And none of that explained the noise.

Maisie moved closer as Dot entered the clearing behind her.

"Dot, it's a truck, and . . . ," Maisie began, but broke off as she peered under the flatbed to the far side and gasped. Five or six logs had spilled off the side of the truck and were lying like a game of jackstraws, one on top of another in a jumble, as if waiting for some giant to pick them up one by one. One was still leaning precariously against the side of the truck.

Clunk . . .

Maisie jumped. The sound was weary and halfhearted . . . and so close. It came from beyond the truck. Running around the front of the cab, Maisie had to catch herself, forcing her feet to a stop, before she went headfirst over a log.

No, not a log. A body.

No, a live person, and it—*he*—was moving.

The man was lying awkwardly on his back, his head tilted down into a deep tire rut and his legs trapped under a crossed pair of logs. Blood stained the knee of his trousers, almost as dark as the mud, not fresh and red.

The muscles in the man's forearm strained with effort of lifting a long fat stick up toward the metal door, but the stick fell back to the ground silently after rising only a few inches. Maisie realized that he must have been hitting the metal door, again and again, but now he was too weak even to reach it.

"Dot!" Maisie yelled, rushing to the man's side, "Over here!"

She knelt by the man's shoulder, and he groaned. Before she put her hands under his head and lifted it gently so she could see his face, she already knew who it was. Her sprinting pulse and churning stomach had understood long before her mind.

It was John.

His eyes were open, and though he was looking at her now, she wondered if he could see her. She was as close to him as she'd been when they'd danced, yet his eyes looked quite blank, the dark pupils so wide there was almost no hazel around them. And then that familiar frown appeared on his forehead. He *had* seen her, he knew she was there. Hadn't that frown appeared upon his face so often since they'd first met?

"John?" she said. "It's Maisie. Can you hear me?"

The frown did not change, but his lips moved soundlessly.

"It's fine, John. I'm here now. Don't talk. It'll be fine." She heard Dot running around the corner. "Dot and I are both here now."

"Oh!" Dot cried.

"The logs must have fallen," Maisie said. Not daring to take her hands from under John's head, she nodded down to his legs. "Look! He's trapped."

Dot was kneeling beside her now, and Maisie went to lay his head back down.

"Careful, Maisie!" Dot shrieked. "You shouldn't have moved his head at all. What if he has a broken neck? You might have killed him."

Maisie froze. "I didn't know," she whispered. "So what do I do now?"

"Hang on a sec." Dot dropped her satchel at her feet and stripped off her coat. Then she pulled her sweater off over her head and folded it into a neat square. "Hold him as still as you can while I tuck this under his head, but be very careful how you lay him down again. Nothing sudden, all right?"

"Nothing sudden." Maisie did as she had been told and was relieved to be able to lay John's head gently onto the pillow of Dot's sweater. John's eyes closed as she did so, and he let out a deep sigh, as if it were a relief to have his head comfortable at last.

Then his lips began to move again, still no sound, only breath.

Maisie laid one hand against his cheek and was shocked

at how cold his skin felt on her warm palm. How long had he been lying here like this? It was only just sunrise, after all. She took his hand in hers and the fingers were freezing. Had he been trapped here all night?

He was trying to speak again, so she bent her head low to get her ear as close to his mouth as she could. She could feel a stirring of his breath on her ear, but still she couldn't make out what he was saying.

"One more time?" she asked. "I'm trying to understand, I really am."

This time she not only felt his breath but heard his single word.

"Elliott!" she cried. "Dot! He's saying Elliott!"

Was Elliott here too? Of course! The men never worked alone, always in pairs at least. The same rule applied to the lumberjills, so she should have thought of that.

John squeezed her fingers momentarily, as if telling her she was right.

Maisie scanned the mismatched pile of logs. Finally, she spotted something.

"There!" She pointed frantically toward some logs by the rear tire of the truck. "Elliott's under there!"

Dot rose and ran to where Maisie was pointing.

"Be careful!" called Maisie. "Don't disturb the logs—they could roll again, or fall."

"I know, I know!" said Dot as she squatted down beyond the largest log, peering under it.

"Is he . . ." Maisie choked off her words. She had almost asked *Is he dead?* but couldn't bring herself to say it. "Is he all right?"

Clearly deciding not to risk crawling under the huge log balanced precariously over her head, Dot backtracked and then disappeared behind the log. The silence was torment for Maisie.

"Dot?"

"Shhhh! Trying to find a pulse," Dot hissed back, and again Maisie waited, feeling her own pulse pounding. "Got it," exclaimed Dot at last. "He's still with us. But it's faint."

"Thank God," Maisie breathed out in relief. "Elliott's going to be all right, John." She hoped against hope that was true, but looking again at the weight of wood hanging above him, teetering on the edge, she knew they needed to move quickly but carefully if they were to save either of the men.

"He's caught by the legs too," said Dot, in that same curt and authoritative tone she'd used when Lillian had cut her hand open on the sawmill blade. "And he's frozen. Exposure can do more damage than broken bones, so we need to get him out of here as fast as we can. Both of them."

Dot's head reappeared, and as their eyes met, Maisie knew they were both asking themselves the same question.

But how . . . ?

"We need Clyde." Maisie said. "You and I might be able to lift one of these logs between us, but I doubt we'd be able to keep the rest from tumbling and making things worse. What do you think? Wee Susan might be on her way up with him already, so if I go and chase them, will you be all right here on your own?"

Dot didn't immediately reply.

"Dot, will you be all right?" Maisie asked again, and then answered her own question. "Of course you will, I'm sure you will. And I'll be as fast as I can."

Dot nodded her head slowly, her eyes settling back on Elliott. Her shoulders drooped as if her confidence was visibly fading. "But what if I don't know—?"

"Stop, Dot. You'll know what to do, I promise you will." Maisie tried to sound kind instead of panicked. "You have the arm patch to prove it, remember."

Dot looked down at the red cross embroidered onto a white circle on her sleeve and drew in a deep breath. "Yes, I *do* know. First, I need to get them warmed up."

"Good idea. I'll give John my coat," Maisie said, putting John's hand gently down onto his chest so she could unbutton her coat and shrug out of it. "John, I'm going to go for help now, but here's my coat. Dot will stay here with you and Elliott—do you hear me?"

John's face didn't move and his eyes remained closed, but she saw his fingertips lift slightly off his chest to acknowledge her words.

Maisie stood, careful not to touch any of the logs in her haste, and spread her coat on top of John. Then she crept over to Dot, scared that even the vibrations of her footsteps could start another log slide. She stripped off her sweater and held it out to Dot. "Here, Elliott needs it more than me. I'll be back with Clyde and the others as soon as I can."

Dot looked up at her then. "Please, hurry."

And Maisie ran.

What if the others hadn't even set off yet? How long would it take her to get back down to camp, and then back up again? She tried to work it out, but her heart and head were pounding so hard, she gave up. She just had to keep pushing herself.

But she needn't have worried, because as she rounded the bend onto the main track, the most beautiful sight appeared far down the hill.

Clyde. And Wee Susan, walking alongside him, and Nancy . . . and was that Beth? Yes! Beth was there too.

Maisie lifted both her arms to wave over her head. "Hurry!" she cried, still waving. "There's been an accident!"

She saw Nancy look at Beth, who shook her head, and each girl held a hand to her ear.

"AN ACCIDENT!" Maisie yelled at the top of what little voice she had left. "COME QUICKLY! WE NEED YOU!"

She waited long enough to see Nancy say something to Beth and Susan, and the three of them quickened their pace. Even Clyde seemed to sense something was amiss, because he suddenly tugged harder at the reins that Wee Susan held in her gloved fists.

Maisie turned and ran back the way she'd come. She waited only long enough to make sure they'd seen the side track leading to the accident site, then ran toward the truck.

"They're almost here—they were on their way anyway.

It's going to be fine," Maisie babbled as she burst back into the clearing.

Dot was holding Elliott's wrist. Gingerly, Maisie crouched down beside them. Now, she was close enough to see how deathly pale Elliott's skin was, and now she was also close enough to see the tracks of shiny tears carving their way down through the dirt on Dot's distraught face.

Eighteen

Nancy was the first to race into the clearing, her face anxious. "What happened? Is Dot all right?"

It was only then that Maisie realized that telling their friends to run toward such a precarious situation had been foolish, and she threw up a hand in warning. "Careful! We can't risk shifting these logs."

Thankfully, Nancy was already skidding to a stop at the sight before her, but she still looked fearful. "Who's hurt? Maisie, for God's sake! Is it Dot?"

"Nancy, I'm fine," Dot shouted from the far side of the truck. "It's the men."

Nancy skirted the truck toward Dot, but at that moment, Clyde thundered around the corner, hooves thumping into the soft mud and gravel, dragging Wee Susan along as she ineffectually pulled back his reins. Maisie shrieked at Nancy to stop him before he got too close, but Clyde was intent only on reaching Nancy, and so she was able to hold him at a safe enough distance from the truck. Wee Susan looked relieved to hand over his reins to Nancy just as Beth ran in behind her.

Beth. Maisie found herself inexplicably thankful to have her sister there.

And now that they had assistance, Maisie knew there were decisions to be made.

"It's John and Elliott," she explained to the newcomers. "They got trapped under a log fall, maybe last night. They're injured, we think, and freezing cold, and we need to get them to hospital before they"—she swallowed hard against the tightness in her throat—"well, we need to get them to hospital as quick as we can. But Dot's worried about them being moved too, in case we make things worse."

"So what's your plan?" asked Nancy.

A plan? Maisie was thrown. She had no plan. She'd expected whoever came to help would take over and tell *her* what to do, but here was Nancy, clearly awaiting Maisie's instructions, as were Wee Susan and Beth.

Maisie glanced back at Dot, torn by uncertainty. To get the men to safety, they would need to lift them up onto the flatbed and then drive them to the hospital in Grantown-on-Spey. For that she needed someone to drive the truck.

"Susan," Maisie said, attempting to control her voice, which was desperately trying to squeak, "I need you to run back down to Carrbridge as quick as you can. We need a driver."

"But who—" Wee Susan was still gasping for breath after running up the hill.

"Find Haven or any of the NOFU drivers," she began, but Nancy shook her head.

"They're not in Carrbridge today," she said, "the trucks already picked everyone up for the Nethybridge job. There may not be anyone left at their camp but the cook, same as ours."

"Damn! Would there be someone from the village? There must be one driver down there, surely."

Nancy shrugged. "I'm not sure. The boys down at the farm can drive, but maybe not something this big."

"If they can drive a car, they can drive a truck," replied Maisie, repeating what her driving instructor had said, even though she still wasn't sure she believed that. "It's all just a matter of scale."

"Scale?" replied Susan. "Are you sure?"

"Go, now, please." Maisie could feel her panic rising again. "Try the Newfoundlanders' camp first, just in case someone stayed behind, then the farm, and then the village. Just bring back someone who can drive anything bigger than a bicycle."

Wee Susan looked doubtful, but with a swift *good luck*, she sprinted off.

What now?

Maisie drew in a deep breath and looked into the expectant faces in front of her, and she knew it was up to her. They couldn't just wait around for a driver to arrive. A storm was coming, and the men were already at risk from the cold. So should they try to lift them onto the truck themselves?

She knew if they lifted the men, there was a chance they might die. And without doubt, if they left them there, they *would* die. Given these odds, Maisie realized, the lumberjills needed to clear away some logs, and quickly.

So a game of jackstraws it was.

The first few logs were easy to remove. They were the ones scattered around, mostly flat on the ground. Once Nancy had attached a log to Clyde's harness, a clap on his shoulder was all he needed to pull it away without disturbing the rest. The huge Clydesdale worked slowly and steadily, following Nancy's every command.

That left four logs still precariously balanced. Two were across John and another was on top of Elliott. The fourth— the largest—had by some miracle remained propped against the side of the truck, suspended over Elliott's unconscious body. It had caught on one of the wide metal loops used as lashing points to secure loads for transportation, but had stayed relatively stable as the girls removed the other logs. However, Maisie could clearly see that if she moved that one next, the larger of the two across John's lower body would also shift, perhaps injuring him even further, and the thought of her causing him even more pain tore at her insides.

As Maisie tried to visualize how to move the logs but still keep John safe, Dot left Elliott and came to sit beside John, pressing her hand to his forehead and her fingers to his wrist, talking to him quietly as she did. With a grimace, she looked up at Maisie. "Where's Susan with our driver?" she asked anxiously, then dropped her voice lower. "We're running out of time. John's in and out of consciousness and Elliott's barely hanging on. We need help, soon. Where are they?"

Maisie had no answer. Looking down at John, lying covered in her heavy coat, she felt her stomach twist. His skin was gray now, his eyelids closed and shadowed. Where *were* Susan and the men? Surely they should have been back here by now. But even if they were on their way, Maisie could not forget what Dot had just said. They had no time spare to wait for them. She must do something. Now.

Trying to ignore the chill that thought brought to her heart, Maisie called to Nancy and Beth so they could help her work out the options for removing the remaining four logs.

"All right, once I've braced this top trunk against the truck so it doesn't shift," Maisie summarized a minute later, to make sure everyone was working to the same plan, "Nancy will get Clyde to lift that one off Elliott. Then Beth, I'll need you and Dot to guide it away to the side. Once it's clear, Nancy, you'll get Clyde to back up and lay the log down in that space beyond Elliott. Does that sound like it'll work?"

Beside Maisie, Beth nodded. She looked pale and sweaty.

"Beth, you won't be in any danger, because I'll keep this log where it is, but you'll need to stay calm and do exactly what Dot or I tell you. Do you understand?"

Beth nodded again, and Maisie wished she'd taken a

moment to hug her before all this, to reassure her. Beth was, after all, completely out of her depth here. Beth wasn't whining though, just bravely helping the other girls, and Maisie suddenly felt very proud. But the hugging would have to wait—there was simply no time now, and they still had so much to get done.

Maisie braced her back against the hanging trunk to prevent it from falling, and Nancy ran to lash one end of a chain to the log lying across Elliott, and attached the other end to Clyde's harness. Then she clucked to Clyde as he took up the slack. Inch by inch, the tree trunk rose up, and since Clyde was doing the heavy lifting, Dot and Beth were easily able to guide it off Elliott's body and swing it over to one side.

Once the log was down, Dot immediately checked Elliott's pulse again, then ran her hands lightly over his chest and legs, searching, Maisie presumed, for any obvious breaks.

Maisie didn't dare move away from where she was pressing against the hanging log, but she talked encouragingly to Beth as her sister rolled the log a few feet farther away.

Maisie looked up the track for the hundredth time, and then up at the glowering sky. Where were the men? And how long before the storm arrived?

"We'll have to move Elliott before we can think about freeing John," said Nancy, standing with arms crossed and gazing at the scene as if it really were no more than an intriguing puzzle to be solved.

Dot yelped. "But we can't move Elliott. We don't know what his injuries are. If there's damage to his spine, we could . . . he could . . ." She didn't finish, but they all knew what word she didn't say. Elliott could die.

"If we leave him where he is," Maisie pushed back, "he's going to get even colder. It's not only Elliott at risk of exposure—John is too. And we can't get John out while this bloody Sword of Damocles is hanging over Elliott." She gestured to the trunk behind her back. "We are not going to stand here like damsels in distress doing nothing, watching these two men . . ." Maisie didn't dare say that word either.

"Maisie's right." Nancy walked over and laid her hand on Dot's shoulder. "We have to get Elliott out from under there now."

"But we're not strong enough to . . ." Dot's words faded away in the heat from Maisie's glare.

"Has the last eight weeks taught you nothing?" Maisie would not let Dot get away with that. "We are lumberjills and we are strong enough to do whatever we need to do. There are three of us—"

"Four." Beth sounded half-aggrieved, half-terrified as she corrected Maisie.

"Yes, sorry, Beth, *four* of us, and we've got Clyde. If we are careful, and if you tell us what we need to do to protect Elliott's spine, we can get them both out of danger. Dot, we have no choice."

Dot eventually nodded her head, and Nancy and Beth started pulling the wide wooden ramp panels from their storage rails under the truck, and hooking them onto the narrow end of the flatbed. Meanwhile, Dot splinted Elliott's left leg with two sturdy sticks and bandages from her first aid satchel, and Nancy formed an impromptu stretcher from their coats by chopping off the sharp metal ends from their cant hooks and threading the poles through the arms.

Maisie regarded the homemade litter and swallowed back a rush of bile that threatened to choke her. What if she had been wrong? What if leaving the men where they were was a better and safer choice? What if she killed one or both by moving them? She looked again at John's face, all trace of his rich tan bleached pale and wan, his closed eyes gray ringed, his lips almost blue with the cold.

No, she couldn't stand by, doing nothing. She had to try.

There was a sudden thud, making Maisie jump, but it was only Beth and Nancy pushing one of the three logs still on the flatbed off onto the ground on the far side of the truck.

"Be careful," she cried, bracing harder against the angled log behind her back. "Leave the other two logs up there, so we can strap over the top of them to keep the stretchers in place. Yes?"

Nancy nodded, and she and Beth ran down the ramp and around to where Dot was kneeling again beside Elliott. Beth looked almost green.

"Beth, are you feeling all right?" Maisie asked, and Beth smiled unconvincingly.

Maisie wondered if she was asking too much of her sister. For all Beth's assertion of there being *four* of them there, Beth hadn't done the training and she'd never been as physically strong as Maisie, even before that. And she was only fifteen.

"Beth? I need you to do something for me." Beth looked at Maisie, eyes wide. "Will you come and take over? Keep this log braced against the truck while Nancy and I lift Elliott. You're not taking its weight—the lashing points are doing that; but by pressing back on it, you'll make sure it doesn't shift while we are working under it. Can you do that?"

Beth stared numbly at Maisie but didn't reply.

"Beth!" Maisie raised her voice a little. "Can you do this for me?"

"Yes," Beth croaked, but then Maisie saw her straighten, and she said with spirit, "Yes, I can! I'll make sure it doesn't fall."

"That's my girl!" Maisie grinned, and as they swapped positions, she gave Beth a swift kiss on the cheek. Taking over her sister's role, Beth suddenly looked older and more confident than Maisie had ever seen her.

"That's my girl!" she said again, before turning to Dot. "Come on then, Dr. Thompson, you're in charge."

For the next few minutes, no one spoke except Dot. She gave specific instructions to Nancy and Maisie on every step of the lift, all the while holding Elliott's head steady. Inch by careful inch, they moved Elliott's unconscious form onto the stretcher and strapped him with lashing straps they found in the cab. Then with a one-two-three, the three girls hefted the stretcher.

John roused again as they passed him to climb the ramp. "For God's sake, be careful!" he croaked.

"We're doing fine, John." Maisie growled through

gritted teeth as she fought off the pain in her hands and shoulders. Elliott was heavy, and even though they'd each lifted more weight than him in logs, this was harder. "You need to trust us."

Maisie could see her own pain and effort mirrored in Nancy's face, but they both held firm until they'd laid Elliott down between the two huge logs on the flatbed. Once they got John up there too, they'd strap across the two tree trunks to keep the men secure for the drive.

For the drive. If Susan ever brought a driver back, of course.

"Well done, Nancy," Maisie said, dabbing gently at the blister on her palm torn by the cant pole. "And you too, Beth."

Nancy was already covering Elliott in Clyde's thick and rather smelly saddle blanket and didn't respond, but Maisie was surprised to see a blush come to her sister's face, though perhaps it was just the cold wind.

Now for John.

His head was resting back on Dot's sweater, his eyes were shut, and Maisie hoped he was still conscious. If they could get him up beside his friend by the time a driver arrived, there'd be no delay in getting them to hospital.

This next bit would be easier, now that Elliott wasn't lying under the hanging log. Even so, Maisie joined Beth to lean against the trunk to keep it steady while Nancy attached the chain linked to Clyde's harness and led the huge Clydesdale away. As soon as Maisie felt the tree trunk lift from its precarious position, she and Beth ducked under it and pushed it away from the last log, which was currently pinning John's legs, until it dropped with a soft thump onto the moist loam beyond.

John's legs, or rather, John's leg. Maisie had been pushing those thoughts to the back of her mind while she concentrated on everything else, but now she had no choice but to draw them forward. John had told her that his right leg was the false one—or at least she thought he'd said it was the right—and therefore that one should not be hurting him. But his left leg, his real one, could already be badly injured, and Maisie knew that if she got the next lift wrong, John could lose that leg too. Or worse.

Once Nancy had reattached the chain to the last log, they raised it slowly. Maisie didn't take her eyes from John's face to see if it registered any pain. But he had no more than the usual wrinkled frown across his forehead. Once the log had gone, she breathed a sigh of relief, and she could have sworn she heard him sigh too. His left foot moved a little, as if he were testing to see how damaged it was. And though John groaned as it did, Maisie was reassured. If he could move it like that, then surely his leg, or his back, couldn't be broken.

"Good work, girls, well done," Maisie said. But as she stepped forward, the others all cried out.

Maisie glanced up in time to see the log that had been lying on the near side of the flatbed topple off the side and fall toward her.

As Beth grabbed Maisie by the arm and yanked her out of the way, Maisie felt the punch of the log glancing off her calf.

She yelped and fell to the ground gripping her leg as nausea swept through her. Even so, she did not miss the grunt only a few inches away as the log landed on top of John. After all they'd done to keep him safe, John had once again been crushed.

"No!" Maisie cried out as she saw John was trapped again. "No, no, no!" Tears of rage and frustration sprang to her eyes. Why hadn't she strapped that log immediately, or at least checked that it was secure?

Dot had scrambled to John's side and was studying where the log had smashed down on his right leg. Maisie pressed hard on the pain in her own calf. But her head started to spin, so she squeezed her eyes closed and rested her dizzy head on the ground.

As she heard Dot muttering quiet comforts to John, Maisie felt someone grab her leg and looked up to find Nancy's hand was adding more pressure to the injured muscle.

"Come on, Maisie," Nancy said. "We can't carry you out of here too."

The pain soon began to recede, and Maisie tentatively stretched out her leg. It was still desperately sore, and she'd have a nasty bruise, but she would not let it stop her getting these men off the hill. As she pushed herself up to sit, her head began to spin again, and she took a deep breath in an attempt to clear it.

"You'll have to cut it off," she heard John say even through the buzzing in her ears. "We can't waste time—for Elliott's sake, you'll have to use your knife to cut it off."

"What? No!" Dot sounded truly appalled by the suggestion.

"Maisie, tell her," croaked John. "She just has to use her knife."

Even through her dizziness, Maisie knew it was important for her to focus on what was being said, but the world was still spinning.

"Shhh, John, shhh." Dot sounded panicked now. "We'll get the log off you in a second or two. It'll be fine. We have Clyde."

"There's no time . . ." John sounded determined. "Elliott needs . . . quicker to cut it . . . Maisie knows . . ."

Maisie forced herself to concentrate, and as she opened her eyes, she saw Dot staring at her, aghast. "Maisie, what's he talking about? Of course I can't cut off his leg."

Before Maisie could make her mouth work to reply, John breathed, "Then let Maisie do it. Please. For Elliott."

And Maisie knew he was right—they were running out of time to get Elliott to safety. Shaking off the last of the fog from her brain, she pulled her knife from its sheath on her belt.

"Maisie, no!" Dot shrieked.

Maisie tried to tell Dot that she knew what she was doing, but her tongue still felt thick and uncooperative. But even if she couldn't speak, she could act. She stuck the sharp end of her knife into the wet fabric of John's right trouser leg, between where the log lay on top of it and where she judged his knee should be. Then she began to cut. Behind her Dot gasped, and Beth whimpered, but Maisie kept the blade moving inch by inch until she uncovered what she knew to be inside.

Pulling the fabric away from the leg, Maisie could see a polished wooden column, with a dark leather band around the top. And as she continued to cut upwards, the fabric fell back to reveal two more bands reaching up John's thigh, both attached to a thick strap that buckled at the side and pulled tight around his well-defined muscle. Maisie grabbed the loose end of the leather and pulled until she felt the metal buckle release and she could pull the strap away from John's thigh.

"But . . . ," she heard Dot whisper, "I don't understand. John, what happened to your leg?"

From the corner of her eye, she saw John bring his hands up shakily to cover his face, as if to block out Dot's question. Maisie needed to help him.

"Dot, later," she said, though sure she sounded clumsy and inarticulate, "he can tell you later. But we need to get him out from under here now. This leg is not our biggest problem, but that leg might be." Maisie held out the handle of her knife toward Dot and indicated that she should cut into the other trouser leg. "We have to find out how badly that one's been hurt."

After only a second's hesitation, Dot nodded silently, took hold of Maisie's knife, and began to cut.

Nineteen

By the time they'd safely lifted John up beside Elliott and draped over them a tarpaulin that Maisie had found in the cab, the storm was well and truly upon them. The heavy blanket of cloud was smothering all light and warmth, the wind was whipping around the clearing, and a fine drizzle had already soaked through the thin fabric of her shirt. But worst of all, it was also now clear, even to Maisie, that no other help was coming.

"It looks like the next bit's down to us girls too," Maisie said, glancing up at the cab. The idea of driving a vehicle of this size filled her with absolute horror. She'd only had a couple of hours' instruction, and on a car about one-fifth of the size. What if she crashed? They might all die. "Although I'm not sure if I can—"

"Yes, you can, Maisie," Nancy said, softly but firmly. "You must. Dot has to stay with Elliott, Beth's too young, and they trained me as a cook, not a driver. And I have to get Clyde back before the weather gets any worse. Anyway, it's only a matter of scale, isn't that what you said?"

"But what if Susan is almost back here with—"

"But what if she's not?" Nancy's tone had turned sharp. "And anyway, you'd meet them farther down the hill, and they can take over. But the weather's getting worse by the minute, and if we don't leave soon, we could *all* die of exposure."

"Don't say that, Nancy!" Beth wasn't fighting back her tears anymore, and she was shivering hard.

"It's all right, Beth. Of course I'll drive," Maisie said. "But let's pray we meet someone who can actually drive this thing before we reach a proper road."

The rain was falling for real now. As they worked to secure the tarpaulin, Maisie kept thinking about John's left leg. Dot was certain it was broken, so they'd done their best to splint it to keep it from moving on the journey, but Maisie had no doubt that John was still in considerable pain. She just had to hope the improvised tarpaulin tent would stop them from getting completely soaked before they reached the hospital. Peering into the dim interior, Maisie might have believed that Elliott was simply asleep. John's eyes, however, met hers, but as he tried to say something, his throat caught and he coughed, and groaned.

But then he tried again. "You promised me," John

croaked, though his mouth twitched as if he were trying to smile, "something more stylish than this for our next date."

"What, like a potato wagon?" she replied, but John's eyes were closed again, and he didn't respond.

Maisie clambered down to where Beth was waiting, holding the last of the straps. She looked ghastly.

Maisie took the strap from her and pulled her into a hug. "Thank you, Beth, for everything. I'm so grateful you were here. We couldn't have done this without you."

Beth sniffed and squeezed Maisie back even tighter. "I'm glad I was here too—otherwise I wouldn't have seen you do all this." She sniffed again. "I wish I could be brave and strong like you, Piggly."

Maisie had to swallow before replying. "You *are* brave and strong, Lilibet. You're here, aren't you? But for the next bit, we are going to have to be even braver. I need you to keep John safe for me, will you?"

"And Elliott," replied Beth.

"Yes, and Elliott." Maisie hesitated only for a moment before adding, "But particularly John."

Beth nodded seriously, then climbed up and crawled under the tarpaulin beside John.

Maisie turned and saw that Nancy was giving Dot a hug, and her hands were rubbing Dot's back as she whispered in Dot's ear. Maisie was ready to tie the final strap to the lashing rings once Dot was aboard, but still the two girls did not let each other go. Maisie yearned to feel someone's reassuring arms—John's arms, she admitted to herself—tight around her like that.

Then Nancy kissed Dot's cheek and the two broke apart. Before Dot could walk away, Nancy had shrugged off her grandfather's leather jerkin. Although Dot protested, Nancy laid it around Dot's shoulders and held it there until Dot relented and put her arms through the holes. Nancy did up the three heavy buttons, gave Dot another quick hug, and then strode over, without looking back, to where Clyde was waiting for her.

Dot watched her go, and when she turned toward Maisie, her eyes were filled with tears. Maisie felt a rush of embarrassment at being caught gawping at such a private moment, but Dot just smiled as she climbed up the ramp.

"Come on then, Flash," Dot said to Maisie, "show us how it's done."

As soon as Dot was settled beside Elliott, Maisie pulled the tarpaulin back down and secured it. Then she unhooked the ramp panels and stored them under the flatbed. She strode to the cab door, thinking that if she *looked* confident, she might somehow *feel* confident. As she reached for the handle, Nancy was suddenly there.

"Good luck, Maisie," Nancy said, squeezing Maisie's arm. "Please look after them, all of them."

The ferocity in Nancy's voice, and the pressure from her fingers, gave Maisie some reassurance. Nancy was right: she *could* do this.

Saying nothing more, Nancy walked back to where Clyde was ripping at the tall grasses, apparently oblivious to the raindrops glittering along his back. Grabbing the bridle, Nancy gave Clyde two hard claps on the shoulder and pushed him away from the truck and up the track.

Maisie suddenly felt very alone.

Starting the engine wasn't a problem, and she managed to put it into first gear with only the requisite grinding of metal on metal, though her calf muscle felt like it was tearing every time she pressed hard on a pedal. And once the truck had moved forward a few yards, she even managed to get it into second gear.

But Maisie couldn't relax yet. The track was so steep at times, she was pitched forward, and as the truck banked and rolled on the pocked and rutted track, she was also being thrown around in her seat and had to cling to the steering wheel for dear life. If it was this bad up front, in the relative comfort of the driver's seat, how bad was it back there on the hard wooden bed? She wished she could shout back to apologize for every bump, but she couldn't even have heard her own voice above the engine's roar if she'd tried.

As she drove, it also became increasingly harder to see. The cloud layer was so dense and dark, and the rain . . . not just rain now, but sleet, with fat, wet snowflakes hitting the window. The wipers could barely clear the glass with each screeching sweep.

The temperature was dropping too, even within the protective bubble of the cab. How could Elliott survive this brutality? Maisie felt sick at the thought. And was John cursing her for every bump and turn she made? How bad was the pain in his leg?

Maisie wrenched the wheel to one side to miss a particularly deep hole in the track, and cursed again the blackout covers stuck on the headlights, which narrowed the light down to only a fraction of what she needed to see. Even though it was midmorning, the forest was in a soaking twilight, and yet she was driving with barely a flashlight's beam to guide her.

There was an explosion from the trees to Maisie's right, and something huge flew across the track in front of her. Instinctively, she slammed her foot down on the brake and twisted the steering wheel hard to the left to avoid hitting the thing, and the truck was suddenly careering toward a wall of dark pines. A ditch ran between her and the trees, and Maisie was driving them straight into it. Maisie pulled the wheel to try to bring it back to center again, and the flatbed behind her skewed away. Even as she fought its momentum, she saw an enormous roan stag with magnificent antlers caught in the headlights' glare, just before it vanished into the underbrush as quickly as it had appeared.

Maisie's arm muscles were screaming with the effort of holding the steering wheel, but abruptly it released and the truck's weight pulled back toward the middle of the track. Maisie desperately spun the wheel the other way, and then back again, searching for the point of midline and balance and safety.

Finally, she found it and felt the truck stabilize, centered on the track, and Maisie could breathe again.

And there was the main road down below her, the real flat road, not this steep and rutted track. The worst of her nightmare was over.

Or was it? She thought of the injured men behind her. Was John still conscious? And Elliott, was he still alive?

Twenty

Every single part of Maisie's body hurt, and she couldn't keep lying in the same position for much longer, since there were sharp ridges and knobs digging into her already-tender hip and back. When she opened her eyes, she found she wasn't lying on a bed but on a row of hard metal chairs set around the walls of a dingy room. The single lightbulb hanging unshaded from the center of the ceiling shone so dully, its light barely touched the dark corners.

Then Maisie remembered. The accident, John's leg, and the harrowing drive all the way to the hospital. When she'd pulled up outside the doors, Dot had run inside to get help, and within a few minutes, the porters had stretchered John and Elliott inside. Elliott had still been unconscious, but somehow alive. John had been ashen faced and clearly in a lot of pain.

Dot had immediately started briefing the nurses about what had happened, but when Maisie and Beth had tried to follow her inside, a battle-ax of a nurse had turned them away, barking that they must wait in the waiting room. And then a policeman had come in, demanding to know which damned fool had blocked the driveway to the hospital, and most of the road besides, by parking a bloody great timber truck right outside the door. So Maisie had been forced to leave Dot to deal with the nurses about admitting the two injured men, while she and Beth went to repark the truck.

By the time they'd walked back into the hospital, Beth had clearly been struggling to stay upright. Maisie had put her arm around her sister's shoulder and led her to the waiting room, where they'd sat, cold, wet, and rather dazed, until a nurse with a kinder face and quieter voice gave them towels and even some soap—a whole bar, which was something they hadn't seen in a while—to go and wash all the dirt off their hands and faces. Then she'd brought them each a large mug of tea and two slices of warm toast. She'd only just heard about the rescue, she'd said, and had thought the girls deserved a hot drink at least for their bravery. Then she'd told them she'd bring them news when she had some.

Within a few minutes, the nurse had reappeared, not with any news, but carrying a heavy green greatcoat, just like Maisie's.

"I just remembered," she'd said, "your friend left this at

the nursing station. Once the patients were into the warm, she thought you'd probably need it again. You're M. McCall, yes?" She'd turned the inside of the collar around so that Maisie could see the label where her name had been written in black ink.

As the nurse had handed it over, Maisie could feel the fabric was a little damp, but it was still warm and comfortable, and Maisie had been sorely tempted to put it on immediately. But Beth had been so brave, especially when she'd saved Maisie from the falling log, and she was clearly cold and exhausted, so Maisie had encouraged her to lie down across the chairs and get some sleep. Then Maisie had laid the big coat over her sister before sitting down herself, suddenly bone weary. At some point, she must have lain across another set of chairs and fallen asleep too.

Groggily, Maisie now looked for Beth, but there was no sign. Her mud-caked greatcoat fell to the floor as she sat up, and the sudden loss of its warmth made her shudder. How long had she slept? Whatever time it was now, she must find Beth, and Dot, and ask someone about John and Elliott.

Tentatively, she stood up, stretched her aching muscles, and wobbled toward the door. Her legs would have ached from pounding the heavy clutch and brake pedals on the drive down the mountain, but with the added discomfort of her bruised calf, each step was a challenge. Her clothes were dry, but the insides of her shoes still squelched with each step.

As she reached the door, it suddenly opened toward her, and she staggered back, falling into one of the metal chairs.

Coming in was possibly the last person Maisie had expected to see. Carrying a small plate of sandwiches on top of two large mugs was Maisie's mother.

If Maisie hadn't already been sitting, she would have collapsed. Finding Beth on her bed that night had been one thing, but this . . . this was surreal.

"M-m-m-mother," she stammered, "what are you . . . ?"

Maisie instinctively braced herself for a sharp, snide comment. But instead, her mother smiled, almost bashfully.

"I came to get Beth," her mother said, placing everything on the only table in the room. She held out one of the steaming mugs to Maisie. "She's had quite the adventure, but it's time for me to take her home again."

"But why?" Maisie asked, ignoring the tea. "I told Dad that I'd put her on a train back to Glasgow on Sunday, so why would you bother to come and get her?"

Her mother studied Maisie for a moment. "Because I missed her. I couldn't bear it any longer, so I had to come to see that she was all right." She sounded like her throat was tight. "To see that you were both all right."

Maisie huffed. "And of course, on Saturday you were *so* worried that your younger daughter had run away, you went straight out to the hairdresser, to help you deal with the grief." She knew she was being vicious, but she didn't care.

"The hairdresser? When did I go to the hairdresser?" Maisie's mother pulled her brown hair away from her collar as if to show off its length. "I haven't been to the hairdresser for weeks, not since you left home. So I have no idea what you're talking about."

"When I called Dad after breakfast on Saturday morning," Maisie said, "to let you know that Beth was here and safe with me, he said you'd gone to get your hair done, and that's why you weren't there to talk on the phone."

"He told you I was getting my hair done?" Maisie's mother looked shocked, and then angry. "I didn't go anywhere on Saturday except back to the police station to report Beth still missing. Oh, the nerve of that man! I was distraught when I realized she hadn't gone to school on Friday, and then found that she'd taken her schoolbag, some warm clothes, and her stout walking shoes. I ran straight down to report her missing, but they said she'd come home when she was hungry. So on Saturday morning, I went back down there at dawn and sat for over four hours until that ridiculous policeman would finally listen to me."

Maisie was starting to wonder if she'd been a little unfair to her mother, but she couldn't quite bring herself to apologize. "Well, Dad said—"

"And that makes complete sense now." Her mother was talking faster as her fury grew. "It was only when I wondered out loud if she might have run away to see you that he even told me you'd called. And that was hours later. How long would he have let me worry that Beth was lying dead by the side of the road, or worse? That bloody man!"

Maisie was startled. She had thought exactly the same

thing about her dad on many occasions, but she could not believe she was hearing it from her mother.

"Of course, I wanted to come up here to get her at once, but he was insistent that she deserved to be punished, and a few nights sleeping in a freezing-cold shed would do it, and then she'd find out quite how comfortable her life was. And part of me rather agreed, but then he started saying the most awful things . . . well, let's say that your father and I had words, and not very nice ones at that. So yesterday I followed Beth's example and caught the train north." She sounded extraordinarily proud of this achievement, as if she'd become a world explorer by getting on a train to Inverness. "But when I got to your camp, they told me that you were both in the hospital—"

"The message we sent back to Auchterblair"—it was Maisie's turn to be annoyed now; whoever had taken down the telephone message at Auchterblair Farm and walked it to the camp had not been listening properly—"was that we were *at* the hospital, Mother, not *in* the hospital!"

"But your friend Violet said that there had been a dreadful logging accident and that you'd been saved in a daring rescue from a mountain in a blizzard. She made it sound like you and Beth, and another girl, were fighting for your lives."

"Bloody Violet!" snapped Maisie. "She made all that up to be spiteful. Beth, Dot, and I weren't even there when the accident happened to some of the lumberjacks camped near us. We came across them by chance, and we were the *rescuers*, not the rescued."

"I realize that now, and from what the nurse says, you saved those men's lives. And Beth told me that—"

"But where is Beth?" interrupted Maisie, suddenly remembering her sister ought to have still been there.

"She went back to your camp with the very nice Canadian chap who drove me down here."

"What very nice chap?" Maisie couldn't help but ask, because she'd never heard her mother refer to another man like that, and had certainly never seen a blush rising in her mother's face as it was now.

"Oh, I forget his name, I think he's the man in charge, but anyway, when I got here and found—"

"The man in charge? Who? You mean the big one with the bald head and grumpy face?" Her mother was definitely blushing right now.

"Well, yes, he is large, and a little balding, I suppose, but he certainly wasn't grumpy. He had a very nice smile, and he was very kind. And polite. He even held the door open for me, and it made a nice change to be treated like a lady." Maisie's mother looked lost in thought, a smile playing around her mouth. "Oh, I wish I could recall his name."

"Haven?" suggested Maisie, doubtfully. "You can't be talking about Haven, surely?"

"Haven! That was it! A very nice chap." Maisie's mother suddenly seemed to realize what she was saying, and to whom, so she continued with her story again. "He and another chap gave me a ride when they came to check on their friends, and then they decided to take the truck back to the camp. Beth went with them so she could pack her things, but I said I'd wait for you to wake up, and Haven has sweetly offered to drive your sister and me to the station to catch the evening train tonight."

This was too strange. This blushing woman could not be her tight-lipped and miserable mother.

Maisie was caught off guard yet again when her mother reached out and touched Maisie's face, running a gentle finger across her cheek. It was a gesture of warmth and affection so unfamiliar that Maisie couldn't remember the last time it had happened, and she wasn't sure if she wanted to pull away or sink into her mother's arms.

"You've got a nasty scratch there, Margaret. Perhaps I should ask the nurse—"

Maisie winced. "It's Maisie. I choose to be Maisie here, not Margaret."

"Oh yes, of course. I forgot that when I first reached the camp last night. It caused a bit of confusion when I asked for Margaret." Maisie's mother smiled.

"But does Beth even want to go back with you?"

"Marg—I mean *Maisie*, you've got to remember that Beth isn't like you, much as she'd like to think she is. Of course, she's very proud of herself for having made it here, and that you let her stay and help, but I think that the accident this morning frightened her. It was nothing like anything she'd ever dealt with before . . . and she thinks that she let you down somehow."

"Let me down? How could she have let me down? She

was excellent. She did exactly what she was told to do, and she pushed me out of the way of a falling log. I could well have been *in* the hospital if it hadn't been for her, Mother, and certainly we could never have got the men onto the truck without Beth's help."

The men. On the truck. Suddenly the fog inside Maisie's mind cleared in an instant.

"John and Elliott! How are they? *Where* are they?"

Twenty-One

Maisie was up and scrambling for the door. She shouldn't be sitting there talking to her mother, she should be asking after John and Elliott. But her mother was on her feet too, blocking Maisie's way out of the waiting room.

"Hush now. All is fine. Inverness has a much bigger hospital, and the doctors there can treat all manner of serious injuries."

Inverness? Maisie swallowed down a lump of disappointment that she had missed seeing John before they'd been taken away. How long had she been sleeping, for goodness' sake?

"I met Dot," Maisie's mother continued. "She's a lovely girl, isn't she? And she was telling me before she left in the ambulance that although your friend was in a bad way, the doctor hoped that if they could get him to the surgeons in Inverness quickly, he'd get fixed up good as new."

Surgeons? Maisie felt sick, visualizing John surrounded by surgeons plunging scalpels into his mangled left leg. Poor John.

"And the other young man, John, is across the hall sleeping now, and the nurse said—"

"What? John's still here?"

"Yes, dear, *Elliott* went in the ambulance with Dot, but *John* is still here." Maisie's mother said his name with a particular emphasis, and Maisie immediately knew that Beth must have blabbed. "His leg isn't broken, only very bruised. They're going to keep an eye on it to make sure something-or-other nasty doesn't develop. But the nurse said that thanks to you, his leg should be fine."

"Oh, thank God!"

Maisie sat down again hard on the nearest seat and tried to catch her breath, and before she knew it, her mother was beside her, wrapping warm arms around her shoulders. Maisie almost pulled away, but it felt so nice to have that comfortable pressure around her back, stabilizing her and binding her in a moment when she felt she was about to fall apart. So instead, Maisie leaned into her mother's embrace and rested her head on her mother's shoulder.

They sat there until Maisie's breathing was regular again. Then her mother released her shoulders and took both Maisie's hands, squeezing them tight.

"I know you probably don't want to hear this, Ma—*Maisie*.

Especially not from me. But I wouldn't feel right going home without having said something."

Maisie could not imagine what was about to be said, but she knew it would not be something she wanted to hear.

"You're still young, dear, and I hear that you and this fellow, John, have become, well, close—"

"I'll kill Beth for blabbing!" Maisie growled under her breath.

"No, not Beth. Not only Beth, anyway. Dot mentioned it too, just to warn me that you might be especially worried about John because you and he had recently become close."

"Will you stop saying it like that? We're friends. We're not *close*."

"Of course, of course. But all I was going to say was that there might come a time when you, and he, start thinking about becoming—"

"Don't say 'close' again. I couldn't bear it!"

"Fine, then I'll say 'something more than friends' then, is that better?"

"Barely."

"Whatever you want to call it, please think carefully. You're seventeen. You should be looking forward to university and to all the opportunities that are there for you. Opportunities that I never had. When I was your age, I couldn't continue my education and have a career. Women like me were trapped into marriage too young, and paid the price for the rest of their lives."

Maisie's mother's green eyes were suddenly teary, and

Maisie realized that she wasn't speaking about random women—she was talking about herself.

"But Mother, you're only, what, thirty-five now? Because when you were my age, you were—"

"By the time I was eighteen, I was already married, with a baby on the way. I was expected to know how to run a house and look after a baby and be everything my husband wanted me to be. And that was hard. Very hard. There were wonderful times, like when you two girls were born, and when you first smiled, and walked. . . . But sometimes it felt like my wings were clipped. I was nothing like your auntie Jenny. She took to married life and motherhood like she'd been born to it, but I couldn't help wondering if there might have been more to my life."

Maisie was struggling to see her mother as a caged bird instead of the straitlaced homebody she'd always thought her to be.

"But if you've always wanted an adventure, Mother, then why did you try to stop me from having mine? Why wouldn't you support me when I joined the Timber Corps?"

Maisie's mother sighed. "Because it's a short-term solution. The war might be over by Christmas, and then there won't be a Timber Corps anymore because the men will want their jobs back. And then where will you be?"

Maisie knew she didn't expect an answer.

"I didn't want you joining up because I wanted you—I still want you—to have all the education I never had, so you can support yourself. That way, you need only get married because you *want* to get married, not because you have no other choice. And you can have some fun before the hard work of being a wife and mother begins."

"But—" began Maisie.

"But I'll admit"—her mother patted Maisie's arm—"I was a wee bit jealous too. If it had only been about me, I would have been right beside you in line to join the Timber Corps too, or the Land Army, or one of the services. I'm sure I'd have loved it. Seeing the newsreel this week, of you working up here, so fresh and free, it made me feel quite young again."

"You saw the newsreel?"

"Of course. Twice!"

Maisie looked at her mother. And she saw that her mother was still young, relatively speaking, barely older than Phyllis or Anna. And Maisie felt a smile come of its own accord.

"Mother, listen, why not have your own adventure now? I'm here, and Beth is determined to join up as soon as she can, so why don't you? You're not too old, you know, and you're quite fit, and—"

"Oh, Maisie, I couldn't. It would mean leaving your father to . . . well, it would mean leaving your father."

"So what? Why would that be so hard? It's not like you even love each other."

"Don't say such a thing! Of course I love your father—I'm his wife. And he's looked after me very well, all three of us."

"But that doesn't mean you *like* him. He's a bully and a bore, and a miser, and getting away from him and his house was the best thing I ever did. Yes, Mother, *his house*, because that's what it is. It's his house, he paid for it, he's in charge of it, and you are simply his housekeeper, so I really think you should leave too. Maybe not now, but certainly when Beth is ready to leave home. Then you'll have nothing to stay for, and you'd have so much to give to the Timber Corps or to the Land Army or even the Nursing Service."

"Maisie, that's silly. A woman can't leave her husband and disappear. . . ."

"You wouldn't be the first. We had quite a few older women train with us. I know you'd be so much happier."

Maisie's mother sat silently for a moment, but then she shook her head and put her arms back around Maisie's shoulder.

"I hate that you think so poorly of your dad. He's not the same man I married, perhaps, but he's had a lot to deal with. When your grandmother died, instead of inheriting what she had always told him was 'a small fortune,' he was left—we were left—with all her debt, and it almost killed him. It took years of working long hours, and scrimping and saving, to recover, but he still tried to give you two a happy home, don't you remember? Those holidays on the beach at Prestwick, and, oh, what was that other place called . . . ?"

"Ardrossan," offered Maisie quietly.

"Yes, that's it, Ardrossan. We went on the train, do you remember? And it rained all week, but we still had fun. Remember?"

"Not really," Maisie lied, feeling only a little shame.

"All those years, your dad was struggling to find any joy in life."

"He had us, though."

"Yes, he had us, only that wasn't quite enough for him. And then, when it became clear that the war was coming, your dad almost became like himself again. You might not remember when he went to join the army. They wouldn't take him, said there was too much damage to his lungs from the tuberculosis he'd suffered as a child. So instead he tried the RAF, the navy, the marines, the fire brigade, and even the police, but still no one would take him. He wasn't yet forty, and all he was fit for was to volunteer as an air-raid warden, as if he were an old man."

She shook her head sadly.

"The disappointment tore him apart all over again, and he became very bitter, and a little nasty."

Maisie's throat felt tight. Had her father been so awful when she joined up because he was *jealous*? But that didn't explain her mother's reaction. "But why did you have to become so nasty too, Mother?" she whispered.

Her mother sighed. "I didn't mean to be. It's just that life can be a little disappointing for me too sometimes. I'm sorry, I really am. I know it doesn't make it all right, but I'd like it if you and I could try again. Perhaps we could be friends from now on? And you know, your dad didn't always disappear into his study for hours, so I'm still hoping that one day soon, he'll realize all the good things he's missing, and he'll come back out and join us again."

"I won't hold my breath for that," Maisie began, but her mother shushed her gently.

"And in case he does, I need to be there. It was fun to think that I might be young enough or brave enough for this exciting life you've decided to lead, for a little while anyway. But now I think I need to get back to your father, and get that sister of yours back into her own bed, don't you?"

She leaned in and kissed Maisie tenderly on the temple, holding her tight as she did. Maisie felt some of the misery and uncertainty release from her chest. Her mother was proud of her after all, something that even yesterday she wouldn't have thought possible.

"Now, from what I hear," Maisie's mother whispered, "sleeping across the hallway is a rather handsome young man with dark hair and strapping shoulders. So why don't you go over there and see how your *friend* is doing."

And this time, it was Maisie's turn to blush.

Twenty-Two

Maisie hugged her mother good-bye and went across the hall to find John. He was already awake, but when Maisie tried to ask how he was feeling, he thanked her almost perfunctorily for rescuing him and for saving Elliott's life without once looking up at her. His response flustered Maisie, but she sat in a chair by his bed anyway, awkwardly assuring him that anyone else would have done the same, and that she'd been lucky she hadn't had to do the rescue alone.

And then silence fell between them.

After some time, John murmured, "Maisie, you're staring at me."

Maisie started. Had she been staring? For how long? And given that John had yet to look at Maisie even once, how had he known she'd been staring at him? He'd been finding the weave of his blanket far more interesting than her.

"Staring? No, I wasn't. At least, I wasn't meaning to."

"Well, you were. And I wish you'd stop."

"All right."

The awkwardness settled in again as Maisie struggled to think of something to say.

"Actually," she said finally, "I was wondering whether you realize how much time you spend frowning."

When he didn't reply, she glanced at him again. His eyes were still on his blanket.

"I mean"—she'd started now, so she might as well go on—"you don't seem to have any neutral expression. You either frown or you smile. Sorry if that sounds rude."

"No, no, I understand. A simple observation."

Maisie was aware that if she let her eyes return to his face, she could be accused of staring again, so she looked instead down to the other end of John. Or at least, to where she assumed the other end of John must be, under the green hospital blanket that stretched across a metal cage that kept the weight of the bedclothes off his damaged legs. Or rather, his leg.

And that was the thing they were both determinedly *not* talking about. His leg. But that made no sense, so Maisie decided to be brave. Only gradually.

"Out of interest, how much do you remember of the accident and the journey here?"

"You've scratched your cheek," John said.

"How much do you remember, John?"

John's frown deepened, as it so often did.

He seemed to be sifting through memories to decide what his answer should be. "Not much," he said at last. "I remember Elliott and me climbing onto the truck to settle the load, and then I remember *not* being on the truck anymore, and the logs falling . . . and the dark . . . and the cold, and Elliott was . . . But then nothing, until . . . until . . . no, nothing more."

He closed his eyes, and Maisie knew he wasn't telling the truth.

"And what about when we got Elliott out from under the logs, and it was only you stuck?"

Pause. His eyes were now open and back on the knitted blanket.

"Not much."

"You don't remember what you told Dot to do?"

His eyes flicked up now to meet hers, then back down.

"No."

"You told Dot to . . ." This was harder than she'd expected. "Dot knows about your leg now, and so do Nancy and Beth."

John pushed his elbows down into the mattress, lifting slightly so he could turn his body to face away from Maisie.

"And I forgot to tell them not to mention it to anyone else, so it's likely that everyone at Auchterblair knows by now too." Maisie reached forward and laid her hand on his arm. "I'm sorry—I didn't think about swearing them to keep the secret before we left."

John rubbed his palm across his face, the way a child

might rub sleep away, and in doing so pulled his arm from under Maisie's hand. She didn't want to move away from him, so she let her hand rest gently on his ribs, though he didn't seem to notice.

"You had your mind on other things at the time," John said matter-of-factly, "so don't worry about it. Someone was sure to find out sooner or later, and I'll just have to deal with it. I only wanted it to be secret because I refuse to be 'John Lindsay, the cripple.' I don't want to be pitied, I don't want to be treated like I can't pull my weight . . . or like I can't defend myself."

Maisie winced at the jibe.

"And even if my leg's gone, I'm still a real man, and I want to be treated as one. Though perhaps . . ."

Maisie waited.

"Though perhaps," he continued at last, his voice dropping to barely more than a murmur, "that's just naive."

Maisie pressed her hand on his chest. "Of course you are a 'real man,' John, whatever that means. For goodness' sake, in all those weeks, I had no idea that you haven't . . . that you'd lost . . . that anything was wrong. You work harder than anyone else, lumberjack or lumberjill, and you're always first to volunteer, even for the heavy work, so who do you think would waste their time pitying you? Listen to me. Losing a . . . Not having . . ."

"You can't even bring yourself to say it." John's tone was suddenly acidic, and Maisie was surprised how much that hurt her.

"Of course I can say it," she snapped. "Losing a *leg* is nothing to be ashamed of."

John grunted.

"A man with only one leg is still a man," Maisie continued. "Just as not having a uniform doesn't mean you're not a man. What kind of old-fashioned attitude is that?" A thought struck Maisie then. Of course! Why hadn't it dawned on her already? "Your leg is why you couldn't join the army, isn't it? And why you got so upset when Violet was being such a cow about it?"

John lay still and silent. Maisie could still feel the rise and fall of his breathing under her hand, and she pressed down a little harder to offer comfort. He did not respond.

"John?"

Nothing. Eventually Maisie pulled her hand away and stood up. "That's all right—you don't need to talk to me if you don't want to. But you know where I am if you change your mind."

Maisie returned the chair she'd been sitting in back to the wall and walked to the door. "I'll be back to see you tomorrow, in case you want to not talk to me then too."

She didn't wait, knowing he wouldn't respond to that either, and walked to the nursing station, where she found the kind nurse who had given them tea earlier.

"I'll come back in the morning," she said to the nurse, "though I doubt he'll be bothered if I do or not."

The nurse patted Maisie's arm. "Of course he'll be pleased to see you, dear. You were the first thing he asked about when he woke up. But he's had an awful shock, and he's been very badly bruised. And we've still to hear from Inverness about the other lad, so let's give him a little more time to recover his humor. We'll have him back on his feet in no time."

Maisie tried not to wince at her insensitive wording, but she did feel reassured all the same. John had faced death up on the mountain, Elliott's and his own, so she ought to give him more time. And it wasn't as if she was going anywhere, except back to camp.

Maisie gave the nurse as much of a smile as she could muster. "Do you know how I might get back to Auchterblair camp? I don't think I could sleep another night on your waiting room chairs."

The nurse chuckled.

"I don't think you need to worry," she said, pointing across to the waiting room. "Your chauffeur and lady-in-waiting have been hoping to escort you home for a wee while now."

Maisie turned to find Nancy walking toward her, arms wide.

The relief at not having to think any further about how to get back to camp overtook Maisie, and she let Nancy wrap her in a hug, then lead her outside to a van Maisie recognized as belonging to the butcher in Carrbridge. Behind them trailed the butcher's lad, a shy boy who sometimes delivered to Auchterblair.

Nancy smiled apologetically as she made an impromptu cushion of her own greatcoat and Maisie's in the back of the van. "Sorry, it was the only transport I could find. I didn't think you'd want to cycle all the way home."

Maisie waved away the apology. True, if she hadn't been so tired, she might have been slightly disgusted by the idea of riding where all the bloody carcasses normally traveled, but since the van still reeked of Jeyes disinfectant and was clearly spotlessly clean, she told her friend not to give it a second thought.

"But thank you for coming, Nancy," she said as she laid her head down onto the bundle of coats. She didn't know the boy's name, but she was still grateful he was there. "And will you thank him too?"

The boy must have heard, because he replied, but Maisie barely heard it. Even before she'd felt the van pick up speed along the main road toward Auchterblair, toward home, the soft relief of sleep engulfed her.

"I'm so sorry, Maisie, I really am. I thought I'd ruined everything."

"It's fine, Susan," said Maisie as she kicked off her dirt-caked boots. Susan was apologizing for about the fifth time for getting lost on the way to find reinforcements, which had been the reason Maisie had had to drive all the way to the hospital herself. "Really, it all worked out in the end, and I know how easy it is to get lost in the forest. I'm just glad you found your way back eventually."

"But I was sure I knew where I was going, and I thought that if I cut off the main track, I'd save so much time getting to the men's camp."

"Yes, I know, Susan, you said. I understand." Maisie pulled on her thick flannel pajama trousers and then her thick bed socks. The hut was noticeably colder than it had been before that morning's storm.

"And when I did finally find it, Haven was there after all, and we rushed back up the hill again, but you'd already gone. With the truck. And Haven started swearing. A lot. And it was snowing, or at least, sleeting, and—"

"Susan! Really, it's fine! Please don't keep apologizing." Maisie was trying not snap at her. Wee Susan was clearly distraught that losing her way might have resulted in someone's death, but really, five apologies were surely enough. "Nothing bad happened. We got them to hospital and they're both going to be fine." Maisie hoped to God that was true—she still hadn't heard if Elliott was even still alive.

"But Violet said that Elliott could still—"

"Pay no attention to anything Violet says. Dot's with Elliott, and you know she'd never let anything happen to one of her patients. Not our Dot."

Maisie used her sleeve to wipe a tear from Wee Susan's cheek and wished she could find the energy to cry too. All Maisie wanted was a cup of tea and her bed. The last twenty-four hours had been so hard.

As if she'd read Maisie's mind, Nancy appeared at her elbow, pressing a steaming mug of tea into her hands. Maisie smiled gratefully and sipped at the rich brown liquid, letting it scald her tongue with both its heat and its strong tannins. "Sergeant major's tea" was what Phyllis had always called it.

Phyllis. Suddenly Maisie wished that Phyllis had been there with them on the hillside. She would have known better than anyone what to do. But then again, Maisie had somehow known what to do too, and she knew that Phyllis would have been proud of her.

Maisie took another sip of tea and wondered how she might describe all that had happened today when she next wrote to Phyllis and Helen. The tea was sweet. Nancy had put sugar in it, or perhaps honey, and it was wonderful. It was a taste from when she was a little girl, from before the war, from before the time when her parents had become so miserable with each other and with her. Aunt Jenny would let Maisie sip cool sweet tea from her saucer. Now the sweet tea was hot, but still Maisie gulped another mouthful down, relishing the heat rolling into her chest and through her body. How could one gulp of tea bring warmth to her whole being?

Suddenly, the roar of an approaching engine made everyone look toward the door. It didn't sound like a truck to Maisie, so what was it?

"Oh my God, look!" someone cried, and Maisie moved with the others to peer out of the window. A Tilley lamp hung outside, and a motorcycle now stood in its pool of yellow light. The rider, a young man Maisie didn't know, sat astride the bike as Dot stiffly swung a leg over the back and gingerly stood upright. She was wearing an enormous leather coat, which she shrugged off and handed to her chauffeur. He put it on, then swung the bike away into the dark, the narrow beam from its blacked-out headlamp vanishing long before the sound of the engine.

As Dot turned to face them, Maisie noticed she was still wearing Nancy's leather jerkin. Even so, she looked frozen and close to collapse. Nancy got to her first, supporting Dot as she led her into the hut and onto a chair beside the black potbellied stove.

"Get her a blanket, quickly, please," Nancy called. "She's frozen, poor thing. And can someone get her a cup of tea? There's some still in the pot, and make sure you add in a couple of spoonfuls of honey too."

"Two spoonfuls?" Violet's scandalized voice cut through the hum. "Since when does one person get *two* spoonfuls? That's not—"

"Oh, piss off, Violet," retorted Nancy, Maisie, and both Susans, all at once, and surprisingly Violet did what she was told.

"Here, Dot, have the rest of mine," said Maisie, handing her almost-full mug to her friend. Dot's teeth were chattering, her whole body racked with shivers, so Maisie kept her own fingers wrapped around Dot's, pressing them against the warm mug. She even helped Dot lift it to her mouth to sip, and Dot smiled gratefully as Nancy threw one blanket, then another, around Dot's shoulders.

"Thank you," Dot said when the shivering began to subside. "And if I *ever* tell you that I fancy a ride on the back of a motorcycle again, you have my permission to shoot me!"

There was some laughter from the women around them, but Maisie got the feeling that Dot was entirely serious.

"Are you all right?" she asked Dot quietly.

Dot nodded. "I'm tired, that's all. And cold."

"And what happened to . . . ? Is Elliott . . . ?" Maisie couldn't find the words to ask.

"He's alive," replied Dot, "though I thought we'd lost him outside Inverness. He had some sort of fit, a seizure. It was awful to watch, knowing I could do nothing to help him. They're still worried about the bump on his head."

"His head?" said Maisie. "I didn't notice a bump on his head. I thought it was only his chest and legs where the logs were crushing him." So Dot had been right when she'd told them to be careful with Elliott's head and neck when they'd transferred him onto the truck. Maisie felt sick at the thought of how much damage her ignorance might have caused if Dot hadn't been there.

"We think he banged it on one of the other logs as he went down, and it's caused an edema," said Dot. "That's where fluid builds up around his brain. They're operating on him in the morning, to drain some of the fluid off."

"Dot! Enough details!" Maisie shuddered.

"But you asked." Dot looked put out.

"I know I did, but I only wanted to know if he was all right."

"It was a close call, and to be honest, we'll have to wait and see. He was in quite a mess, but they said they'd let me know what happened with the operation if I call tomorrow from the post office. It's all we can do, Maisie, but Elliott's in good hands." Dot took one hand from the mug and laid it onto Maisie's arm. "And how's John?"

Something about Dot's tone suggested she was asking about more than just the state of John's injuries, but there were too many flapping ears around for Maisie to answer with more information than a simple update. "They think his left leg's only bruised, and his ribs too. So physically, he's going to be fine. . . ."

She shrugged, and perhaps it was what she didn't say that made Dot squeeze her arm in response. Dot understood.

"When was the last time you ate?" Nancy asked as the other women began to disperse back to whatever they'd been doing before.

"I'm not sure," said Dot. "A while ago, I suppose, but all I want to do is to get out of these disgusting clothes and into my bed. And then sleep for a year." Dot smiled at Nancy. "But thank you for caring."

"You can't go to sleep on an empty stomach," Nancy said, leaning in to rub Dot's back. "Or you'll leave a void for the devil to fill. Or at least that's what my grandma always used to tell us."

She stood and hooked one hand under Dot's arm, helping her to her feet.

"Come on, let's get you a piece of toast at least. And a fresh cup of tea. Then you can sleep."

"That sounds good, actually," conceded Dot. "Maisie, will you come with us?"

Maisie was about to follow Dot and Nancy, but something about the way Nancy was holding Dot up, and the look on Dot's face showing how much she was cherishing that support, made Maisie stop.

"That's all right—you two carry on," she said. "I'd better lie down before I fall down."

As she watched her friends go, Maisie wished John would look at her the way Nancy looked at Dot. But when John looked at Maisie, it was almost always with a dark and sad frown.

Twenty-Three

Maisie slept badly that night, and found herself awake in an early-morning silence, punctuated only by the soft snores of the other women in the hut. Knowing that sleep had deserted her, she got up and dressed quietly. Pulling on her boots, she noticed a strange light was filtering through the window, giving the air an unpleasant yellow tinge, and she wondered if they'd get another storm later on; so she decided to go for a walk right now, before anyone else was up, to try to walk off her melancholy before it took hold.

Within a couple of minutes, she had on her heavy coat and her flashlight in her hand. The yellow light had intensified, though the ground at Maisie's feet was still almost in darkness. It was cold again, but the air felt thick and moist, and Maisie couldn't decide whether to keep or shed her coat, feeling both chilly and sweaty at the same time.

She had no particular route in mind as she set off—she only wanted to feel the comforting repetition of putting one boot in front of the other, even if her bruised calf was protesting each step.

After she'd been walking a little while, a verse of John's unfinished poem entered her head, the one he'd read out to her on the hill, and two of the phrases began turning themselves over and over, like a scratched gramophone record catching at the needle.

As from sweet heaven, the angel flies to gather you in silk,
And lead you to your final hour.

She couldn't quite remember the exact words as he had read them to her, but she thought she was close. And there was something about their lyricism that drew them from her memory, as if roused by the predawn heaviness in the air.

She was no closer to interpreting the poem's meaning than before, but she wondered if the poem might be an elegy for his lost leg. She was still baffled that she hadn't guessed sooner—immediately—about his leg, especially as his dancing had been so dreadful. God! How had he even *tried* to dance with her? But it had been so easy to dismiss the signs because John was always so competent. He was so physically strong, and, to Maisie at least, invincible. Yet, he doubted himself. He could not believe that she could ever want him, even though she had wanted him so much that she'd tried to sit on his lap so she could kiss him even more.

That memory made her shudder. She was not a small girl, after all, and the extra pressure her weight would have put on his knee, and on the wooden leg attached to it, would have been so uncomfortable, or even painful, she was sure. The false leg had been designed to take one person's weight, not two, and had looked so slender in comparison to the huge tree trunk under which it had been trapped . . . Wait! Under which it must *still* be trapped. They'd been so frantic about getting John and Elliott to the hospital, they hadn't had time to retrieve John's false leg. It hadn't even occurred to her to try, she thought now with shame. That wooden column, with its leather straps at the top, and presumably some kind of false foot at the bottom so it fitted into his big work boots, was a vital part of John's life—his most important tool. It was of far more value to him than any ax or saw, and yet she'd left it stuck in the mud on a rain-soaked hillside. What had she been thinking?

Looking around, she found that, perhaps instinctively, she'd been walking in the direction of the accident site. She was already more than halfway there. Pushing herself even harder, she reached the turn off the main track within another fifteen minutes and ran down the slope to where the jumbled pile of giant logs still lay scattered across the slant of the clearing.

Maisie quickly found the largest log of all. And there, wedged tight under it, was John's leg. She gave it an explor-atory tug, but the leg wouldn't budge. Presumably John's boot, which must be at the bottom of the leg and therefore under the log, was preventing its release, though she couldn't see it from where she crouched. The trunk was too heavy for her to move alone, and anyway, she wouldn't risk yet another log roll that might injure her. She'd tempted fate too many times of late.

Tentatively, she pressed her fingers into the mud under the leg. After yesterday's rain, it was softer than it would have been in midsummer, but still too hard to dig in with her fingers. Damn! She'd dressed so quickly, she hadn't brought any tools with her. What she really needed was something sharp, like a knife or a cant hook.

A cant hook! Nancy had broken the metal hooks off the two cant poles yesterday to make the stretcher. Maisie dashed over to where Nancy had smacked the tools into submission, and there they were, the two-pronged hooks that would be perfect for digging.

Soon Maisie was scratching deep gouges into the sticky mud. She glanced almost proudly at the hard calluses on her hands. If she'd done this kind of scraping and digging during her first week of training, her hands would have been bleeding and raw within minutes.

The sun was fully up, and all signs of incoming rain had vanished by the time she freed the leg. As it came away in her hand, she fell backward, the muddy boot falling into her lap. John's leg was not what she had expected at all. She remembered a line drawing in the copy of *Treasure Island* that she and Beth had loved to read to each other as children. It was of

Long John Silver, the one-legged pirate, whose leg had been drawn as nothing but a gnarled stick. But this one looked so realistic, so, well, like a leg.

It was slimmer than she supposed John's real flesh-and-bone leg must be, given his size and build, but its beautiful deep-brown wood—oak perhaps?—had been carved and polished into a calf-muscle shape. From its widest point, it narrowed down to where it disappeared inside his mud-caked boot. She felt the boot move in her hands, even though she held the leg still, and realized that the leg and foot must be jointed at the ankle in some way. She was tempted to pull the sock out of the boot so she could see how it worked, but somehow, that felt like a deliberate invasion of John's privacy.

At the top was a smooth wooden cup into which, she supposed, John would place his . . . his stump. Was that the right word? She wasn't sure. The cup had been lined with leather, which she could feel was beautifully soft from wear, even if it was rather damp from sitting out all night. Thankfully she hadn't needed to sever any of the straps in the rescue, and running her fingers along the wide leather now, Maisie wondered how tightly he had to buckle the strap to keep it secure. Remembering the blisters she had suffered from the chafing leather each time she'd worn her new work boots, she wondered how painful it had been for him to wear these straps until they didn't rub and blister the soft skin of his thigh anymore.

But perhaps the pain from blisters and chafing skin were as nothing to the unimaginable agony he must have suffered when he'd lost the leg itself. And then it occurred to her that she hadn't had a chance to ask him *how* he had lost it.

Meeting John in another situation, and if she hadn't known he'd come over from Newfoundland as a lumberjack, she might have assumed that he'd lost it in the war, injured in action, as so many other Allied servicemen had. One of the girls at school had brought her uncle to talk to the class and be the guest of honor at the prize-giving back in June. He'd been an RAF Spitfire pilot and had lost his leg when he was shot down over the English Channel during the Battle of Britain in 1940. Maisie recalled how embarrassed she'd been that this handsome and dashing man was having to work so hard simply to stand upright when presenting the prizes. Mrs. Packham had clearly noticed too, because just as he was about to present Maisie with her book—the prize for winning the diction competition—Mrs. Packham had suggested that he might be more comfortable presenting from a chair. But the squadron leader had proudly straightened his back, squared his shoulders, and declared, "These young ladies deserve to be honored in the appropriate fashion, not by some chap lounging around." Then he'd wiped his forehead with a pristine white handkerchief from his pocket and had shaken hands with Maisie as if nothing were amiss.

She'd thought of that pilot a lot after the ceremony, about his recovery and rehabilitation, having to learn to walk all over again, and she wondered what a pilot would do if he couldn't fly a plane anymore.

Maisie shook the memory away and tucked the cant hooks

carefully through her belt loops. The prongs were sharp, but the hooks were too valuable to leave up here. Then she picked up the leg again, and with the warm, smooth wood and the heavy and filthy boot held tightly in her arms, she headed down the hill toward camp.

She'd promised to go back to Grantown to visit John later today, even if he hadn't asked her to, so she'd return the leg to him then. And perhaps then she'd summon up the courage to ask John what kind of man would have the determination to become a lumberjack even though he'd suffered as devastating an injury as losing his leg. But she knew the answer to that already. The bravest kind.

Back at camp, Maisie told Violet why she would not be working that day, and to her surprise, Violet didn't argue with her. She didn't even tell Maisie that she'd have to count it as one of her days off for the month. It was as if any mention of John made Violet run for cover.

After breakfast, Maisie walked down to Carrbridge and caught the bus going to Grantown. With a booted foot and wooden leg lying across her lap, she raised more than a couple of eyebrows among the driver and other passengers. Before leaving camp, she'd done her best to get as much of the mud off John's boot as possible, but even so, the nurse looked entirely unimpressed at Maisie's arrival, although that might have been because Maisie had forgotten to clean the mud off her own boots too.

With a sigh, the nurse handed her a sheet of newspaper on

which to lay the leg on the floor and sent Maisie to wash her hands yet again, telling her especially to lose "the allotments under those fingernails." Then the nurse escorted Maisie—with John's leg wrapped up in newspaper in her now-clean hands—down to the ward.

John was sleeping as they approached.

"He's had a bit of a rough time, according to the night staff," the nurse said, pausing at the end of the bed to have a look at the charts hanging there. "Awful nightmares, she said. But then, a lot of them do, you know."

Maisie was puzzled. Lumberjacks? Newfoundlanders? Men, in general? She wasn't sure who the nurse meant. "A lot of *who* do?"

"The lads who've come back from over there," replied the nurse, dropping her voice so only Maisie might hear. "Those boys have seen some dreadful things, and some, like this one, have been injured into the bargain."

"Back from over where?" Maisie asked, feeling very dim.

"Over *there*." The nurse sounded frustrated. "Over on the front line, fighting in France or wherever. You know, soldiers, or—"

"No, I think you're mistaken," Maisie interrupted. "He's a lumberjack, not a soldier."

The nurse's eyebrows rose as she regarded Maisie. "He might not be a soldier now, dear, but there's not many young men of his age who end up with his sort of injuries, both in his body and in here"—she tapped her temple with one finger—"without having seen service, whether it was army, air force, or navy."

Maisie stared at her, and then back at John. But he hadn't been a soldier. He would have told her about it. And he would have put Violet in her place when she'd taunted him about being a coward because he wasn't in uniform. Surely.

But then again, he'd kept his leg secret, and she supposed she'd never actually asked him if he'd seen service.

Perhaps her shock showed, because the nurse patted her shoulder gently.

"Your lad has had some medicine to help him to sleep awhile longer. And you look like you could do with a cuppa. I was about to make one for myself, so why don't you park yourself in that comfy chair and I'll go sort that out. Go on now. The doctor won't make his rounds until after lunch, so you'll not be disturbed."

In a daze, Maisie sat down in the comfortable chair beside John's bed and laid the leg, still wrapped in the newspaper, under it. The nurse pulled the screens around the bed and then clicked softly away.

Maisie looked at John. Last night, he'd deliberately turned his back on her, but now she had a perfect view of his face. In sleep, he looked younger. His features were relaxed, with neither smile nor frown creasing the tanned skin across his brow and around his eyes. A dark shadow of stubble had grown on his chin and under his nose, framing his dark-pink lips, for once at rest, but, not for the first time, incredibly inviting. Without even thinking about what she was doing, Maisie lifted one finger to her own lips and kissed it. Then she reached out and placed her kiss, barely, onto John's soft lips.

Astonished by her boldness, she froze, her finger barely touching him, waiting to see if she had woken him, but his breathing didn't alter and his lips didn't move to acknowledge her kiss. At once, Maisie felt both relieved and ashamed. He'd made it clear yesterday that he didn't want to talk to her, let alone do anything else. A wave of misery suddenly engulfed her. This strange sweet man in front of her had been her first . . . not her first *love*, she didn't know him well enough yet for that, but he had been her first . . . *possibility*. But now? Now he was her first loss. She had reached out for him and he had turned his back.

Maisie suddenly shivered and pulled her arm back so she could wrap it around herself for comfort. As she did, however, her elbow caught the nightstand beside her, knocking something to the floor with thud. Maisie saw it was the little black notebook that John had been carrying when she'd met him up at the croft, the one he'd read from.

The notebook had fallen open beside her chair, and as she reached down to retrieve it, something caught her eye. The page was full of John's tightly scrawled handwriting, the thick unsharpened pencil line almost indecipherable. But one name, scattered several times around the rambling text, was unmistakable.

Maisie, Maisie, Maisie, Maisie.

Twenty-Four

Maisie stared at the page. Had John written about her? She ran a shaky finger along a line that might have said *in her eyes*, followed by something that had been crossed out and replaced with *shines the dawning of* something something. Within the tight scrawl, she could also decipher the words *heart* and *strength*, and that one might have been *beauty*, though probably not.

She tilted the book toward the light to see if she could make out anything more. It was so hard to read though, especially in the dull curtained-off space, she began to turn the pages to see if she could find her name written any clearer elsewhere. Flicking back toward the front of the book, Maisie found other pages of clearer poems with fewer crossings out.

And there were doodles too, little scribbled drawings in

the margins and across the head of the page—not really scribbles, more beautifully drawn studies of trees and birds. Maisie turned a page and found a penciled landscape she recognized. It was the view from the abandoned croft, and on either side of the page, he'd drawn a pair of golden eagles. One flew high and proud, while the other rocketed to earth, wings outstretched and terrifying, the ultimate hunter. The lines were so simple in their construction, but so vivid.

And still she turned the pages. Toward the front of the book, the writing became even more difficult to read, with lines scored through several times, the pencil angry, and the blanked-out lines abandoned and unreplaced. And on these pages, the tiny sketches and studies were different too, broken-down walls, shell holes, and receding parallel lines of men with rifles. And there were cannon and what looked like fireworks, though they were more likely shells exploding. There were planes too, some flying, some dropping a staccato pattern of pencil-jab bombs down the page, and one was falling, its spinning silhouette repeated several times down a spiraling line until only its tail was visible above the bottom of the page.

These were pictures of the war. The nurse had been right. John had been a soldier, though he hadn't thought to share that little detail with Maisie, any more than he thought she ought to know about his lost leg. What could she make of that? At times, she had thought he liked her as much as she liked him, but time and again, she was proved wrong.

And yet . . .

Maisie flicked back to the page where he had written her name, her name, her name. After a moment, she turned the right-hand page to see what had come after.

There was a portrait, a pencil sketch of a girl.

At first Maisie thought it was of her. The girl did have hair swept and pinned up under a scarf, and she had a dimple at the edge of her smile on her left cheek but not her right, and she might even have had Maisie's arched eyebrow. But no, the girl in the drawing was far too pretty, her eyes too striking, her mouth too full, to be Maisie.

And yet . . .

"Do you like it?"

Maisie looked up from the book straight into John Lindsay's dark-brown eyes. He'd been watching her as she'd nosed her way through his private notebook. Maisie was mortified. A rush of embarrassment coursed through her, burning up her neck and face. She slapped the book shut immediately but then wasn't sure what to do with it. She went to lay it on the nightstand, changed her mind, and instead held it out to him.

John stretched his hand out, and yet he didn't take the book from her. Instead, he laid his fingers over hers, sandwiching them between his skin and the soft leather. His gaze never left her face.

"I owe you an apology," John said. "And an explanation."

"No, really, you don't," began Maisie, her heart racing. "You don't owe me any—"

"Maisie, I do," he interrupted. "You saved my life, and

Elliott's. So please listen, for a moment." John's other hand appeared from under the blanket, and he folded it over hers. "If you and Dot hadn't found us, if you hadn't brought us down, Elliott would be dead, and probably I would be too. So please, let me explain."

Flustered by his intensity, Maisie withdrew her fingers from his grasp, put the notebook on the shelf beside her, and put her hands in her lap. "I only did what I thought was right, and so did Dot. And we would have done the same thing whether it had been you or Haven or that big bloke, Eric, the one with the red beard. . . . All right, maybe I would have thought twice about Eric."

Although John didn't laugh, Maisie felt the atmosphere between them lighten a little.

"I can see that," he said. "And I might have thought twice about saving Eric too."

"Perhaps you're still here because I helped you, or perhaps not, and the same goes for Elliott. But none of that is a good enough reason for you to tell me something you don't want me to know. Of course, I'd love to know more about you, about your life in Newfoundland before the war, and about how you . . . about your leg. But you must tell me because you want me to know you better, not because you think you owe me something."

John sat silently for several seconds, then reached out and took her hand again, drawing it toward his face. Maisie thought he might kiss it, but he didn't. He simply laid the backs of her fingers against his forehead and closed his eyes.

His skin felt very warm against hers, and she wondered if her cool fingers were soothing some pain away.

"First," John began without moving, "I didn't come over here as a lumberjack, I came—"

"As a soldier." Maisie tentatively filled in, and he nodded.

"And second, which I know I told you before, I'm not a Newfoundlander. I'm from Halifax, in Nova Scotia, meaning I'm a Canadian."

With his eyes closed as he said this, he looked so serious, almost as if he were in a confessional box, that Maisie wanted to smile. Instead she nodded, just as seriously.

"In that case, I'm not sure you should be holding my hand. I mean, what would my mother say if she found out I'd been seen holding hands with a *Canadian*?"

John eyes opened.

"I'm joking," Maisie reassured him with a smile. "You could be from America or Australia or Timbuk-bloody-tu and it wouldn't make a difference. Why does it matter whether you're a Newfoundlander or not?"

"Have you ever felt you were expected to fill someone else's very big shoes?" John asked, and Maisie shrugged.

"I'm not sure."

"My dad served in the Great War, like my Uncle John. He wasn't much older than I am now when he went over to Belgium and France in 1917, but unlike my Uncle John, he managed to stay alive long enough to come home again after the Armistice, which was just as well really, for me anyway, seeing as I was born about nine months later.

"All my childhood, people told me stories about what a great guy my dad was, and what a hero he was. And he was. He used to tell us all these stories about his time in the war, about his buddies and the scrapes they got themselves into. He made it sound like it was all a big adventure. He'd served under Colonel Willis, a man who could have walked on water according to my dad. Then Colonel Willis appeared again, quite out of the blue, in 1939, and said that since things where heating up again in Europe, he was getting together a bunch of lads from Halifax to go over there to help. Dad virtually threw me at him.

"Not that I didn't want to go, I was more than ready to get away from Halifax. Life had been tough for my parents—tough on everyone—and there weren't many jobs around. University was out of the question, since we couldn't afford it, and I reckoned it would help them if they had one less mouth to feed. So I joined Willis's group. And it was great. Me and my pal Walt—Walter Clarkson, that is—joined together. Of all the men Willis sent over, about a hundred of us, Walt and me were the last ones to go, and the youngest. The colonel had served with a British regiment in the Boer War and the Great War, and he'd arranged for us to be part of his old regiment when we arrived, so by the end of September, we were with the 2nd Manchesters. The training was bloody hard, but I loved it, even the parade square drill and ten-mile runs—especially the runs, because if you got back in a decent enough time to please the sergeant, you'd get a pass to the pub on Saturday night. I'd always played rugby and hockey, so this was like having rugby training for weeks on end."

Maisie watched John transform as he talked. This was a man Maisie had not met before. Gone was the introspection and uncertainty. This was a man revisiting the excitement he'd felt as a young and untested recruit. And Maisie could see how little of the real John she'd ever known.

"And we learned how to fire machine guns—the 2nd Manchesters is a machine-gun regiment—and it all seemed like a load of fun to us. It got even better once training was done and we were sent to Aldershot to join our company. Walt and me had both signed up for seven years, but were already talking about doing another seven after that. This was a job we would enjoy for a long while. Or so we thought.

"But then, as Willis had predicted, all hell broke loose. The Germans went into Poland, and Britain declared war. Then Canada did the same, and suddenly the fun and games of training were behind me, and I was on my way to France, like my dad and Uncle John before me."

He paused, as if gathering his thoughts, but Maisie knew she should not to try to fill the gap. He seemed to be talking from another time and place, so she sat quietly and waited.

"And I was scared," he continued eventually. "I don't think I've ever admitted that before. We worked our way across northern France and then hunkered down in the trenches we'd dug, waiting for the Germans. We were with D-company of the 4th Infantry Brigade by that time, and we thought the waiting, the anticipation, was harder to deal with than any fighting would be, but we were wrong. It took the Germans long enough, but when they came, they came at us hard. And we fought back hard, but they had too much firepower, too many men, and nothing seemed to go right.

"Then word came down the line that we were to retreat, not far, just until we got to the Albert Canal, and we had to hold the canal to allow everyone else to get back to the English Channel.

"That was our only hope of escape, to reach the sea. We were ordered to do anything we could to keep the corridor along the canal open, and we managed it, for a while anyway, but eventually we had to fall back, too. In the end, it was only us Manchesters and some French units, facing the whole of Hitler's army."

John fell quiet, as if he was working something out in his mind before he put it into words. They sat so long in silence that Maisie was wondering if she should prompt him after all, but instead she moved her hands until they were wrapped around his.

"It was a Stuka," he said suddenly, looking into her eyes for the first time since he'd begun to talk, as if willing her to understand. And she did. Or at least, she thought she did.

"A fighter plane?" she asked.

"Worse, a bastard dive bomber. Those Stukas would come screaming out of the cloud like banshees. You knew it was a Stuka by that damn noise." Suddenly John's muscles tensed, his forehead creasing and his hands forming fists inside hers. "We'd had the order for the final retreat and we'd been pull-ing back for three days, always making sure we stayed ahead of the German artillery coming in behind us. We'd heard there were boats evacuating troops from the beach and harbor at Dunkirk, so that's where we headed. But we moved slowly, doing as much as we could to keep the Germans back, to give the guys on the beach more time.

"But they kept pushing us, and eventually, our backs were to the water. It was complete chaos, men everywhere, abandoned artillery and vehicles scattered around, and men wading out to all these tiny little boats. I'm serious—it was pathetic, really, to see an army as strong as ours being rescued by the kind of boats you'd see at the seaside. But hell, it was working! The little boats were taking men, some as few as half a dozen at a time, to bigger boats sitting out in deeper water, and once those were packed full, they'd turn for home.

"And you'd think the men left waiting on the beach would have been panicking and fighting for space on the next boat, but they weren't. They were mostly forming orderly lines, like they were waiting to buy a loaf of bread or something. That's the British for you, isn't it? You people do love to join a queue."

He looked up again, and though it had sounded like he was making a joke, his face showed no humor, so Maisie gave him a small tight-lipped smile in return but said nothing. This was the most that John had ever told her about himself, and she was desperate to hear more.

"They waited in line because they were sure the boats would come back again," John continued. "And they were right. I heard later that some of these crews had been going back and forth across the Channel in what the boys were all calling the 'little ships' for almost three days. They came again and again, under constant air attacks and even knowing that there were U-boats in the Channel that could torpedo that crappy little rowboat right out from under them. Brave bastards!

"And still the Germans came on, us 2nd Manchesters to the east of the harbor, the French to the west. One last line of men, standing there like King bloody Canute, thinking we could turn back the tide of German artillery.

"And then came that Stuka. I didn't see it, and for once I didn't even hear it. The Luftwaffe had been bothering us for days, coming back time after time to strafe our columns along the canal, and there was almost nothing we could do to stop them. We'd had to leave behind the big ack-ack—the anti-aircraft guns—in the retreat, and although we still had the Vickers guns we could carry, they weren't powerful enough to hit the planes. So we ended up on that beach, ducking and praying to God we wouldn't be hit.

"And eventually, even God gave up on us, or on me at least. I suppose God chose to answer the Stuka pilot's prayers that day, and not mine, and I was left with—"

John gestured angrily down the bed, his face creasing in pain, and Maisie wasn't sure if his leg was hurting again or if the pain was only remembered. She reached toward his hand in concern.

"Can I get you some—"

John didn't seem to have heard her, remaining lost in the

memory. "I only realized I'd been hit when I was facedown on the sand and couldn't get up again. I tried to stand a couple of times before it dawned on me why I couldn't support my own weight. And that was when I saw that my"—John hesitated for only an instant—"that my boot was lying a yard away in the bloody sand and that my foot was . . ."

Maisie's stomach heaved and her head swam. John, too, looked like he was struggling to keep talking. All the color had drained from his face as he spoke, and dark-blue smudges encircled his eyes, the days-old stubble shadowing his sickly pallor. But John also looked like he needed to keep talking.

"Being the brave chap that I am," he continued, "when the pain eventually came, I passed out."

To Maisie's astonishment, John chuckled. It was a dark sound, and unsettling.

"Yup, I went straight off to sleep like a baby, leaving my buddies to pick me up and carry me. I woke up as Walt and Lofty McGinnis were waist-deep in the water, loading me onto a motorboat. I told those stupid bastards they should have left me where I was and saved themselves."

His face twisted at the memory, but Maisie was surprised that he was being so hard on himself. He would have done the same for his friends, she was sure.

"Your friends wouldn't have left you," she exclaimed.

"Your friends wouldn't have left you." John sent Maisie's words back at her with such a vicious mimicry of the pitch of her voice and even her Glasgow accent that Maisie sat back as if he'd slapped her. "Of course they should have left me. I

was almost dead already. And if they hadn't wasted precious time strapping my thigh to stop me from bleeding to death and carrying me down to the boat, they would both have made it."

"Made it?" Maisie asked cautiously, braced for another angry retort.

"Made it onto a boat. Made it back to safety. Made it home." John was looking at her again, but she wasn't sure he was seeing her. He was seeing Walt and Lofty instead. "But no, not them. They dumped me into one of those crappy, brave little boats, and I told them to get in beside me. There was more than enough space for all three of us, but then they both . . . they both turned back to the beach."

Maisie held her breath. Lofty and Walt hadn't got into the boat beside John. What had they been thinking?

"They went back to try to save more men. The Germans were up on the road above the harbor by then. We could see them from the boat, so I know Lofty and Walt could see them too. They were marching down toward us like a long, black wall. A long, black wall of the devil's infantry."

Goose bumps had risen on Maisie's arms. "And Lofty and Walt, did they . . . ? Did they . . . ?"

Did they escape? Did they survive? Did they reach a boat in time? She didn't know which of these questions she'd begun to ask, but she desperately wanted a positive answer to them all.

John's gaze was thick with despair as he shrugged. "Did they rescue anyone else? Yes, they got another guy onto our boat—he barely had a face left, and the ungrateful bastard was dead within an hour, so what was the point?"

"But did Walt and Lofty—"

"Did they die? Of course they died—they were facing the entire German infantry. After they brought the last man on board, the captain of the boat gunned the engine, turned us out to sea, and left Walt and Lofty behind. And do you know the worst thing of all?" He looked at Maisie as if he really wanted an answer, but all Maisie could do was shake her head. What could be worse than what he'd already told her? "The worst thing is that I couldn't stay conscious long enough to watch my friends die. I passed out and woke up in a hospital bed hours later."

John squeezed his eyes tight shut. "How can I admit that to Walt's mother?" he whispered. "'I'd like to tell you that your son died the hero, Mrs. Clarkson, but I was fast asleep on a boat at the time.'"

Suddenly, John shoved his elbow down angrily onto the mattress, trying to sit up, then groaned in pain. Shaken out of her grief-soaked daze, Maisie jumped forward to help him lift himself up, but as soon as he felt her hands around his arm, John yanked it back out of her grasp as if her touch had burned him.

"I can do it myself!" John barked. "For God's sake, just let me do it myself. I'm not a bloody baby!"

Twenty-Five

Maisie was stunned at John's outburst. "I was only trying to . . . ," she began. "I'll get the nurse instead."

"Don't!"

"But you—"

"I said don't!"

With a furious groan, John slumped back against his pillow, eyes tightly closed, breathing hard. "Whatever you do, don't call the bloody nurse."

His voice was quieter now, and he reached his hand out toward her, but Maisie kept her own hands firmly in her lap, to stop them from shaking.

"I'm sorry, Maisie," John said softly, opening his eyes. "I shouldn't have shouted at you again. It's just . . . I don't like nurses very much."

"I'm not a nurse."

"I know you're not, but . . . well, you acted like you were. And the other night too. . . ."

"The other night, when I punched a sailor before he could punch you? You think I was acting like a nurse then too?"

"No, of course not. But you were protecting me when I didn't need it. You were suddenly driven to look after me, out of pity."

"I did not punch him out of pity, I promise you. I punched him out of fury."

John looked up at her, his eyes sad. "Perhaps. But it was fury at seeing him about to punch a man you had just learned needed to be looked after, to be nursed."

"That's not—"

John lifted his hand up to interrupt her protest. "Look, I know this is a poor excuse, but I've spent a lot of time in hospitals and in a rehabilitation home, trying to recover from . . ." John gestured again in the direction of the cage over his legs, though this time with no vehemence, only apparent resignation. "So I've met a lot of nurses, and they all wanted to pull me and prod me, stick me with needles, or stuff me full of tea and pills and God knows what else. When you're a patient, it's like they think you're a baby again. They treat you as if you have no mind and no will of your own. And it'll happen in here too—I'll lay money on it. If they're not forcing you to shave and dress when all you want to do is sleep, they're telling you to go to sleep when the pain is keeping you awake. Either that, or they're shoving ice bags where the sun doesn't shine."

Listing these affronts seemed to exhaust John more than his furious outburst, and as his voice weakened, Maisie tried to contain her own annoyance. Whatever turmoil lay inside this man, he had clearly exhausted all his stores of calm and patience. She couldn't blame him for that, but why should nurses bear the brunt of his guilt and rage? And why should she?

Maisie leaned forward, ladling on the sarcasm. "And did all these dreadful nurses try to help you sit up in bed, like I did, even though you could clearly do it yourself? How disgraceful! No man should have to put up with all these per-petually helpful, and probably quite pretty, women feeding him, plumping his pillows, taking away his pain, and offer-ing to put ice on his bedsores. You *poor* thing." Maisie could feel her initial mockery softening as she spoke, but still, she remained alert should he explode again.

He didn't. Instead, John gave her a rueful grimace. "You have simply no idea"—his voice sounded calm again, with a twinge of irony—"how difficult it can be to deal with 'per-petually helpful, and probably quite pretty, women.'"

Maisie was relieved to hear some humor in John's voice again, and she fought to find it in her own. "I can imagine it must have been a great trial."

John gave her an apologetic smile. "I'm not making excuses, but when I was recovering, I wanted to prove to myself, and to the nurses and doctors, that I didn't need their help. It took me a long time even to get out of bed, first into a wheelchair and then onto crutches. And when I finally got fitted for the prosthesis—the false leg—I discovered that the only thing that would get me walking again was sheer bloody-mindedness. That was when I decided I would never be reliant on other people again, that I will never again be somebody's burden."

Maisie could sense how much it was costing him to admit all this, and she felt her anger diminish completely. Sliding forward to the edge of her seat, she took both his hands and leaned in close so he had no choice but to look into her eyes.

"How could you possibly be a burden when you are so capable? Until you told me, I'd never even suspected that you were injured, let alone that you were hiding such an enormous secret inside your trousers."

John froze for a second, then slowly raised one eyebrow in question, and Maisie realized what she had just said.

"I meant your leg," she sputtered. "I meant you were hiding your leg inside your . . ."

She grabbed her hands back from his and pressed them to her burning face to cover her embarrassment. John began to chuckle, and it was such a reassuring sound that Maisie found herself laughing too.

And their laughter quickly turned into hysteria, so that when the nurse came in a minute or two later, they were both still wiping tears from their eyes. Maisie felt heady, watching the trauma of John's memories recede under the onslaught of hilarity, even if only for a little while.

"Oh good, you're awake, Mr. Lindsay," said the nurse

officiously as she came through the door. "It's time to get you shaved and dressed before the doctor arrives, and I thought you might need another ice bag to put on your—"

And Maisie and John were off again, dissolving into choking giggles.

The nurse stood there a few moments longer. Maisie couldn't see what expression the nurse wore through her haze of laughter-stoked tears, but she soon heard some very loud tutting and the nurse's shoes clicking away down the hall again.

As she tried to get her breath back under control, Maisie rummaged around in all her pockets to find a handkerchief to blot her tears. It felt good to laugh so hard.

And John was still laughing, the bed frame shaking, as he pressed the crisp almost-white sheet to his eyes. And he didn't stop laughing, even as Maisie's own giggles seeped away. Still he laughed, though the sound of it, Maisie slowly realized, had changed.

And Maisie knew that John was not laughing anymore. He had curled over to one side, and he was weeping.

Maisie didn't know what to do. She wanted to help him, to reassure him, but would he even want her interference and comfort, or would it embarrass him? Would it add to his belief that she felt sorry for him? She'd never seen a man cry, and she was sure her father would rather have died than ever cry in front of her and her sister. But then again, when she was crying, it was reassuring to know that someone was there who cared.

After only a moment's hesitation, she perched on the edge of John's bed, and laid her hand on his back and rubbed in small circles. This time, he didn't push her away, so she wrapped her arms around him and kissed his cheek, just in front of his ear, the only part of his face not hidden by the sheet.

"Shhhh, now," she whispered as his shoulders heaved under her. "Shhhh."

Gradually, the shuddering of his rib cage slowed and gave way to occasional heaving sighs.

"I wish there was something I could do," she said, "to take away some of your pain."

"Will you . . . ," he whispered, "will you stay with me awhile?

Maisie pushed the sweaty hair back from his forehead. "I'll stay as long as you want me."

"Thank you."

"It's nothing."

"It's not nothing."

They huddled together for a while, and as Maisie felt his breathing settle into a regular rhythm, her own eyelids began to feel heavy. The early start and the effort of her climb that morning crept up on her, and with the reassuring warmth of John's shoulder under her cheek, she felt her own body relax, hypnotized by the slow rise and fall of his breathing.

"Goodness me!"

Maisie heard the nurse's sharp exclamation, and she sat up immediately.

"It's as well Doctor Cameron has been delayed this morning, otherwise there might have been all sorts of trouble."

Maisie struggled to sit up, embarrassed to have been caught in John's bed. Well, not *in* the bed, but certainly *on* it. And she had all her clothes on, even her boots. Small mercies.

"Erm, sorry, we . . . that is, I . . ." She couldn't explain this one away.

But the nurse didn't seem to be judging her. Rather, she was watching Maisie rearrange her rumpled uniform with some amusement, even if she was trying to hide it. In the bed, John was again trying to push himself upright, gasping as he did so.

"Hold on a second," the nurse instructed him, striding over to the bed. "Let me help you."

"I think he'd rather do it himself," said Maisie quickly.

"Nonsense!" the nurse said, jabbing her hand under John's arm and lifting him up, with surprising strength and ease, into a sitting position. "We can't risk burst stitches in your leg at this point. You should be fine to get up into a wheelchair today if you're careful, but dragging yourself around the bed won't do that wound any good at all, will it, Mr. Lindsay?"

It was clearly not a question she expected him to answer, because she turned and disappeared out of the door, coming back almost immediately with a wooden stand on which sat a tray with a water bowl, a razor, a bar of shaving soap, and a rather worn shaving brush. "So, Mr. Lindsay, will you shave yourself or would you like me to do it?"

John glared at the nurse and then sideways at Maisie. "I

told you, didn't I?" he said. "They just can't help themselves."

Maisie pressed her lips together to suppress a smile, but John seemed absolutely serious.

"Well?" said the nurse.

"No, thank you, nurse," John almost growled. "I don't need a shave."

"But Doctor Cameron much prefers to see his patients once they are clean and—"

"Well, Doctor Cameron will have to put up with it, won't he? I will bathe and shave when I choose to bathe and shave, and in the meantime, please do not treat me like I'm an invalid." John did not seem to be getting angry, but his tone was still sharp.

The nurse glanced at the shaving kit, then back at John. "I'm not treating you like an invalid, Mr. Lindsay. I'm treating you as I would treat any one of the patients in my care. But if you choose to sit in your own filth for another day longer, then that is your choice. I do, however, suggest that tomorrow you put your girlfriend's sense of smell ahead your own pride before you refuse to undergo basic and decent ablutions again." With that, she picked up the shaving tray and its stand and marched out of the door.

"I'm not . . . ," began Maisie, but the nurse had gone before Maisie could explain than she wasn't John's . . . that he wasn't her . . .

When Maisie looked back at John, he was still frowning.

"You shouldn't have talked to her like that," Maisie said gently. "She was only helping."

"Interfering, more like," he snapped, but when Maisie held him in a hard stare for a moment or two, he dropped his eyes from hers. "I know, I'm sorry."

"That's all right," Maisie said with a terse smile. "But if you did want to have a wash and a shave, I could go and get us a cup of tea for once you're finished."

"Not you as well! God save me from all the perpetually helpful and exceptionally pretty women like you! Seriously, I will bathe and shave when I can walk to the bathroom myself. But in case you'd forgotten, it's hard to walk to the bathroom—or anywhere else for that matter—if you've only got one damn leg!" John grabbed at his blankets and threw them off the bed with a magician's flourish, uncovering both the metal cage straddling the bed and his legs.

Maisie couldn't help but look. John's striped hospital pajama trousers had been rolled up to his thighs. His left leg, all the way down to his foot, was almost entirely deep purple and red. A wide bandage had been strapped around his calf muscle. The white fabric had been spoiled by a dark-brown stain that lined up with the gash Maisie had seen once Dot had cut away the fabric of his left trouser leg. In contrast, his right thigh, from the fabric to the knee, was perfectly bruise-free, with pale skin and black hair over solid muscle. But by a couple of inches below his knee, the skin became smoother, shinier and pinker before coming to a smooth, rounded end.

Maisie wasn't sure what she'd expected, but compared to the bloody damage all down his left leg, the end of his right leg was somehow less shocking to look at.

Cautiously, Maisie reached out her hands toward John's legs, but as her fingers touched his skin, she heard him breathe in sharply, so she withdrew, just a fraction.

"I won't hurt you," she said quietly.

"I know," John replied. "It's only that no woman . . ."

Maisie snatched her hands back. What had she been thinking? Of course he wouldn't want her to touch either his painfully fresh wounds or the older scars. She couldn't go around touching a man's legs whenever she felt like it, even a man she liked as much as John—*especially* a man she liked that much.

"I'm so sorry, I really am. I shouldn't have . . ." She was feeling panicked now, and flamingly embarrassed, and looked quickly around her as if there was something she should be picking up, a handbag or a coat, anything. "I think I should go back now—the girls will be wondering where—"

"Maisie, stop," John said, reaching out to her. "It was only that apart from the nurses, no . . .

"But the bus will be leaving—"

"Maisie, please! You said you'd stay."

Maisie hesitated. She wanted to, but in her embarrassment, the room had become so stuffy and suffocating.

"All right, but it's so hot in here," she said, patting her glowing cheeks with the cool backs of her hands while studiously avoiding looking at John's legs. "Can we please find somewhere else to talk? Somewhere a little cooler perhaps? We can have that cup of tea."

"Of course. Although . . ." John paused as if waiting for her to understand an obvious point. "Perhaps there's a wheelchair somewhere?"

Maisie suddenly realized what he meant.

"Oh!" she cried out. "I forgot! You were asleep, so I put it . . ." She reached under the bed and brought out his prosthetic leg and laid it beside him on the bed. "I tried to clean it up as best I could, getting all the mud off, and I don't think it's damaged. You might not remember, but we didn't even have to cut the straps, thank goodness."

John ran his fingers over the wood and the leather straps, and Maisie could see emotions warring on his face.

"So you rescued this part of me too." His voice was soft and earnest. "Thank you. I'm grateful."

"I'm only glad it wasn't damaged when the log fell." Maisie drew in a deep breath, feeling her anxiety recede. "Because I'm sure wooden legs don't grow on trees." She waited for her attempt at a joke to sink in, and was rewarded when she saw the corners of his mouth lift a little.

"I'm sure they don't," John said. "And does your invitation to get a cup of tea in the lounge still stand?"

Maisie smiled. "Of course. Shall I help you with—" Maisie stopped herself in time. "Shall I go to find the tea while you get dressed?"

"That sounds like a good plan," John replied, and his smile filled Maisie's heart.

Twenty-Six

"I thought he was going to kill me. Seriously. He was the biggest bloke I'd ever seen and I'd knocked his beer all down his front. Accidentally, of course. I still wasn't all that steady on my new leg, and I'd had a pint already."

Maisie raised her eyebrows.

"All right, maybe a couple of pints. Or three. But it still wasn't deliberate, and even though I apologized, I could do nothing but wait for the first punch to land." John pretended to brace himself for an imaginary punch, squeezing his eyes tight shut and lifting his hands to protect his face. It was such a ridiculous expression, Maisie couldn't help but laugh. They were seated in the lounge over a cup of tea. John had tried to use his prosthetic, but ironically it was his new injuries that prevented him from walking, and he had used the wheelchair instead. But in spite of that disappointment, he'd been telling Maisie darkly funny stories ever since, his bruised leg resting on a soft cushion, his other knee jiggling as he talked.

"But the punch never landed." John continued. "Instead, the big bloke very delicately put one finger under the bottom of my glass and tipped my beer all over me. I couldn't believe it."

"And that was Haven?" Maisie asked.

"Yup. And he told me later, once we were both nursing our hangovers with sausage and eggs the next morning, that if I hadn't apologized, and if he hadn't heard my accent, he would have knocked my head right off. Turns out Haven's grandmother was from Nova Scotia originally, and she'd never lost her accent even after fifty years or more in Newfoundland, so he knew it well. But I suppose he didn't expect to find a drunken Canadian bum in a pub at the Liverpool docks. And before I'd finished my breakfast, he'd persuaded me to cash in my ticket home and sign up as a NOFU lumberjack."

Maisie was enjoying John's stories, which included seasickness and vomiting over the side of the Dunkirk rescue boat and the strange itch in his nonexistent foot for months after that foot had been shot off. And now he was telling her stories of all the falls and trips and nurse baiting during the months of his enforced rehabilitation at a converted manor house in the wilds of Yorkshire.

"We called it rehab prison. They threatened to lock up our wooden legs and wheelchairs at night to stop us from escaping, but ultimately they decided that since we were so damn far from the nearest main road, pub, or train station, we'd most likely die before we'd got more than a couple of miles across the moors. Either that or the Hound of the Baskervilles would get us."

It was wonderful to see him so talkative and funny, but even so, Maisie could see a brittleness to his energy. It was uncomfortable to witness again and again the speed at which he could shift from despair and misery to the excited high of storytelling. She had never seen anyone's mood change so quickly or so dramatically before. Of course, her father had a temper, but his anger was a slow burn, a mood that darkened with unhurried menace, like storm clouds rolling over the sea. John could switch lightning fast from down to up and back again. She realized that because of this, she was finding it hard to relax, constantly anticipating the next shift from one extreme to the other, never sure what might trigger the change.

But right now, he seemed so alive, so happy. Perhaps knowing that he wasn't keeping such a huge secret anymore had come as a relief.

"But when you joined up with Haven in the pub, did you even know how to be a lumberjack?" she prompted.

"Hell, no!" John declared in delight. "I could handle an ax, of course, from childhood chores of splitting wood for the stove at home, and my upper-body muscles had developed their strength again from all the work I did walking with crutches in the rehab hellhole. But all the real knowledge came to me from Haven. He'd been a lumberjack for twenty-five years, and was generous to share his knowledge with a rookie, even a one-legged one. Of course, a couple of the other guys guessed about my leg, but you know, they never mentioned it more than once. I'd expected some ribbing, but as long as I kept up with the work, they let me get on with it.

"And then Elliott joined us a few months ago when the next batch of men arrived, and we got to be friends, and Haven seemed happy to let us work as a team. Some of the older guys were more jaded, but Elliott and me, we were up for whatever Haven could throw at us. That was why we went up the hill the other night, to try to get the truck loaded and cleared. But I guess we messed up. God! I don't even know what happened. All I remember is Elliott shouting, and I turned to see that the logs were . . ."

Maisie could almost hear the click. Within one sentence, John's mood had plummeted, his head went down, his shoulders drooped, and he fell silent. Maisie's heart sank.

John said nothing for a while, and Maisie couldn't think of what to say without sounding trite and falsely bright.

"I think he's dead," John said suddenly. "Elliott. Exactly like Walt and Lofty. And guess what? I didn't get to say good-bye to him either."

Maisie was horrified. "Elliott's not dead. The nurse said she told you he was alive."

"Of course they're not going to admit to me that he's dead, Maisie, not while I'm recovering. But I know it, in here." John thumped hard on the left side of his chest with his fist.

"I leave all my friends for dead—Walt and Lofty, and now Elliott. I as good as killed them myself, all because of *this* piece of carpentry." He leaned down and slapped at the wood of his right leg.

"John, stop! Don't say that. You were seriously injured both times—and there was nothing you could've done. You didn't kill them. You know you didn't."

"All right, I didn't, but I certainly didn't stick around to save them, did I? Did I?" John suddenly looked up at her, glaring at her, challenging her to contradict him. "And I don't even know where they are."

"Of course you do. Elliott's in Inverness at the Royal Inf—"

"But I don't know where Walt and Lofty are buried. Or even *if* they got buried. Maybe the Germans left them there on the beach to rot, or to float away, or to be pecked to nothing by the gulls."

"John, stop!" cried Maisie, the bile rising in her throat. "You were seriously hurt. Leaving your friends at Dunkirk wasn't your fault. And with Elliott, it was an accident. You have to believe that none of it was your—" Maisie choked on her tightened throat.

John lifted his hand to swipe away her argument and his chin dropped again. He suddenly looked like an old man, sitting there slouched in his wheelchair.

"I think you should leave," he said finally.

Maisie wondered if she'd even heard him correctly. "I should . . . ?"

"You should leave. And you shouldn't come back."

"You don't mean—"

"I do mean. I don't want you to come back. I don't want you in my life anymore. In another time, this might have worked out between us, but—"

"In another time?" Maisie couldn't believe what she was hearing. "In another time, there wouldn't have been an 'us' to work out. If it hadn't been *this time*, I would still be at school in Glasgow, and you would be at university in Canada, and I would never even have known that you existed. Surely we should be making the most of the gift we've been given, John, the gift of *this time*."

"No."

"*No?* That's all you can say? Just *no*?"

"I can't."

"Why not? Why do you keep pushing me away? Why won't you let me in?"

"Not let you in? For God's sake! For weeks, you've never been out of me. You're in there, all the time, in my head and in my . . ." He punched hard at his chest again, and Maisie winced as if it were her own heart under the blow. "And I can't let you be in there any longer. I can't let you take over and force them out."

Maisie had lost all sense of what he was saying. "Force *who* out?"

"Force *them* out. Walt and Lofty, and Elliott. Out of *here*." And again his fist hit his chest, and again, even harder. "When *you're* in here, I can feel myself losing *them*. They're slipping away from me, and you're taking their place, filling me up. And I can't do that to them. I owe them too much."

Was he so desperate to keep hold of his guilt that he would push away every hope of being happy? And push away her happiness too?

"And anyway," he was whispering now, "it's only a matter of time before I lose you too."

"But you won't lose—"

"Yes, I will. And if you don't leave because you're fed up with me—I've seen how you look at me sometimes, Maisie— then I know that something will happen to you, something awful, and I won't be there to save you. Just like the others."

Maisie dropped to her knees beside John's wheelchair, ducking her head so she could see into his face. She wanted to stop him from talking, to keep him from saying these awful things.

"Listen to me." Maisie reached up under his hair and took his face between her hands, trying to lift his head so she could see into his eyes, so he could see into hers.

Reluctantly, it seemed, John raised his chin from his chest an inch or so, and Maisie could see his eyes awash with tears. She knelt up and gently pulled his face toward hers.

"Please, John, believe me . . . ," she whispered. "I won't leave. I won't die. I'm right here, and I'll never hurt you."

Maisie placed her mouth gently against his, tasting the tea they'd been drinking, tasting John. And as his mouth began to move against hers she opened her lips slightly. And for a moment, she thought that he had believed her.

Gently, she slid her hand behind his neck so she could pull him closer and deepen the kiss, but as she did, John suddenly tore his lips from hers and pulled her hand from his neck. Caught by surprise, Maisie lost her balance and toppled sideways against his injured leg.

John shouted out as she crashed against his bruised shin, and Maisie desperately tried to twist her body away from him before she did any more damage. As she did, she hit the side table with her arm and crashed to the floor along with the china teacups. Lying there, Maisie tried to make sense of what had happened in the space of three seconds.

She had promised that she never would hurt him. And then she had.

But she was hurt too. Her shoulder was aching, and she could feel something warm trickling down her cheek where a shard of china had hit her, either blood or tea. But more than that, she hurt most because he had rejected her comfort, her kiss. He had pushed away her act of reassurance and love. Again.

Maisie had tried to understand how much John had suffered and was still suffering, but maybe he was right, she was only making things worse for him. Perhaps someone else was meant to help him heal, because it seemed that every time she tried, she only hurt him more.

Maisie scrambled to her feet but could barely stand upright for the ache deep inside her.

"Maisie?" John sounded uncertain, but she would not share her pain with him. And she would not stay to comfort him out of pity, because he was pitying himself enough for both of them.

Without even looking in John's direction, Maisie walked through the open door and down the hallway. The nurse was rushing toward the lounge and asked what had got broken. Then she offered to have a look at the cut on Maisie's cheek, but Maisie didn't stop. She needed to get out of there, and quickly, before she was drowned in John's misery. He'd said he didn't want her there. She would give him what he wanted.

As she reached the main door at the far end of the hallway, Maisie heard John's shout, loud and wretched.

"Maisie!"

She threw open the heavy wooden door.

"Maisie!"

She didn't stop. She couldn't stop. She just kept walking.

Twenty-Seven

In the weeks since Maisie had fled John's side at the hospital, her heart breaking even more with every step she took away from him, she had found little to smile about. It was as if the morning frosts that had chilled the Cairngorms had also settled inside Maisie.

After days and days of miserable and unbroken autumnal rain through the early part of November, winter had now arrived with a vengeance. Hoar frosts sparkled each morning across the newly bare branches of the trees, the grass crackled underfoot, and Maisie had been forced to use the poll of her ax to crack open the layer of ice on the water trough outside Clyde's stable every morning before she could give him a drink.

Like the other lumberjills, Maisie had taken to wearing

more clothes to bed than she did going out into the woods to work each day. At least when she was chopping and sawing, snedding and hauling, she was working up some warmth, but at night the temperature fell below freezing, and Maisie's bed was one of the farthest away from the heating stove.

But that was all right; for the last four nights in a row, Maisie had used the cold as an excuse to get into her bed early and pretend to go to sleep. She lay curled up within her cocoon of sweaters and blankets, with her greatcoat pulled over the top, listening to everyone else settle gradually into the rhythmic peace of sleep. And she did her best not to think about John. It wasn't easy, but at least in bed she wasn't forced to talk to anyone else. She didn't have to face Dot and Nancy, who insisted on gazing at her with such painfully sympathetic eyes. She knew they understood her misery, at least some of it, but what could they do to lessen it? Nothing. Every day, at every turn, she was reminded of John.

But at least she hadn't had to see him, or even the other Newfoundlanders, in the past few weeks. The NOFU lumberjacks and WTC lumberjills had not worked alongside each other as much recently as they had before the accident. Instead, as the days grew shorter, each group had been concentrating on smaller tasks like undergrowth clearing and hedgerow maintenance.

Another good thing to happen in the last few weeks was Violet's disappearance. She'd left to become the recruit liaison officer back at Shandford Lodge. Her absence was a gift to the aching Maisie. And what was even better, Rose had been promoted to team leader at Auchterblair after Violet's departure. And Rose was happy to assign Maisie to work anywhere the NOFU men weren't working.

One night, Maisie lay curled in her bed, wishing away thoughts of John. That day she'd had some good news. She'd applied for a reassignment and it had just come through. And Dot had agreed—after some thought—to come with her. Soon the two of them would be in Perthshire, far away from any memories of John, at the Struan sawmill, near Blair Atholl. It would be a fresh start for Maisie, and also a reunion, since Phyllis and Helen were still stationed there. And Maisie would tell Dot to say nothing to them about the accident or about John or . . .

So much for not thinking about John.

Maisie felt a tap on her shoulder. Sticking her head out from under her blanket, she found Nancy's face only inches from her own, one finger held up between them, beckoning to Maisie.

"Come with us," Nancy breathed into Maisie's ear. "To the kitchen, to get warm."

Looking beyond Nancy, Maisie saw that Dot was by the kitchen door. They were both wrapped up in coats, boots, hats, scarves, and gloves, and draped in their blankets. Dot was also holding on to the thin mattresses off their metal bedsteads.

Of course, the kitchen would be much warmer than the dormitory hut, since the range was left burning low overnight. Part of Maisie—the part that was still shivering even under all the layers—could have laughed aloud at this brilliant plan, but the not-wanting-to-talk-to-anyone part of her wasn't so sure.

Nancy seemed to anticipate Maisie's hesitation, because she smiled and whispered, "And there might even be a nice cup of tea, if you're lucky."

Maisie nodded and even managed a small smile back. That was Nancy's cure-all, a nice cup of tea. And as Maisie struggled to get her feet, which were currently swaddled in all three pairs of woolen socks she owned, into her boots, it occurred to her that the smile had felt good—perhaps it had even been her first smile since leaving the hospital, and certainly since the arrival of John's letter. . . .

No! She would *not* think about John. Or the letter he'd sent. She would not let herself think about that again.

The wooden floor of the kitchen and mess hut wasn't exactly cozy, but the main oven did keep the room warm all night.

"Wasn't this a fine idea?" squeaked Dot as she tossed her mattress down, adjusting it to lie parallel to Nancy's. She gestured to Maisie to lay hers beside them. "Why didn't we think of it earlier? And if we stuff the bottom of the doors with our towels against the drafts, we'll be as warm as July."

Maisie dropped down on her mattress next to the oven, tucking her blanket tight around herself, as Dot finished blocking the drafts and sat back down. Nancy was pouring out three mugs of thick black tea from the heavy teapot on the counter.

"Nancy's other brilliant idea," said Dot, in a loud whisper, "was to make a pot of tea before bedtime, so it would be perfectly steeped by the time we got back here."

"More stewed than steeped, I'm afraid." Nancy handed one of the mugs to Maisie. "It's more like tar, and there's no milk left either. But at least it's warm."

"Thanks, Nancy," said Maisie, wrapping her grateful fingers around the warm china. "This is perfect. And thanks for letting me to join you."

"Of course. You have to be here too," said Dot. "Did you think we would have done this without you?"

Maisie didn't know how to answer that without hurting Dot's feelings. Even though she'd found it hard recently to talk even to Dot, and she knew they were both concerned about her, Dot also hadn't been clamoring to spend much time with Maisie either. She was, of late, inseparable from Nancy. They'd been working side by side in the stable, since Dot had somehow arranged to be put on stable duty, and regularly walking and cycling to and from the village in their limited free time.

And Maisie had noticed that Dot had changed. Since the rescue, Dot seemed to have grown taller, acting more confidently in front of the group. Part of that was clearly because Nancy pushed Dot to do things she was nervous to do, but another factor had been the news that Elliott was recovering well. A message had arrived from the surgeon in Inverness saying that Elliott's survival was entirely due to the expert care of WTC first-aider Dorothy Thompson, as she and her colleagues rescued him from the forest. And Dot had even received a letter of congratulations from HQ, saying how proud the whole Timber Corps was of her. Maisie was happy for Dot. She couldn't begrudge Dot her newfound purpose nor the praise, and she couldn't even feel jealous of Dot's friendship with Nancy, even if Maisie sometimes felt she was losing their friendship. In fact, Maisie was pleased to see Dot find another close friend. She remembered how shy and nervous Dot had been when they'd first met. How much had changed since then!

Maisie realized that Dot was still waiting for Maisie's response. Well, would Maisie have been surprised if they'd snuck off without her? No, not really.

Maisie shrugged. "I wouldn't have blamed you if you had."

Dot didn't reply, but Maisie didn't miss the look she exchanged with Nancy, and Maisie was sure then that there was more to tonight's midnight gathering than finding warmth.

Sure enough, Dot opened her mouth to speak, but then closed it again.

"Go on, say it," Maisie said. She'd suspected this conversation was coming for a week or so now. "I think I can guess what you're going to say."

"Maisie, it's only that . . ." Again, Dot looked to Nancy for help. "I'm sorry, but . . ."

"You're sorry, but you're not coming with me to Struan"— Maisie finished Dot's sentence matter-of-factly—"because you want to stay here with Nancy."

Dot nodded, uncertainly. "But how could you know that?"

"I think I knew," she said quietly, "as soon as I saw the look on your face, and on Nancy's too, as she arrived with Clyde, like the Seventh Cavalry, on the day of the accident. It was as if you both knew she had come to save *you*, not Elliott or . . . or John."

Why was it still so hard to say his name, even now, with weeks of silence lying between them?

"But—"

"I shouldn't even have asked you to come with me in the first place. That was me being selfish. And it meant a lot that you said you'd come, even though I think I knew you'd stay here in the end." Maisie leaned forward and laid her gloved palm flat against Dot's cheek. "We'll always be friends, Dot. But I also know that being around Nancy makes you happiest of all, and that since you came here, you've become so much more than you ever thought you could be."

As Maisie sat back, she reached out her hands to her two friends, and then they took each other's hands too. Maisie felt warmer than she had done in weeks.

"Thank you, Maisie," said Nancy, squeezing Maisie's hand. "Dot has been so worried that you'd be upset, after all that you've been through, you know, with John."

It wasn't any easier to hear his name spoken by someone else either.

"Of course I'm sad." Maisie gave what she hoped was a reassuring smile. Even if she did have to go to the next camp alone, she'd never risk losing Dot's friendship by being nasty about it. "But we can write, and maybe visit sometime. And who knows, after the war, perhaps we'll all end up living right next door to each other."

"In matching cottages, with one long white picket fence all along the front." Dot giggled, the anxiety fading from her eyes.

"And a shared green out the back where we can raise chickens and horses," said Nancy with a soft laugh.

"Horses in a garden?" Maisie joined in. "They'd eat all my lovely flowers and trample on my vegetables."

"We'll buy a field at the back then, for Clyde and the others, a big field—"

"Clyde?" squealed Dot.

"Of course, Clyde," replied Nancy, laughing hard now. "You don't think we could keep horses and not have Clyde as one of them, sweet old man that he is."

"All right, you can bring Clyde, but only if I can get some kittens, and Maisie can get a dog, and we could . . . Maisie! What on earth's the matter?"

Only then did Maisie realize that she was crying, as weeks of tension and anxiety were suddenly released by thirty seconds of laughter with her two wonderful friends.

"Nothing's the matter," she sniffed and choked out through a thick throat. "They're happy tears, really."

"Are you sure?" said Dot doubtfully. "They don't look like happy tears."

"They are, but I'm going to miss both of you so much." The three girls came together in a big hug, from which Maisie pulled away only when she urgently had to retrieve her hankie from her pocket to wipe her runny nose. "Though perhaps you'll regret not coming with me after all. The rumor is that the girls at Struan are billeted in a proper house, with real beds, and an actual bath."

A few minutes later, once Nancy had cleared the mugs to the countertop and had poked at the embers under the stove to release some more heat, the three of them settled down on their mattresses. Maisie heard Dot and Nancy whispering for a few minutes more, but she didn't try to make out the words. She was exhausted, and tomorrow, she would have to pack up all her belongings—not that she had much to pack, of course—and a truck would be picking her up early on Saturday to take her to the station at Boat of Garten to catch the train to Aviemore, where she'd change onto the Highland Line for the journey south. With any luck, she'd reach Blair Atholl, and then Struan, in time for tea.

For the first time in ages, Maisie felt calm as she let sleep creep in to ease her mind. With it came snippets of poetry, words by the poets Burns, McCrae, and Lindsay, tangling into a soothing lullaby. Maisie fought to keep her eyes open only long enough to think back to the minutes she'd spent listening to those words spoken in John's deep and resonant voice, and to regret that she would never hear him read them again. For Maisie was not the only one leaving the Highlands. John would be back home in Nova Scotia by Christmas.

He'd written to tell her that, and Maisie had spent the weeks since then refusing to think about John, and about that letter, because if she let herself recall what it had said in its tight scrawled script, she would have to accept that by Christmas, John would truly be lost to her forever.

Maisie shifted on the thin mattress. She would not think about John, or his letter, not now, not after she'd seen some light tonight shine through the gloom of the last few weeks.

But tomorrow, perhaps she would let herself think about John then.

Twenty-Eight

Rose appeared at the end of the bed as Maisie packed for her next day's departure. Band music was playing on the wireless set at the far end of the hut, and Rose began swaying in time as she watched Maisie fold up everything she owned and try to force it all into the suitcase she'd brought from home.

"Well, at least you won't have to try to fit your thick sweaters and coat into your suitcase," Rose said, "since you'll need them for your journey."

Maisie smiled up at Rose. Other than Dot and Nancy, Rose was the friend from Auchterblair who Maisie would miss most. She was so straightforward and drama-free, and undoubtedly the type of leader the women at Auchterblair deserved. And despite everything, Maisie was pleased to see that Rose and Robert from the NOFU camp had found each other, and seemed so happy whenever they had a chance to be together.

"And talking of your journey," Rose said, holding out a brown envelope to Maisie, "here's your travel pass and train ticket. And there's a ten-bob note in there too, in case of emergencies."

Maisie thanked Rose and took the envelope, tucking it into her handbag so as not to lose it.

"We'll all miss you, Maisie," Rose said. "*I'll* miss you especially." She wrapped her arms around Maisie and squeezed. "I so wish you didn't have to go."

Within Rose's hug, Maisie shrugged but could not find the right reply. She didn't want to hurt Rose's feelings, but she could not say her good-byes yet, not today. Tomorrow, Maisie would be leaving at dawn, so the good-byes would have to be short and sharp, which was certainly preferable to this long-drawn-out agony.

Rose sniffed near Maisie's ear. "I know, I know, no tears allowed," she said, and letting Maisie go, Rose turned and hurried out of the door toward the mess hut.

Maisie sighed and looked at what she still had to fit into her suitcase. There were her books, her letters, and the single picture frame, holding a photograph of Maisie, Beth, and their mother, in Sunday-best dresses and polished shoes, looking awkward and serious. It had been the only photograph in her bedroom when she had packed to leave home all those weeks ago, and looking at it now brought a strange burst of sad nostalgia for home. She supposed she'd be given enough leave sometime to go home for a visit. Or perhaps Beth, and even their mother, might come to visit her at Struan.

Beth's last letter had said that life at home was much better since they'd returned from her northern adventure. Mother seemed to be dealing more positively with Dad's moods, and Dad was even spending less time shut away in his study. Beth's letter was also full of her plans to apply for either the Women's Auxiliary Air Force or the Women's Royal Naval Service as soon as she turned eighteen. That would allow her to travel and see the world, she said, not like Maisie, who was, apparently, "stuck in boring old Scotland doing nothing but chopping wood all day." Maisie had smiled at that because, of course, Beth's week as a lumberjill had been *so* boring.

As Maisie lifted two of her books from the nightstand, a letter fell out from between them, folded notebook paper with her name scrawled across the front in John's erratic sloping handwriting. Maisie picked it up, and for a moment, she was tempted to open it again. But what was the point? She'd read it so often when it had first arrived, she could even now have recited it from memory as if it were a poem.

It had been hand delivered by Rose's Robert, the day after John had been released from the hospital and returned to Carrbridge.

According to Robert, John's duties around camp had been restricted to light tasks for a few weeks while his injuries healed fully. Elliott, however, wouldn't be coming back anytime soon. He'd been moved to a rehabilitation hospital—a rehab prison, Maisie had thought—to the north of Inverness. Maisie missed Elliott. He had always been sweet and fun to be with, but even so, when Dot had said a week or two ago that she planned to visit him, Maisie had turned down the invitation to go too. Maisie could not hope to distance herself from John Lindsay if she was actively seeking out his friends.

And distance from John had been what she most wanted, until, of course, the letter arrived to tell her that she would soon have exactly what she'd wished for. Having been given the medical discharge he'd requested, John was booked to travel on the *Empress of Canada*, a luxury transatlantic liner that was now a troopship. He would be sailing from Belfast to Halifax in early December, and Maisie knew the risk he would be taking, sailing across the U-boat playground of the North Atlantic, where so many convoys had been torpedoed.

John hadn't mentioned any risks in his letter, but he had again repeated that she deserved better than him, and that he was sure that she would find happiness with someone more stable, someone who could give her everything she needed. Everything she needed? What *did* she need? She had no idea, but John seemed to think that was a man who could take her dancing, or sit her on his knee. A man who could still wear a uniform with pride.

Why was John always so focused on her wanting a man in a uniform? She'd never even hinted at having any such interest, but still he came back to it again and again. Maisie supposed she knew why now. John had worn his uniform when his body was at its strongest and fittest. When he'd lost his uniform, he'd lost all that, and more. He'd also lost his vocation and his closest friends.

Maisie sighed. John had lost so much more than his leg on the beach at Dunkirk, and he was still suffering. But she was clearly not the right person to help him heal.

Maisie slid John's letter and the books into her case and picked up a second letter from the nightstand. This one was heavy and official-looking, and it had her name and address neatly typed on the front of the thick cream stationery and the War Office crest in the top left corner. It had arrived only a couple of days before, but Maisie had yet to find the courage to pass it on. But she knew she would have to— John deserved to know the truth it contained—and since she was leaving early tomorrow, giving it to him tonight was the only option she had left.

Despite all her previous promises to never see John again, when this letter arrived, Maisie knew she would have to go and see him one last time. She would return his uncle's beautiful book, give him this letter, and say good-bye.

Maisie closed the lid of her suitcase, and as she put her coat on, she slipped John McCrae's red book and the long cream envelope into one pocket, her flashlight into the other. Wrapping her long woolen scarf around her neck, Maisie let herself out of the hut door and into the cold gloom of the late afternoon.

The sunlight was almost gone, the moon low but bright, and Maisie could feel the impending frost descending as she walked down the track to the road. Once she was beyond the range of the band music from the wireless and the lumber-jills' chatter, the silence of the countryside enveloped her, the crunch of her boots on the gravel the only sound in all the world.

She walked briskly, and it wasn't long before she could see the lights from the men's camp filtering through the trees. She recognized the faint strains of big band music and smiled to know that the lumberjacks were tuned in to the same wireless program as the lumberjills. It was Vera Lynn's request show, *Sincerely Yours*, on which she played music and read out messages to the troops abroad. Seeing the men sitting outside the huts on stools, cigarettes dangling from their lips, Maisie wondered if the songs were making them think of their homes so far away in Newfoundland.

She was thankful that these were not the men she'd run into before, red-bearded Eric and his friends. Instead, it was Robert, and she thought the other man sitting across from him, dealing out playing cards onto a wooden crate, was called Sid—or was it Stan? Yes, Stan. Probably. Either way, she'd worked alongside him only once or twice.

Robert leaped to his feet as she approached, almost knocking over the crate in his rush, and Stan swore loudly. When Stan noticed Maisie, he had the good grace to act sheepish. "Sorry about that—I didn't realize we had a visitor of the female persuasion," he said.

"Please don't worry. I'm sure I've heard all the swear words you've got," Maisie replied, trying to push past the tightening in her gut. "And I've probably used most of them too. But why are you two out here playing cards when it's so cold?"

"Oh, it makes inside feel so much warmer when you go back in," replied Robert, and Stan nodded in agreement with this strange logic. "But what can we do for you, Maisie? I doubt you've come to let me beat you at cribbage." He gestured to the cards, and Maisie found herself smiling. She liked Robert and could see why Rose was so taken with him.

"Not tonight, no, but thanks anyway," replied Maisie. "Actually, I was hoping to see John Lindsay. I have a book to return to him, and I haven't seen him since . . . since the accident." She patted her pocket, as if she needed to prove her story with the dull thud of her hand hitting the hard cover.

There was no chance that she could miss the way the two men glanced at each other. It wasn't a worried look or a humorous one, but it was enough to make Maisie's stomach start to churn again.

"Isn't he here?" she asked quickly. "I thought he wouldn't be leaving to catch his boat home for a few more days yet."

"No, it's not that," said Robert. "He's still here. It's only . . ." Again, that same look passed between the men.

"It's only that John's not been quite the same since he got back from the hospital," Stan said, picking up Robert's explanation. "That's all Robert meant."

"Not the same?"

"I'll go tell him you're here, but I thought you should know, before you see him."

"I still don't understand what you mean."

"Look, let me get him, eh? Then you can give him the book and it'll all be done."

Before she could respond, both men disappeared through the door to the hut, leaving Maisie to shrug her woolen shoulders up to her ears and stamp her feet to keep the cold at bay.

It was less than a minute before John appeared at the door, but he took only a step or two outside before stopping. He was dressed no differently from how she'd always seen him, but Maisie was shocked. The trousers, shirt, and sweater-vest were ill-fitting and overly big. It had been barely a month since she'd seen him, yet in that time he'd become so thin, almost fragile, a shrinking shadow of the strapping and handsome man she'd met in the summer. Had that only been in September? Sometimes it felt like she'd known John so much longer. But not this John.

He looked at Maisie for a few seconds, appearing unsure of whether to move toward her or to retreat back inside.

Maisie heard someone, perhaps Robert, saying John's name, and John half turned. A hand appeared and pushed a heavy brown coat into John's hands before vanishing again. Then the door was quickly closed behind John, and Maisie heard the latch drop into place.

"John," said Maisie.

"Maisie," replied John, still holding on to his coat.

When he said nothing further, she pulled the book from her pocket. "I was packing, and I realized that I still had your uncle's poetry book. I did try to return it a while ago, but—"

She held it out to him, but he didn't take his eyes from her face.

"Packing?" he asked.

"I'm leaving early tomorrow. I've been reassigned to another camp in Perthshire. They asked for volunteers to go, and, well, I thought it might make life easier for us both if I wasn't here anymore."

"But—"

"But you're leaving too, I know. I got your letter. But even so, it'll still be easier this way. But before I left, I wanted to return your book." She held it out to him again, and this time he took it. Their fingers touched for only a moment before she withdrew her hand. "And there's something else I need to tell you. Two things, actually."

"Maisie, I . . . ," John began, but seemed to run out of steam.

A movement behind him caught her eye, and Maisie glanced to where at least five faces were pressed against the hut window, watching them. God! Men were more nosy than women.

"Excuse me, gentlemen," she said very loudly, "may we please talk without an audience?"

John followed her gaze over his shoulder to the windows, and the faces immediately withdrew. Even so, Maisie still walked a few steps farther away, and after a moment or two, John followed, pulling on his coat. She waited for him to catch up and was horrified to see how uneven his gait had become, now a profound limp, each step seeming to roll his hips from one side to the other, as if he were walking across a furrowed field.

John stopped in front of her and seemed to be waiting for her to continue.

"Oh yes, the two things," Maisie began, but then hesitated. He looked so gaunt, so frail, that she wasn't sure she should have this conversation with him after all.

But if not now, then when?

"Well, the first thing is that I wanted to apologize for pushing you too hard, and for expecting things that you weren't in a position to offer. I understand a little more now, and I need you to know that I only wanted to make things better for you. I just want to see you happy. I'm proud that you came to trust me enough to tell me about your leg, but I think that trust wasn't quite enough. Perhaps I was naive. I'd hoped that I might help you heal by giving you comfort, and time, and . . . and love."

Maisie held her breath after that word, but John did not seem to have even heard it. "But I realize now," she eventually continued, "that I'm not the right person to do that for you. But one day, I feel sure you'll find someone who can help you get past all the pain. Someone who'll make you happy."

John's frown deepened and he opened his mouth to reply, but Maisie lifted one finger toward him so she could finish what she had to say.

"And don't tell me that you don't deserve to be happy, because you do, we all do, and you more than most. Look what you have already sacrificed for the sake of your country, and for mine. Please don't continue to throw your happiness away because of some misplaced guilt. You have so little to feel guilty about."

John reached out for her raised finger and gently pushed it away from between them.

"Maisie, you can't tell me I have nothing to feel guilty about," he said softly, his voice rough as if little used of late. "You know that's not true. Walt and Lofty died because of me, and then Elliott—"

"But Elliott didn't die," Maisie replied, "though he might have if you hadn't banged on the truck until we heard you. And do you know how I particularly know that Elliott didn't die?"

John could not help the quick curious glance he gave her at that.

"I know that because Elliott spent a whole afternoon last week moaning to Dot that you haven't answered any of his letters, let alone gone to visit him."

John looked again at Maisie, then away.

"Elliott is stuck in a rehab prison, less than an hour from here by train, which you would know if you'd read even one of the dozen letters he says he's sent you. He's being terrorized by all those—now, what was the phrase?—'perpetually helpful and probably pretty nurses,' and you haven't even visited him."

This time, when John looked at her, he held her gaze. She'd hoped he might smile at her attempt to find some humor in this difficult moment, but his face remained disappointingly blank.

"Elliott misses you." Maisie was close enough to reach out and touch John, but she didn't. "And he certainly doesn't blame you for what happened. Quite the opposite. Dot told him how we heard your signals, and he's telling anyone who'll listen that his best mate saved his life. So if Elliott isn't blaming you, then what gives you the right to blame yourself?"

John lifted his hand to his face and rubbed it over his eyes.

"And Lofty and Walter—" she began.

John threw out his hand, palm flat toward her as if he was trying to shield himself from whatever she was about to say.

"Don't!"

"You need to hear this too."

"No, I don't—"

"Yes, you do!" Maisie had to get him to listen, so she pulled the thick cream envelope out of her pocket and held it out to him. He immediately snatched his hand back, as though the paper might burn him.

"You told me that you didn't know where your friends had been buried," Maisie said quietly. "Do you remember?"

Slowly, John nodded.

"Well, after that, I wrote to the War Office to find out. I asked where Privates Clarkson and McGinnis of the 2nd Manchesters were buried after being lost on the third of June on the beach at Dunkirk. But the War Office never replied"—Maisie pulled the envelope back and held it up so he could see the typescript and crest on the front—"until this week, when this arrived from a Captain Andrews. In his letter, he says that there are no graves registered for those two soldiers, either in France or in Great Britain."

John's shoulders visibly sagged.

"But Captain Andrews also said," Maisie continued quickly, since she knew this must be torturing John, "that he checked some other records, and miraculously, he found both Private Clarkson and Private McGinnis on those lists instead."

"Which lists?" John said doubtfully.

"The Red Cross lists for prisoners of war. Your friends didn't die, John. They were captured, not killed, and they're both being held in a POW camp somewhere. It's all in here." Maisie held out the letter to him again, and this time he took it. "Walt and Lofty are still alive."

With trembling fingers, John opened the letter, and Maisie watched him read both sides of the page once, and then again.

Maisie stepped forward and laid her hand on John's arm.

"John, I'm so glad I had the chance to get to know you a little. You're a truly wonderful man, but I wish you believed that as much as I do."

"Wait—" John began.

But Maisie knew if she stayed any longer, she would never be able to leave. "I hope you have a safe voyage home, and that you find some peace within yourself soon."

"But Maisie—"

"I really do wish you all the very best, John." Her voice cracked on his name, and she had to swallow hard. "And perhaps you were right. If only we had met in another time."

Maisie had expected to feel her eyes fill with tears as she walked away from John for the last time. But they didn't. Or at least not until she was almost past the NOFU hut, and whatever song was playing on the wireless finished, and another started.

Even before Vera Lynn had begun to sing, Maisie knew what her first words would be.

We'll meet again, don't know where, don't know when.

Maisie couldn't bear it, and she began to run.

But I know we'll meet again some sunny day.

She ran until she couldn't hear the music any longer, because she knew that there would be no sunny day still to come for her and John Lindsay.

Twenty-Nine

"O holy night! The stars are brightly shiiiiiiiiiii"—Phyllis took in a quick breath—*"ning, it is the night of our dear Savior's birth."* She bent to hoist another log up and onto the rollers of the headsaw without breaking off from her not-quite-tuneful, but very loud, rendition of the Christmas carol, during which she was drowning out the entire choir of King's College, Cambridge, singing out from the wireless on the shelf behind her.

"Long lay the world in sin and error piiiiiiiiii"—another ragged breath—*"ning, till He appeared and the soul felt its worth."*

At the other end of the saw table, Maisie grinned at her friend and hummed along with the next couple of lines, realizing that she felt happy today. Phyllis might not have the best voice, but she was certainly filling the sawmill and all its occupants with Christmas spirit, and Maisie knew for sure that this would be a Christmas unlike any other.

Maisie had arrived at her new posting both physically tired, after the early start and long drive, and emotionally wrung out after all the good-byes at Auchterblair—and after that particular good-bye. But almost before she'd clambered out of the van that had collected her from the station, she'd been smothered by her old Shandford friends, Phyllis, Helen, and Cynthia, who'd grabbed her and her suitcase and manhandled her up the steps of the beautiful old house that served as their billet. It was not unlike Shandford Lodge, Helen proudly told Maisie as she unpacked, because it had once been one of King Edward VII's shooting retreats, sitting as it did on the edge of Rannoch Moor. And Phyllis had been telling the truth on her postcard—the lumberjills were sleeping in real bedrooms, with real beds, and there were even three real bathrooms. What luxury after the Blue Lagoon!

Cynthia had apparently left Advie on Speyside to join Phyllis and Helen at Struan only a couple of weeks before Maisie, and the four of them had quickly became almost inseparable. Maisie had loved getting to know her old friends from training even better during the month since she'd arrived, and working inside the sawmill was certainly preferable to being outside for hours each day now that winter had set in. Even so, Maisie missed Auchterblair. Dot had written twice a week without fail, and Rose too, but still . . .

Phyllis pushed the log along the rollers toward Maisie, guiding it onto the saw blade until the teeth caught and it began to cut through the soft wood as if it were sponge cake. Once Phyllis could see that the far end of the log was under Maisie's control, she stepped back and geared up for the bit of the song that Maisie knew Phyllis loved the best, having heard her sing it at least twice a day for six days straight.

"*Faaaaaaaaaaall on your knees!*" Phyllis planted her feet wide apart and slowly raised her arms out to each side. "*O heeeeeeeeeeear the angel voi-ces! O night divine, O night when Christ was born . . .*"

Maisie gathered up the newly cut planks and laid them on the trolley next to her, ready to go through to Helen in the planing shed next door, as Phyllis hit her highest—and her least on-pitch—note.

"*O night dee-vaaaaaa-ine, O night . . .*" Phyllis swiftly brought down both the volume and her arms until she was almost whispering, and her hands were pressed together in front of her as if she were the Virgin Mary herself. "*O night divine!*"

Maisie clapped, and Phyllis clearly appreciated the gesture because she gave her a quick curtsy. Then Phyllis launched into the second verse as she lifted the next log onto the saw table.

The far door to the yard beyond Phyllis suddenly swung open, and a blast of bitterly cold air swept through the shed, lifting swirls of sawdust into the air like snow flurries, wafting them through the archway into the planing shed.

"Shut the bloody door!" Cynthia screeched from the next room, where Maisie knew she and Helen would be working in shirtsleeves because of the heat generated by the plane engines in the relatively small space.

Still, no one came in through the doorway, so once the log was set on the rollers, Phyllis went to investigate, launching into the opening lines of "O Come, All Ye Faithful" as she walked. When she reached the doorway and looked out into the yard, however, her singing died away and she disappeared outside, even though she didn't have her coat on. When it became clear that she wasn't immediately coming back inside, Maisie switched off the saw's motor and pulled the heavy trolley laden with rough-edged planks through into the other shed, where she parked it next to Helen at the edging machine.

"Thank you!" said Helen, raising her voice above the noise of the cranky engine. "And you can take this one for the next load." She lifted the last plank from the trolley she'd been working from, now empty, set the pale cream wood onto the belt, and let it move away from her past a fine-toothed saw that sliced neatly along its edge.

Another cold draft billowed the sawdust through the archway.

"Shut the bloody—" Cynthia began again, but at that moment the main door slammed, and she gave a satisfied nod. "Thank you! It's like living in a bloody barn."

Maisie smiled, knowing that Cynthia's bad mood was entirely caused by a hangover after a night out at the Struan Inn with some of the lads from the Canadian Forestry Corps who were billeted nearby, and who had built this sawmill in the first place. The girls had tried to get Maisie to join them, saying that a night in the pub was always good entertainment, but Maisie had said no, she had letters to write to Dot and to Beth, and she could do with an early night.

She had nothing against the CFC boys, but watching them swagger around in their army uniforms—they were soldiers first, after all, and lumberjacks second—made her think too much of the other lumberjacks she'd known . . . too much about John, and what was the point of that?

By now, John would be home in Halifax. In her letters, Dot had mentioned, more than once, that John had left a few days after Maisie had, and therefore he would have boarded his ship for the crossing to Nova Scotia soon after that. Every day since, Maisie had been the first in line to borrow the newspaper from Mr. Ritchie, the mill manager, so she could scan every page twice, searching for any news of torpedo attacks by U-boats in the North Atlantic, and more particularly, any reported sinking of a troop ship.

By the middle of Advent, however, she was scanning the pages only once, and for the last week, she hadn't even looked at the paper at all, knowing that the ship must have already reached its destination. John was now in Canada and Maisie was in Scotland. And that was how it should be.

Even so, she had wondered briefly if she might ask Dot, in

her next letter, to ask Haven if he had John's home address. She didn't want to call either Haven or Dot's attention to the fact that she wanted to write to John, but she also doubted a letter sent to "John Lindsay, Halifax, Nova Scotia" would ever find its way to him. But then again, perhaps it might. Was Halifax a village or a huge city? She had no idea, and felt rather ashamed at how little she knew about where he came from. Perhaps she'd look it up in an encyclopedia at the library next time they went into Pitlochry.

But then again, why bother? What would she even say in a letter?

"Here you go," said Helen, shoving the empty trolley toward Maisie, interrupting her thoughts. "And try to cheer up a bit, won't you? It's Christmas Eve, and you look as miserable as Cynthia this morning."

Maisie plastered a fake smile onto her face and tried to get herself back to that happy state she had been in during Phyllis's impromptu carol concert. Where was Phyllis, anyway? The wireless choir had already reached the "Sing, choirs of angels" verse, to which Phyllis liked to lend her ballsy descant, yet the choir sang on unaccompanied. Had Phyllis not come back in yet?

Grabbing the handle of the trolley, Maisie had turned to go back through when she saw that Cynthia had turned off her belt saw and was now standing under the archway between the sheds. For some reason, Cynthia was smiling, in spite of her hangover, and then she looked behind Maisie at Helen and gave a sideways nod of her head, as if indicating that

Helen should come see too. Helen switched off the engine of her machine at the same moment the wireless fell silent next door, the choir cut off halfway through a shrill "*O come!*"

Silence.

It was an odd sensation—the mill was never silent—and almost as if the departing sound had left its vibrations in the air, prickles were spreading up the back of Maisie's neck, not least because both Cynthia and Helen were now grinning at *her*. Without the racket of the machines, she could also make out soft thumps and low mutterings coming from the main shed. And still Cynthia and Helen kept grinning.

Phyllis appeared in the archway beside them, and she too looked like she'd won the grand prize at the bingo.

"Oh, there you are Maisie," Phyllis choked out. "I've been wondering where you've been."

Well, that was strange.

"You were the one who vanished outside," replied Maisie.

Phyllis glanced back over her shoulder and nodded to someone out of Maisie's sight.

"What's going on, Phyllis?" Growing anxiety inside Maisie was shortening her patience.

"Well, Maisie," Phyllis suddenly declared loudly, and started to move back the way she'd come, "I rather need your help with something? Something quite important. And urgent. And *in here*."

Phyllis started waving her arms theatrically into the shed, as if she were a conjuror's assistant in a variety show. Maisie pulled off her leather gloves and tucked them into her belt before cautiously approaching Phyllis, suddenly feeling rather nervous and ridiculously suspicious. Peering into main shed, however, she saw that all the fuss had only been about the arrival of a Christmas tree. It was a very pretty little tree, with lumpy balls of silver foil dancing alongside brown paper cutouts of angels and snowflakes. And at the very top sat a gold star, roughly fashioned out of . . . well, it rather looked to Maisie like the paper from inside a cigarette packet.

But strangely, the Christmas tree was also wearing army trousers and boots.

Maisie focused. Obviously, the tree wasn't wearing the trousers and boots. A man in an army uniform was holding the tree.

Maisie still didn't understand, though. It was very sweet of one of the CFC lads to bring a Christmas tree to the saw-mill, but why was Phyllis making such a fuss about it?

But then, several more men in army uniforms appeared from behind the tree, all grinning as much as Maisie's friends. And Maisie knew that they couldn't be CFC, because she knew these men.

It was Haven, and Rose's Robert, and Stan, no, Sid, no, Stan. And damn, what was that other chap's name? Four lumberjacks, gathered around the little tree.

And then she noticed another man off to one side, sitting in a wheelchair, all wrapped up in a coat and tartan blanket, from which striped pajama bottoms and plaid carpet slippers were poking out at the bottom.

"Elliott!" Maisie cried. "What the hell are you—? How did you—?"

And Elliott was grinning too, and pointing at the tree. And Maisie suddenly knew who was holding the tree.

Almost as if she'd shouted his name, the little tree lowered a few inches and John's face appeared behind the golden cigarette-paper star.

"Happy Christmas, Maisie."

But how? Why? How could John be here, safe and well? Why was he not home in Halifax?

Somehow Maisie drew in enough breath to speak, but "Happy Christmas, John" was as much as she could snag from within the maelstrom inside her mind.

And then the tree was being passed into Haven's arms, and John was in front of Maisie, right there only inches from her. He grasped her hands and pressed them against the stiff khaki wool of his jacket. He looked strong and well, not like the last time she'd seen him. Still pale perhaps, and thinner than he'd been when she'd met him, but certainly not frail anymore. In fact, he looked rather wonderful.

"Maisie"—John's voice made even her name sound like poetry, and Maisie's breath hitched—"I came because I wanted—"

His voice seemed to catch in his throat and he coughed.

And then an odd thought struck Maisie. John was wearing a uniform. And a question chimed around inside her head like Christmas bells. *Why was John wearing an army uniform?*

"I came," John began again, a soft smile playing on his lips, "because I wanted to ask you something."

Panic engulfed Maisie, smothering her as completely as if she'd been sucked under water.

WHY was John wearing an army uniform?

"I wanted to ask you if you would—"

"No!" The word was out of her mouth before Maisie was even aware she had thought it.

Snatching her hands out of his, Maisie turned and ran.

Thirty

Maisie was through the planing shed, out of the door, and halfway across the snowy yard before her knees buckled under her and she stumbled. It took two or three more steps before she had regained her balance, and she stood, breathing hard, her hand over her mouth to stop the sobs from escaping.

John had joined the army again. John was going back into battle, and this time he would not come back.

And his question? She didn't care what he wanted to ask her. He was in the army, not safe at home in Nova Scotia. What had he been thinking? Had he joined up because of his ridiculous obsession that she'd like him more in a uniform? Hadn't he listened to a bloody word she'd ever said?

"Maisie?"

She whirled around. John was standing a few feet away from her, his face torn with anxiety.

"What have you *done*?" she demanded.

"I don't understand, what—"

Maisie rushed at him and slapped the back of her hand across his chest, her knuckles catching painfully on a button.

"What possessed you?" she was screeching now, her voice tearing at her throat. "I thought you'd gone home. I thought you were safe. But oh no, not you! You choose to go back into the army so the Germans can do a proper job of killing you this time."

Again she swiped her hand hard against his chest, but this time, John grabbed hold of her wrist and held on to it. Maisie tried to pull her hand away, but he wouldn't release her.

"I'll let you go on two conditions," he said gently, loosening his grip slightly, though not enough for her to pull away. "That you stop hitting me, and that you listen to me for one minute."

Maisie tried one more tug, without success, and she gave in, nodding slowly.

John released her wrist but still looked wary. "I have not joined the army," he said.

"But the unif—"

"Not quite anyway. I have joined the Home Guard. Look." John turned his shoulder toward her and she saw for the first time a crescent patch at the top of his sleeve stitched with the words "HOME GUARD." Immediately below it was another, which read "3RD INVERNESS (NEWFOUND-LAND) BATTALION."

Maisie lifted her hand and ran her fingertips across the patch.

"But why? You swore you'd never wear a uniform again."

"I know, but . . ." John shrugged. "It was Haven's idea. Things at camp have been a little, let's say, rough now the nights are longer. The guys have been feeling cooped up in the camp. They're used to being outdoors most of the time at home, in all weathers, even at night with fires and flashlights. But the rules here say they can't work after dark because of the blackout. A while ago, Haven got talking to some guy in the pub who was in the Inverness Home Guard, and that set him thinking that perhaps we could contribute more than timber to the war effort.

"And it's come at a good time. With the long dark evenings, we all feel like we're doing something useful, now that we can't be up the woods. Things like watching for enemy aircraft, and night patrols around the villages and the air base. Of course, I probably shouldn't be telling you all that. You could be an enemy spy."

John grinned suddenly, and in spite of herself, Maisie felt her heart lighten. But still, she couldn't give in so easily, because saying good-bye had been too damned hard.

"But why you?" she asked. "You should be at home already."

"That was Haven's idea too. Haven's such a nosy beggar,

he was eavesdropping on us that night you left, and he heard the lecture you gave me."

"He *what*?" Maisie was aghast that Haven should have listened to their private conversation.

"He was worried about me, and about you too. He knew the black mood I had been in, and that my leg was still causing me pain. So he followed us to make sure that nothing . . . went wrong."

"Oh!" What else could she say?

"And after you'd gone, he kept your lecture going. No, don't huff like that, you were both lecturing me, and I'll admit it, you were right to. Haven's take on it was that if I scuttled off back to Halifax with my head down and my spirit low, it would be almost impossible for me to deal with what was troubling me, but if I stayed and faced it all . . ."

John seemed to be searching Maisie's face for something, though she wasn't exactly sure what.

"His other bright idea was to drive me the next day to visit Elliott in rehab prison—except that place was more like a luxury hotel—and Elliott introduced me to one of the doctors there, a major in the Medical Corps. We talked for a little while and then Haven drove me back to camp."

"But Dot said you'd left Carrbridge to get the boat home."

"I did leave Carrbridge, for a little while. You probably won't believe this, but I went to stay at the rehab prison with Elliott, voluntarily. It gave me some time for my leg to recover and meant I could talk more to the major. And Elliott and I played a lot of chess, and I wrote some poetry, quite a lot of poetry actually, at the doctor's suggestion. And that's helped a bit. Nights can still be difficult, but, I am starting to feel more like myself again."

"You look a bit more like yourself too," Maisie said. And he did, tall and proud—and handsome—and so different from the last time they'd been together. "And I'm glad about that."

"Me too." John smiled. "I only got back to Carrbridge last week, and Haven had laid my Home Guard uniform out on my bed, without even asking me if I wanted to join. And you know, that was fine too. Somehow, I was ready to wear it.

"But the one thing I haven't been able to get past was the look on your face every time I did something stupid that hurt you. I know I hurt you, Maisie. And I feel desperate about it. I wasn't sure you'd even want to hear that from me."

Maisie felt the urge to tell him not to worry, of course he hadn't hurt her, but she pushed it back down again. John *had* hurt her, and they both knew it. But that seemed to be why he was there, to acknowledge that and to apologize. Would that make it all right, though? Maisie still wasn't sure.

"So," he continued, "when Dot mentioned that you—"

"Wait, you've spoken to Dot about me?"

"She happened to mention that you'd be staying at your new camp for Christmas. And also, that you had sounded a little lonely in your last couple of letters, and you might enjoy a visitor"—he glanced back over his shoulder with a smile—"or six."

"I sounded nothing of the sort—that's just Dot being

meddlesome!" Maisie cried indignantly, though even as she said it, she knew that Dot had been trying to be kind. "But I will agree with her that it is nice to have a visitor . . . or six."

"I'm glad to hear that, because we had a devil of a job smuggling Elliott out of that place from under the noses of all those perpetually interfering, and only occasionally pretty, nurses."

"You *smuggled* him out?"

"Well, maybe smuggling is too strong, but Matron certainly frowned at us very hard as we bundled him into the back of the major's car, lent to us just for the occasion."

Maisie couldn't help but smile at that.

"And did you bundle the Christmas tree into the major's car too?"

"Actually no, that little beauty came from a lovely old church in Blair Atholl."

"You did *not* steal that tree from a church!"

John laughed, throwing his head back. "Of course we didn't! We're lumberjacks, remember—we can magic trees out of thin air, and then adorn them with beautiful hand-made decorations, which might have once wrapped up the breakfast we ate on the road."

"And a cigarette packet too, if I'm not mistaken," Maisie said with a giggle.

"You are certainly a connoisseur of decorative style. And I'm delighted that our mission to bring Christmas joy to this small corner of your country has proved us worthy of your attention." John twirled his hand in the air, but before he could let it lead him into a bow, Maisie took a step toward him, until there was almost no space between them.

"But that's only half of your mission, surely. Isn't it about time for you to fulfill the other half too?"

For a moment, John looked as if he hadn't understood, but then he smiled, not a wide grin but a soft, sweet smile, and nodded his head.

"Of course. My mission. I came to ask you a question, didn't I? If you're ready to hear it."

Maisie still wasn't sure that she was ready, whatever the question turned out to be. Even so, she nodded.

"Well, if you would let me escort you back into the elegant, and much warmer, interior of the shed there, I will certainly ask it." John offered her his arm and they turned to walk back toward the door, which was still standing open. Maisie pretended she didn't see the heads that had been peering around the door vanish the instant she and John were facing that direction.

As they entered the planing shed, the fragrant warmth enveloped them again. But the space was surprisingly empty. Where had everyone else gone?

As John led Maisie across and into the main shed, she got her answer as the crackle of a needle touching a record filled the space, and Maisie saw the gramophone sitting on the workbench beside Elliott, who was *still* grinning. Then the music began, softly at first, but growing with each bar, each phrase.

"*We'll meet again*"—Vera Lynn's voice was sweet, her tone

sincere—"*don't know where, don't know when.*"

Suddenly Maisie was back in Brechin Town Hall, in the moment when a dark and handsome stranger had stepped forward.

But I know we'll meet again some sunny day.

And now here he was again, still dark and handsome, but no longer a stranger. And he was offering her his hand, and finally, after all the explanations, he was asking the question he had come all this way for.

"Not quite the sunny day we were promised, but would you care to dance?"

There was undoubtedly mischief in John's eyes, and Maisie didn't want to say yes, not immediately. She could make mischief too, so she'd make him wait a little.

"But you told me that you couldn't dance," she said, suppressing a smile.

"And I was right, I couldn't dance. Not many one-legged men can. But that was then, and this is now, and it turns out that Nancy is quite an accomplished dancing instructor. Am I right?" He turned, addressing his friends, who all nodded emphatically. "She and Dot have had all of us dancing, even the guy with only one leg. Of course, they might have had a harder time with the guy who prefers to laze around in his chair all day, but I'm sure they'd have given it a go."

From beside the gramophone, Elliott raised up one finger at his friend, and they both laughed. Then Elliott gave

John another signal, a quick "get on with it" wave, and John turned to face Maisie again.

"I'm only going to ask this only once more, and I'll understand if you say no. Then I'll be on my way, taking this lot with me." Again, he held his palm out toward her, and this time she didn't hesitate to lay her hand on his. "Seriously, Maisie, I don't want you to do anything you aren't happy with, but . . ."

Maisie stared up into his beautiful brown eyes and waited. And waited.

"Well, go on then," she whispered.

John chuckled quietly. "Please, Maisie, may I have this dance?"

There was no need to answer. Maisie's body was already against his, their chests and hips pressed tight together, as John placed his right hand in the small of her back and held her hand gently in his left. And then they were dancing, swaying on the spot at first, but then moving into slow and wide circles.

Keep smiling through, just like you always do,
Till the blue skies drive the dark clouds far away.

As she laid her cheek on John's shoulder, Maisie saw that Haven and Phyllis, and Stan and Helen, had started dancing too. Robert looked a little more reticent, perhaps because he was wondering how Rose would feel about him dancing with another woman, but it was only a second or two before he and Cynthia were also spinning around the floor. To one side, Elliott and Malcolm—the other chap's name came to her then—began playing the fools by dancing with each other, Malcolm spinning Elliott's chair around in dizzying circles until Elliott cried out for him to stop before he threw up.

Maisie smiled happily, and she felt John's warm breath as he kissed her cheek. She raised her face up toward John's, and without breaking step, Maisie's lips found his.

It was only as the music died to a crackling silence that Maisie let the kiss end, so she could gaze up into those warm brown eyes.

"Merry Christmas, John."

"Merry Christmas, Maisie."

Epilogue

Even though it was late in the spring, the breeze floating in through the kitchen door still had a nip to it, and Maisie wrapped her woolen cardigan a little tighter around herself. She leaned over to make sure the blanket lying on top of her sleeping son hadn't worked itself loose. It hadn't—that boy could sleep through a hurricane—but she still tucked it tighter down the sides of the baby carriage he was almost too big for now, just to make sure.

She sat back down to finish the letter in front of her on the kitchen table.

Sending lots and lots of love to you and Nancy.
> *Missing you, as always, dear friend,*
> *Maisie xxx*
> *(and Little Elliott)*
> *(and of course John)*

She blotted the wet ink and folded the letter into the waiting envelope, addressing it in her neatest handwriting. As usual, writing that particular address made her smile.

Miss Dorothy Thompson,
Auchterblair Stables,
Carrbridge,
Inverness-shire,
Scotland

Not only had Nancy and Dot bought the Auchterblair huts and land for a song once the war was over and the Women's Timber Corps disbanded, they had also bought Clyde, just as Nancy had said they would. Clyde therefore became the founding resident of the first riding and livery stables in Speyside. Did Clyde realize how lucky he was? Perhaps. The slightly blurred photograph that Dot had enclosed in her last letter suggested the fat old Clydesdale was being spoiled more than ever.

Maisie propped the envelope on the windowsill by the open door, next to the one she'd written earlier to Rose in

London, and gazed across the yard to the jumble of red saw-mill buildings at the far side. The largest straddled the creek above the point where it let out into Second Lake beyond the mill. From where she stood, she had the perfect view of the trees that hugged the lake, sweeping their thickly wooded way up the hills beyond. What was now lusciously green would, in only a handful of months, become a rainbow of autumnal color before vanishing under its annual quilt of sparkling white snow.

Maisie loved her new home. Even the low hum of the machinery in the mill, and the shouts as the men loaded and unloaded the trucks, didn't intrude on its splendor. In fact, the noises gave Maisie such a sense of belonging that she didn't even hear them most of the time. Nova Scotia—New Scotland—was all so different from her Old Scotland, and yet, it was so very much the same.

She knew they'd been very lucky that John had found such a perfect job when he returned to Halifax after the war, given the number of men who were returning and expecting to find employment. But the owners of the sawmill had known John's father for years, and since their manager had decided to retire, they'd been willing to take the chance on a young man returning from the war, even one missing a leg. And because the manager's job came with a house on the mill site, Maisie and John had stepped off the boat from Glasgow straight into their first marital home.

Maisie was so proud of how hard John was still working to move past the injuries he had suffered, both to his leg and to his spirit. The major at the rehab prison had told her privately that it would not be an easy fix, and had likened it to the shell shock suffered by men during the Great War. The anger, the anxiety, and the nightmares would undoubtedly continue, he'd warned, but he'd also said that with her help, John would find a way to cope, even if he never completely conquered them. John was still writing poems, and although he didn't show many of them to Maisie, he had recently met with an old friend of his uncle John's, a retired English professor from McGill University, who'd asked John to send him some of his work to read. So, all in all, Maisie and John's new life, with the mill and with their darling baby son, Little Elliott, was going well.

The move back across the Atlantic for *Big* Elliott, and his new Scottish wife, Ruth—who had been one of Elliott's perpetually helpful and, in Ruth's case, very beautiful nurses from the rehab prison—had not been quite so easy. Having decided to move to Halifax along with Maisie and John, rather than return to Elliott's native Newfoundland, they had been forced to rely on Ruth's nursing qualifications and skills to keep money in their pockets while Elliott went back to university to finish his degree. How often had Maisie heard Elliott joke that Ruth had not only been his ministering angel but his meal ticket too? Of course, Maisie had enjoyed having them live in the mill house's downstairs guest room for the first few months, since it had sealed the friendship between her and Ruth and filled the large gap left in her life by leaving her lumberjill friends behind. Once Elliott had begun teaching at the high school in Halifax, however, he and Ruth had got their own little cottage down toward town, though not far from the mill, and Maisie was sure it wouldn't be long before Ruth started to think about having a baby too.

Maisie knew she'd been so fortunate to have Ruth with her for the move to Nova Scotia. In the same way that she and Dot had helped each other through their lumberjill adventure, Ruth and Maisie had faced the challenges of being war brides, and settling so far from home in a brand-new country with brand-new husbands.

Remembering that it was Ruth's afternoon off from the hospital, Maisie lifted down two jars of strawberry jam from the shelf and put them gently into the basket under the pram so she wouldn't forget them later. Once Little Elliott—she was still having to work hard not to think of him as Baby Elliott, given he was toddling around these days—woke from his nap, they'd go for a walk down to the post office to mail her letters to Dot and Rose, as well as the parcel of maple-syrup fudge to the still sugar-rationed Beth in Oxford, and the birthday card to Mother. Then they'd go to the butcher's, and lastly to the greengrocer's to buy some flowers, since she and John planned to drive into Halifax this evening to lay them on the war memorial.

They'd arranged to pick up Elliott on their way—although he was walking quite well these days, with the support of a stick, the long walk into town was still too much for him after a full day of teaching—and their friend Walter Clarkson had said he would meet them there. Together they would lay the flowers under the new plaque, which had recently been added below the names of those who had fallen in the Great War. This plaque commemorated those from Halifax who had fallen in this war, *their* war, and those names included Private Nicholas "Lofty" McGinnis of the 2nd Manchester Regiment.

John's reunion with his childhood friend Walt had been so happy and so sad all at once. Although they had slotted back into each other's lives as easily as if they'd never been apart, John had also been grief stricken to learn that Lofty had succumbed to pneumonia during February of 1943 while he and Walt were prisoners in the Stalag XXA prison camp near Thorn in Poland.

As a way of paying tribute to their friend, John and Walt had decided not only to mark the anniversary of Lofty's death each year, but also to do something to remember him on every anniversary of the last time the three friends were together—June 3rd, 1940. That was the day that Walt and Lofty had lifted John onto the rescue boat during the evacuation of Dunkirk and had both then returned to shore to help others to escape. That was the day that Walt and Lofty had been taken prisoner. Hard though it was for Maisie to believe, that day had been ten years ago today.

Glancing at the clock, Maisie did a quick calculation. Little Elliott would probably sleep for another half an hour, so she could make the most of the time by making a cup of tea and getting a start on the ironing. Maisie filled the kettle and placed it next to the flatiron on the range, and opened the little door to check on the fire inside. It was getting low, so she reached into the basket for some more firewood. Only one small log nestled in the bottom, so Maisie picked up the basket and, pulling the kitchen door closed behind her, carried it around to the woodpile behind the garage. Replenishing the firewood in the basket was one of John's chores—one he had clearly forgotten about today—and Maisie groaned to see that although there was a pile of off-cut logs, John hadn't yet split them for use in the stoves. It had been a busy spring for John since the melt had finally released all the river timber trapped in the ice in the fall, sending it downstream to the sawmill, so he had a good excuse. Even so, she still needed firewood.

Maisie began toward the mill to ask John to spare one of the men to split some logs for her, but as she walked, a sudden gust of wind ruffled the shallow layer of sawdust under her feet. A familiar scent of wood and resin and mulch and forest enveloped her, bringing on a wave of nostalgia and homesickness, not for Glasgow, but for Shandford Lodge, for Auchterblair, and for Struan. What was it about this scent, the warm sunshine, and the cool breeze that immediately took her back there?

Without another thought, Maisie changed course. From the wall above the workbench in the garage, she gathered her trusty whetstone and her ax—the same six-pound ax she had used throughout her four years as a lumberjill—and walked back to the woodpile, spitting on the blade and rubbing it with the stone to set again the keen edge that she had so neglected of late.

She collected an armful of the logs and dropped them next to the splitting block, then hefted her ax for the first time in far too long. As she swung it in a slow practice stroke, she could feel the neglect in every muscle in her arms, chest, and back, and recalled how she'd moaned to Dot and the others about her aches and pains for weeks on end. But the pull on her muscles now made her feel alive again in a way she hadn't even realized she'd been missing. Of course, she'd have to be careful—she couldn't risk hurting the new baby growing inside her—but it was still early days. She hadn't even told John that they were expecting again, though she suspected that Ruth had already guessed. But being pregnant did not mean she had lost all her strength—lifting a heavy toddler and bags of groceries had seen to that—and now that the ax was in her hands, Maisie wondered how she could have left it hanging on the wall of the garage for so long.

The wooden handle wasn't as smooth as it had once been, and Maisie knew that it wouldn't take long for the soft skin on her palms and fingers to blister and tear. But that wouldn't be the end of the world, would it? A handsome lumberjack had once given her a special remedy for callused hands, and she knew there was a tub of Vaseline in the bathroom and a large tin of pig fat in the pantry. Her hands would be just fine.

As always, the familiar tune of her chopping song went through Maisie's mind—"*We'll meet again, don't know where, don't know when*"—as she swung her ax up and around, reveling in the familiar whine of the blade traveling through the air. *"But I know we'll meet again some sunny day."*

The six-pound ax split the wood with one clean crack, and the two pieces tumbled to the ground. As Maisie Lindsay set up another log, she hummed her chopping song again, knowing that she and John were going to be just fine too.

THE SCOTSMAN, 10 October 2007

Statue to "Lumberjills" Unveiled

The first memorial to "the forgotten army of World War Two"—the 5,000 members of the Women's Timber Corps (WTC)—was yesterday unveiled in the Queen Elizabeth Forest Park, near Aberfoyle in Stirlingshire.

The life-size sculpture of a "lumberjill," as the women were known, was created by Scottish artist Malcolm Robertson and paid for by the Forestry Commission to mark the as-yet-unrecognized contribution these women made to the war effort. Many lumberjills were sent far from their homes, to work and live in spare and often freezing conditions, undertaking all the tasks related to timber production previously done by their male lumberjack counterparts, most of whom had been called up to serve in the Allied forces.

At the unveiling, Scottish Environment Minister Michael Russell said, "I am delighted to help commemorate the hard-working women of the Women's Timber Corps, whose valiant, behind-the-scenes work helped Britain in the war effort."

A number of the lumberjills who are still alive and fit enough to travel—even the youngest lumberjills are now in their eighties—joined the minister for the ceremony. Among those who gathered to pay tribute to their WTC colleagues was Mrs. Margaret McCall Lindsay, known to her fellow lumberjills as Maisie, who had traveled back to her native Scotland from Canada, accompanied by her grandson John Dickson.

Mrs. Lindsay had met and married a young lumberjack from Nova Scotia, John Lindsay, who was serving with the Newfoundland Overseas Forestry Unit following distinguished war service in France. The two were married in Glasgow in 1946 and emigrated to Halifax, Nova Scotia, soon after. Not only did the couple build one of the largest timber companies in eastern Canada, but shortly before his death in 1995, Mr. Lindsay was awarded the Canada Medal for the Arts for his contribution to poetry and literature.

In reply to the Minister's words, Mrs. Lindsay told the assembled crowd, "This beautiful statue is a fitting tribute to all the wonderful girls and women I was so fortunate to call my friends. Thank you to all at the Forestry Commission who have worked so hard to win us this recognition."

The Women's Timber Corps was disbanded in August 1946. Each member received a letter from the then Queen Elizabeth, later to become the Queen Mother, although it took until this year for the members of the Women's Timber Corps to have their contributions acknowledged officially.

The Scottish government has this week awarded a gold medal to each lumberjill still living, in recognition of her extraordinary sacrifice and service.

Sadly, fewer than 100 of the original 5,000 members of the WTC are still alive to receive their medals, but Mrs. Lindsay said she was proud to have been there representing her fellow lumberjills at the unveiling. She said, "We worked too hard—I can still feel the calluses on my hands, you know— to have our contribution to the Allied victory forgotten. Now our children and grandchildren, spread across the world as they are, may return to this beautiful forest and know we played our part."

Author's Note

In Another Time is, of course, an imaginary love story, and both Maisie McCall and John Lindsay are fictional characters (sadly). But there would be no story if not for the real-life adventures of the five thousand women and teenage girls who joined the Women's Timber Corps during World War Two. As an author, I am grateful that there are people and organizations who have understood the importance of gathering the life stories of those who lived through the war and sharing them on the internet and in books.

Maisie is modeled on a dozen or more lumberjills and shares their extraordinary courage and grit, their daring spirits, and their sense of fun. Most of all, she makes the kind of friendships they did, many of which lasted for the rest of their lives.

There were, however, four lumberjills whose stories influenced mine the most:

Bonnie McAdam was already a licensed bus driver when she joined the Women's Timber Corps, and she stayed on at Shandford Lodge as a trainer. Bonnie was the campaigning force for the Lumberjills Memorial Statue unveiled in the Queen Elizabeth Forest Park near Aberfoyle in 2007. Sadly, Bonnie died soon after being shown the initial designs and never saw her bronze lumberjill proudly gazing out over the Scottish hills.

Rosalind Elder joined the WTC at just sixteen. She trained as a horsewoman, working with big chains and even bigger Clydesdale horses. Rosalind was stationed at Advie on Speyside and married Louis Walsh, a NOFU lumberjack, soon after the war. She traveled across the Atlantic as a "war bride." She spent the rest of her life in Canada. She still lives in Vancouver, and I have been thrilled to have been in touch with her and her granddaughter, Amy Hurwitz.

Bella Nolan, from Kingussie, who joined the WTC with her sister, was stationed at Auchterblair Camp, and I was grateful for her memories of the site, including that the ablutions hut had been called the Blue Lagoon. She too married a Newfoundlander, though they raised their family in Scotland.

Christina Edgar was a nineteen-year-old office clerk when she joined the WTC, and she spent most of the war in the woods around Alyth, near Dundee. She eventually returned home to Glasgow, where she met and married a man called, appropriately enough, Jim Forrester. I was thrilled to meet up with Mrs. Forrester, and her daughters Irene and Christine, and to visit the Lumberjills Memorial at Aberfoyle together. She was incredibly generous with her time and her memories, and I'm honored to have spent the whole afternoon with her. You can read Christina's story on the Forestry Commission Scotland website.

As a historical novelist, I place my fictional characters in a world of historical fact. My stories are not so much what *did* happen but what *could have* happened in a particular time and place. What, therefore, were the facts behind this story from a small pocket of wartime, so far from the battlefront?

The Women's Timber Corps was formed in 1942 when Allied shipping convoys bringing timber were targeted by German U-boats. Britain was forced to turn to its own ancient forests, but since so many male foresters were serving in the armed forces, the government recruited women to fill their boots.

Over five thousand women and girls left offices and shops, homes and schools, to become WTC lumberjills. In Scotland, they spent six weeks being trained at Shandford Lodge, near Brechin, before being assigned to a WTC camp, many of which were unheated wooden huts, although some girls were lucky enough to be billeted in local homes. The work was physically challenging and often dangerous, and they spent long hours out in every weather, with only one week off a year.

The camaraderie of working alongside other women, however, kept them going even in the hardest of environments, and they had lots of fun too. The local towns and villages would throw dances, and even though there was a distinct shortage of British men, they could still dance with the lumberjacks from the Newfoundland Overseas Forestry Unit and the Canadian Forestry Corps.

Although the CFC was a military unit, the Newfoundlanders—more than three thousand of them—volunteered to work as civilians. However, many also joined the Home Guard, the secondary defense service made up of men too old or too young to fight, or from reserved occupations. The only Home Guard unit in Britain made up entirely of overseas recruits was the 3rd Inverness (Newfoundland) Battalion.

Many romances developed between lumberjacks and lumberjills, and dozens of marriages resulted. Numerous lumberjills later returned with their new husbands to Newfoundland and to Canada as war brides.

As a side note, although the men of NOFU referred to themselves as "Newfies," I came to understand during my research that these days that term has a strong derogatory sense to it, so I chose not to use it in my story.

In the years before television, Pathé News was the primary source of visual news, with newsreels showing in cinemas before the main picture. There is a real film of the lumberjills—you can watch it on the fantastic British Pathé website, along with other fascinating wartime films—and yes, its narration was every bit as patronizing about the lumberjills as I depicted in my story. In fact, with permission, I borrowed most of the voiceover script word for word.

John's military experience was also based on real-life events. Knowing I wanted to place John as a soldier at the evacuation of Dunkirk, I was frustrated to find that no Canadian units had been there. However, I then discovered that one hundred men from Nova Scotia had volunteered to join the British Army in 1939. Recruited by the charismatic Colonel Willis, and later nicknamed the "Halifax 100," the men had joined the 2nd Manchester Regiment as machine gunners, and they went over to France within weeks of arriving in England. The 2nd Manchesters then played a major part in protecting the men at Dunkirk from the advancing German army. Four of the Halifax 100 were captured and spent years as prisoners of war, and two—Privates Thomas McCarthy and William Adams—were killed and are buried in Dunkirk Town Cemetery.

The evacuation of Dunkirk between May 26th and June 4th, 1940, was a triumph over disaster for the Allies. As the Germans advanced through France, over 400,000 members of the British and French armies became trapped at Dunkirk, their backs to the English Channel. As the men waited to be rescued, they were subjected to attacks by German Stuka dive bombers and mortar shells from land artillery.

With extensive damage to the harbor wall preventing Royal Navy ships getting close, the evacuation instead used over eight hundred small pleasure craft and fishing boats from ports along the south coast of England to rescue men straight from the beach in shallow water. Day after day, what became known as the Little Ships of Dunkirk crossed the

Channel to bring more men home. The evacuation target from the Admiralty had been just thirty thousand men, but after nine days, over three hundred thousand men had been saved. Sadly, almost one hundred thousand more—mostly French—were killed or captured.

Interestingly, twelve of the actual Little Ships involved in the evacuation were recently used in Christopher Nolan's *Dunkirk*, a feature film that I cannot praise and recommend highly enough.

So, did I take any liberties with history? A few perhaps.

Of Maisie's three assignments, Shandford Lodge and Auchterblair were real WTC camps. But while there was a sawmill at Blair Atholl during the war, I sent Maisie to nearby Struan because it's a place that holds very special memories for me from when I was seventeen.

The lumberjills at Auchterblair regularly went to the cinema and to dances in nearby villages and towns, but a long drive to Inverness is less likely. Fuel was rationed, and Inverness was within a restricted zone, with soldiers checking identification and the purpose of any visit. I ignored these restrictions, however, because I wanted John and Maisie to have a long cuddle on the way, and because I wanted to write a good fistfight with a bunch of Navy sailors!

John McCrae's poem *In Flanders Fields* was written on a battlefield during World War I and led to the red poppy's becoming the international symbol of remembrance of that war. Lieutenant Colonel McCrae was a Canadian army doctor who died in January 1918 in a field hospital in northern France, yet his poem is still recited in annual Armistice ceremonies more than a century after it was written. McCrae had no children but regularly sent letters and drawings home to his nephews and nieces. It was with the greatest respect that I imagined John Lindsay as one of those nephews.

In writing *In Another Time*, I have tried to pay tribute to all those who served, to those whose injuries—physical and psychological—were felt for the rest of their lives, and to those who were lost. As a mother of children around the same age as Maisie and John, I hope that we are never again forced to sacrifice our young people to such a war.

However, memories of war service were not all bad. Lumberjill Christina Forrester told me, "I have very happy memories of my time with the Timber Corps and helping the war effort. I grew up very quickly once I was away from home, found muscles I never knew I had; and the friendships I made there lasted for years. All those experiences made me the person I am today."